"I don't have
an incredibly

Zeke began, "but I'm ~~not~~ ....ng. Instead, I'm thinking about ways to talk you into going out with me. Every time you turn me down, it only encourages me to ask you again. If you really want me to stop, say yes."

It was the most convoluted reason Elizabeth had ever heard for going out with a man. "Let me get this straight. I'm supposed to go out with you so you'll quit asking me? Is that what you're saying?"

"Pretty much," he retorted. "Think about it. If we go out, we may discover that we don't even like each other. In that case, whatever chemistry there is between us will die a swift death, and we can forget that we ever looked twice at each other."

If any other man had suggested such a thing, Elizabeth might have thought he was crazy. But this was Zeke McBride....

"All right," she said. "How about Thursday night?"

Dear Reader,

I'm always getting letters telling me how much you love miniseries, and this month we've got three great ones for you. Linda Turner starts the new family-based miniseries, THOSE MARRYING McBRIDES! with *The Lady's Man.* The McBrides have always been unlucky in love—until now. And it's wedding-wary Zeke who's the first to take the plunge. Marie Ferrarella also starts a new miniseries this month. CHILDFINDERS, INC. is a detective agency specializing in finding missing kids, and they've never failed to find one yet. So is it any wonder desperate Savannah King turns to investigator Sam Walters when her daughter disappears in *A Hero for All Seasons?* And don't miss *Rodeo Dad,* the continuation of Carla Cassidy's wonderful Western miniseries, MUSTANG, MONTANA.

Of course, that's not all we've got in store. Paula Detmer Riggs is famous for her ability to explore emotion and create characters who live in readers' minds long after the last page is turned. In *Once More a Family* she creates a reunion romance to haunt you. Sharon Mignerey is back with her second book, *His Tender Touch,* a suspenseful story of a woman on the run and her unwilling protector—who soon turns into her willing lover. Finally, welcome new author Candace Irvin, who debuts with a military romance called *For His Eyes Only.* I think you'll be as glad as we are that Candace has joined the Intimate Moments ranks.

Enjoy—and come back next month, when we once again bring you the best and most exciting romantic reading around.

Yours,

Leslie J. Wainger
Executive Senior Editor

Please address questions and book requests to:
Silhouette Reader Service
U.S.: 3010 Walden Ave., P.O. Box 1325, Buffalo, NY 14269
Canadian: P.O. Box 609, Fort Erie, Ont. L2A 5X3

LINDA TURNER

THE LADY'S MAN

INTIMATE™ MOMENTS®

Published by Silhouette Books

America's Publisher of Contemporary Romance

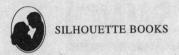 SILHOUETTE BOOKS

ISBN 0-373-07931-1

THE LADY'S MAN

Look us up on-line at: http://www.romance.net

Printed in U.S.A.

Books by Linda Turner

Silhouette Intimate Moments

The Echo of Thunder #238
Crosscurrents #263
An Unsuspecting Heart #298
Flirting with Danger #316
Moonlight and Lace #354
The Love of Dugan Magee #448
*Gable's Lady #523
*Cooper #553
*Flynn #572
*Kat #590
Who's the Boss? #649
The Loner #673
*Maddy Lawrence's Big
  Adventure* #709
The Lady in Red #763
†*I'm Having Your Baby?!* #799
†*A Marriage-Minded Man?* #829
†*The Proposal* #847
†*Christmas Lone-Star Style* #895
‡*The Lady's Man* #931

*The Wild West
†The Lone Star Social Club
‡Those Marrying McBrides!

Silhouette Desire

A Glimpse of Heaven #220
Wild Texas Rose #653
Philly and the Playboy #701
The Seducer #802
Heaven Can't Wait #929

Silhouette Special Edition

Shadows in the Night #350

Silhouette Books

Silhouette Christmas Kisses 1996
"A Wild West Christmas"

Fortune's Children

The Wolf and the Dove

A Fortune's Children Christmas 1998
"The Christmas Child"

LINDA TURNER

began reading romances in high school and began writing them one night when she had nothing else to read. She's been writing ever since. Single and living in Texas, she travels every chance she gets, scouting locales for her books.

Chapter 1

The beat of her windshield wipers echoed the thumping of her heart as Elizabeth Davis gripped the steering wheel tighter and peered through the windshield, searching through the blowing snow for the faded center line of the road. It was nowhere to be seen. Swearing softly in the gathering darkness, she realized too late that she should have shut down the office and left for home at least an hour ago. She'd known a late-winter storm was bearing down on western Colorado, but she'd thought she had plenty of time to finish up some paperwork, then make it home before it hit. She'd been wrong. She'd hardly climbed into her car and left the city limits of Liberty Hill behind when the first snowflakes started to fall.

Even then she hadn't been worried. She'd grown up in the Rockies and knew how to drive in the snow. Her Jeep had four-wheel drive and was as dependable as the sunrise. Granted, she hadn't lived in the area for very long, only three months, but she drove the fifteen miles between town and her small rental house twice a day and could chart every curve and dip of the road in her sleep. Finding her way home shouldn't have been a problem.

But the snow was wet and heavy and fell faster than her windshield wipers could sweep it away. Barely five o'clock, it was already nearly dark. Familiar landmarks quickly became lost in the blowing snow and deepening night, and visibility shrank to almost whiteout conditions. Her eyes trained unblinkingly on what she prayed was the road in front of her, she kept her foot light on the accelerator and inched her way carefully up one hill and down the next.

Her headlights the only light in the all-encompassing darkness, they cut a narrow swath through the storm, illuminating nothing but a tunnel of snow-covered trees that seemed to stretch for miles. With tension crawling up her back, she leaned forward over the steering wheel and strained to see. Had she missed the turnoff to her house? She couldn't, in all honesty, even say if she'd come to it yet. With her attention focused on the road directly in front of her, she could have driven right past it without even seeing it.

Another time she would have laughed at the idea of being lost on the very road she lived on, but there was nothing the least bit funny about a blizzard. She'd heard of people getting turned around in the snow and freezing to death between the walk from their garage to their front door.

"Think, Elizabeth!" she said out loud, breaking the tense silence that engulfed her. "The house has to be around here somewhere. The drive is a half mile past the McClusky place, and even in a blizzard you can't miss those fancy gates of theirs. So have you passed them or not?"

The words were hardly out of her mouth when her headlights picked out a break in the trees that lined the right side of the road. And there in the darkness were the elaborate iron gates that marked the entrance to her neighbor's property. She'd always thought they were more than a little ostentatious, but at that moment she'd never seen anything more beautiful in her life.

The last half mile to her driveway passed in a blur. Tired and hungry, she crept along at a snail's pace and finally spied the oversize mailbox at the edge of her drive. It wasn't until then that she realized she really hadn't expected to make it home at all. Trees went down all the time in storms this bad, and all it would have taken was one across the road to send her back to the office for the night.

Her breath escaping in a sigh of relief, her thoughts jumping ahead to the pot of homemade soup that was waiting for her in the refrigerator, she turned...and misjudged where the edge of the road was under the snow. Her right-front wheel slipped off the pavement and immediately skidded on a patch of ice. Before she could hit the brakes, she bounced up and over a boulder and came to a jarring stop just a whisper from the edge of the drainage culvert on the side of the road.

Her heart thundering, Elizabeth sat there, stunned, her hands locked tightly around the steering wheel and her widened eyes trained on the drop-off right in front of her bumper. Another few inches and gravity would have pulled her right over the edge.

Close, she thought, shaken. That was just a little too close for comfort. The ditch was only six feet deep, but she had no desire to inspect the bottom of it in her Jeep. Carefully shifting into reverse, she eased down on the accelerator. Nothing happened. Frowning, she checked to make sure the vehicle was in four-wheel drive, then tried again, only to swear softly when the vehicle didn't move so much as an inch. She was stuck!

And John Wayne, unfortunately, was nowhere in sight. The road was deserted in either direction, her house, less than a quarter of a mile down the drive, too far to walk in such dangerous weather. So if she was going to make it home tonight, she had to get unstuck all by herself. Great, she thought with a groan. Just great! Grabbing the flashlight she kept stored under the seat, she zipped her down parka up to her chin and stepped out into the storm.

Howling like a banshee, a frigid wet wind immediately slapped her in the face and stole her breath. In the half hour that had passed since she'd left work, the temperature had dropped at least another fifteen degrees, and despite her winter gear, it was colder than hell. Chilled to the bone, she dropped down on one knee and swept the beam of her flashlight under the Jeep to see what the problem was.

At the sight of the rock wedged under the transfer case, she felt her heart sink to her toes. No wonder she couldn't move! One of the front wheels wasn't even touching the ground, and the two back ones were sitting on ice, unable to get any traction. She could sit on the accelerator until doomsday and she wasn't going to go anywhere. Damn!

Sitting at an odd angle far off the shoulder of the road, the Jeep was nearly lost in the dark, blinding snow. Zeke, in fact, wouldn't even have seen it but for the faint glow of the taillights as he swept past. Too late, he realized that it wasn't an abandoned car but probably someone in trouble. Why else would they be parked that far off the road during the worst blizzard to hit Colorado in five years?

Swearing, he touched his brakes and pulled over as quickly as he could manage on the snow-covered road, but he was still fifty yards past the vehicle before he brought his Suburban to a stop. A heartbeat later, he was backing up.

He expected to find the driver holed up in the car with the heater running. Instead, he was down on his knees in the snow near the right-front tire, struggling with a fallen tree branch.

"You okay, buddy?" he called out as he approached the parka-shrouded figure. "Looks like you had a little trouble. Here…let me help you with that."

Even as he spoke, he moved to help the man, but that was as far as he got. At the first sound of his voice, the dark figure scrambled to his feet and whirled, the blinding beam of his flashlight hitting Zeke right in the eyes. It wasn't until the other driver spoke that he realized it was a woman.

"That won't be necessary. My husband's on his way." Her voice was cool and competent and had "back-off" written all over it. "He's the Falls County sheriff. He should be here any minute."

Surprised, Zeke shielded his eyes and tried to see around the flashlight beam, but all he could make out was the dark silhouette of a slender figure lost in a down parka. So she was married to Nick Kincaid, was she? he thought with a snort. And he was Roger Rabbit. He might not have lived in Liberty Hill for years, but he knew Nick, knew that he'd never married. There was only one woman he loved—though it was a well-guarded secret he hid well—and that was Zeke's sister, Merry. As long as she walked the earth, he'd never look at another woman.

So why the devil was this woman pretending to be someone she wasn't? He only had to think about the long, lonely stretch of dark road leading away from them in either direction to have his answer. There wasn't another living soul in sight and not likely to be on such a cold, miserable night.

She was a woman alone and in trouble. And he was a stranger.

He could have told her she had nothing to fear from him, but he doubted she would have believed him. So he did the only other thing he could to make her feel more comfortable—he went along with her lie.

Dropping the hand he held up to shield his eyes from the flashlight, he gave her a charming smile that came as easily to him as breathing. "Begging your pardon, ma'am, but he could be a while in this weather. Unless you want to be here most of the night, maybe you'd better let me help you."

"Oh, but that's not necessary!"

"No trouble," he assured her, and stepped around her to go down on one knee and inspect the underside of her Jeep. "Looks like you're stuck on a rock. What happened? D'you swerve to miss a deer, or what?"

Normally, Elizabeth wouldn't have had a problem admitting she'd misjudged her own driveway. But she had no intention of telling a man she didn't know from Adam where she lived. Just last month, a woman over in Wilson County was raped by a man who stopped to help her change a flat on a deserted road. From what Elizabeth remembered, that man had looked nothing like this one with his rugged, dark good looks, but she wasn't taking any chances.

Standing well back away from him, she said, "Something like that. Look, I don't mean to be rude—and I really appreciate you offering to help—but this really isn't your problem—"

"And you'd feel a lot better if I'd just go on and leave you here to solve it yourself," he finished for her as he pulled back from under the car and shot her a knowing look.

She didn't bother to deny it. "Actually, yes, I would. I don't know you—"

"That's easily remedied. I used to live around here—my family still does. You might have heard of them. The McBrides? I'm Zeke. I've got ID if you'd like to see it."

He reached for his wallet and drew out his driver's license, but Elizabeth hardly spared it a glance. Surprised, she echoed, "McBride? You're Merry's brother?"

He grinned. "Whatever she said about me, it's not true. You know how sisters are—just because a guy put a frog in their bed when they were ten, they hold it against him for life. If you want the real skinny on me, talk to my mother. She'll tell you I'm harmless."

Elizabeth hadn't met his mother—or the rest of his family, for that matter—just Merry, who was a veterinarian with U.S. Fish and Wildlife when her services were needed. Merry had never mentioned her prodigal brother, but then again, they weren't best friends, just acquaintances who waved when they passed each other in town. Not that it mattered. Elizabeth didn't need any testimonials from Zeke's relatives to know just what kind of man he was. She'd recognized him the second he smiled at her.

He was a flirt. The evidence was there in the twinkle in his eyes, in the grin that appeared on his handsome face at the sight of a woman…any woman. And that made him far from harmless.

Her father had that same charm, and when she was a child, she'd thought he was the grandest man on earth. He was fun and loving and had the knack for making her feel as though she and her mother were the only two females on the planet. Then, when she was twelve, she'd discovered that he didn't reserve his intimate, loving smiles for just his family. There were other women.

To this day Elizabeth could still feel the shock, the hurt.

His betrayal shook the security of her childhood to its very foundation, and nothing had ever been the same since. In an instant, her trust in her father was gone, the family unit compromised. She expected her mother to bring up the dreaded ''D'' word, but divorce was never mentioned. Instead, when Connor Davis promised he'd never so much as look at another woman again, her mother found a way to believe him and all was forgiven.

The peace the family found after that couldn't last, of course. Not when her father strayed again. And again. He just couldn't seem to help himself. And each time, her mother forgave him. They'd been together for thirty-five years, and even though her father continued to stray, their marriage seemed stronger than ever.

If that was love, Elizabeth had decided long ago, she wanted no part of it. Oh, she adored her father—how could she not? At sixty, he was still attractive and fun and the life of the party. But he didn't know the meaning of the word commitment, and that was the last thing she wanted in a man.

Which was why she made it a habit to date the serious, studious types. They might not be wildly exciting or make her heart thud wildly with excitement, but they weren't distracted by every skirt that walked by, either. And that was just the way she wanted it. If she hadn't fallen in love with any of them, it was just because she hadn't met the right one yet. He would come along eventually, and when he did, he wouldn't be anything like her father or the oh, so charming Mr. McBride. He would be faithful and dependable, and when he told her he loved her, she could believe him.

But Zeke McBride wasn't asking her to spend the rest of her life with him, just let him help get her Jeep off the rock it was stuck on. And for that, she supposed, she could trust him. Gossip was the main source of news in the area, and if one of the McBride men had a habit of accosting women on the side of the road, she surely would have heard about it by now.

"Mothers tend to be more than a little prejudiced when it comes to their sons," she said dryly. "But there aren't any frogs out this time of year, so I guess I'm safe enough."

"Until spring, at least," he agreed, winking at her. "Now that we've got that settled, let's see about getting you off that rock."

All business, he leaned down again to examine the situation and swore softly. "Damn, that thing's as big as a house and the back wheels are on ice! We need a tow truck, but in this weather, you'd probably have to wait half the night for one."

"What about stuffing some branches under the front wheel that's not touching?" she suggested. "That's what I was trying to do when you drove up. I thought if I could get all four wheels touching, I might be able to get some traction."

Frowning at the wheel, he nodded. "That might work if we can get the front end jacked up and get something under the wheel bigger than that rock. We need a log or something." He glanced around and spied one half-buried in the snow. "There! That should do it!"

She helped him pull the log over to the Jeep, and as they worked, the storm worsened. Gale-force winds buffeted them, while the snow continued to come down in sheets, covering everything in sight, including the branches she'd started to collect when she'd realized she was stuck. The tracks left by both her Jeep and Zeke's Suburban had already disappeared, and visibility was down to ten feet.

As much as she liked to think of herself as a woman who

could handle just about anything, Elizabeth knew she was lucky Zeke had come along when he had. With enough time, she'd have been able to get her Jeep unstuck by herself, but time was something she didn't have tonight. Not when the temperature was already in single digits and conditions were quickly becoming dangerous.

In near silence they worked together, jacking the front end up, then rolling the log under the wheel and wedging it in place. The branches Elizabeth had collected were packed behind the rear wheels for traction, then Zeke was carefully lowering the jack. Half expecting the weight of the vehicle to dislodge the log under the front wheel and bring the transfer case right back down on the rock, they both let out a sigh of relief when it held firm.

They still, however, weren't home free. "The log's in there pretty tight, but it could shift once you start to back up," he told her as she climbed back into the Jeep and rolled her window down so she could hear him if he yelled at her to stop. "Just take it slow and you should be okay."

Her heart pounding, she shifted the transmission into reverse and once again carefully pressed the accelerator. For a second the rear wheels spun, searching for traction. Then, just when she was about to give up hope, the Jeep began to move. Afraid to stop for fear she'd get stuck again, she didn't hit the brakes until all four wheels were on solid ground and she was well back on the road.

Even then she couldn't seem to let go of the steering wheel. She still had a death grip on it when Zeke walked around to the driver's side and grinned at her. "You okay?"

She nodded, then laughed shakily as she forced her fingers to release their grip on the wheel. "Yeah. I was beginning to think I was going to have to spend the rest of the night on that rock."

"That was never an option," he assured her. "If worse came to worst, I'd have given you a lift home and you could have dealt with all this tomorrow." Casting a glance at the storm raging around them, he frowned. "This is getting damn nasty. Maybe I should follow you home just to make sure you get there safely."

"Oh, that's not necessary," she began. "I just—"

She started to tell him she could easily make it the short distance home by herself, only to remember that she'd claimed to be married to the sheriff. With the way her luck was running tonight, he probably knew that the sheriff lived in a homemade log cabin on the other side of town. The second she told him she lived just down the hill, he'd know she'd lied to him.

Still, she should have told him. After the way he'd helped her, he deserved the truth. But it was getting late, she was tired, and she knew a man like Zeke wouldn't be able to pass up the chance to flirt with her once he knew she was single. And that was the last thing she wanted to deal with tonight. Anyway, what would it hurt to let him continue to think she was married? she reasoned. She didn't socialize with the McBrides, and he was probably only in town for a short visit with his family. The chances of her ever seeing him again were slim to none.

"Actually, I drove out this way to check on my sick aunt," she fibbed, and prayed he didn't notice that she couldn't quite look him in the eye. "She just lives a little farther down the road. I'm sure I can make it on my own. Anyway, you've helped me enough, and your family must be expecting you. You should get going before the weather gets any worse. I'll be fine."

For a moment she thought he was going to insist on escorting her to her fictional aunt's, but something in her tone must have warned him he was wasting his time. Giving in gracefully, he smiled. "If you're sure, then I'll be on my way. Stick to the crown of the road and you shouldn't have any trouble."

With a final salute, he turned away, took three steps toward his vehicle, and was swallowed whole by the stormy night. Watching her rearview mirror, Elizabeth knew his truck was somewhere behind her on the side of the road, but she couldn't see it—or him—anywhere in the blowing snow. Then his brake lights flashed in the darkness, and she realized she'd been afraid he'd lost his way in the storm. She should have know better. From the little bit she'd seen of Zeke McBride, he appeared to be a man who knew where he was going.

A few seconds later he tapped his horn at her in a sharp farewell and then he pulled away, his headlights cutting a swath through the darkness as he slowly headed toward Liberty Hill. Alone again in the storm, Elizabeth once again turned into her drive. This time, she didn't misjudge the edge of the ravine.

Zeke had told his mother to expect him around six. Two and a half hours late, he turned off the highway and drove through the entrance of Twin Pines, the ranch that had been his family's for nearly a century. The house where he'd grown up—and where his sister Janey and his mother still lived—was another three miles down the road, but he was home the second he drove onto McBride land. It had always been that way. It didn't matter that he'd established a life of his own in Cheyenne or that his work kept him too busy to come back to the ranch very often. He'd been born and raised there; the red dirt of the place was and always would be in his blood.

He drove by his brother, Joe's, house and wasn't surprised to find it dark and deserted. He would be at the

homestead, along with Janey, Merry and his mother, to celebrate the return of the prodigal. A quick grin of appreciation curled Zeke's mouth at the thought. He was the only
one who had left the ranch and moved away, and it was
always the same his first night back when he came home
for a visit. His mother pulled out the best china, cooked all
his favorite foods, and the rest of the family teased him
about being the favorite. And what, he wanted to know, his
blue eyes twinkling, was wrong with that? Any number of
women had told him he was downright adorable.

Just imagining how Joe would roll his eyes at that, he
chuckled as he topped the hill that overlooked the valley
where the first McBride had started the ranch with a two-
room cabin decades ago. In the near whiteout conditions of
the storm, he could see little but the faint glow of the lit
windows of the house where he'd been born and raised,
but he could imagine every porch and veranda, the mammoth rock fireplaces, the angles and gables of the metal
roof, as clearly as if it was a bright summer day.

It was a rambling place that had been added on to a half
dozen times, a blending of rock and logs and different ar-
chitectural styles that had come in and out of fashion over
the years. It could have been a real eyesore. Somehow,
though, it all flowed together to create a home with a surprising amount of character that was more a result of
chance than design.

And inside, the family was waiting for him. As he
reached the circular drive in front of the house and pulled
up behind his brother's pickup, he could see that the cur-
tains hadn't been drawn in the living room so that they
could see him when he drove up. Before he could even cut
the motor, the entire family was rushing toward the front
door.

Seconds later he blew inside, bringing a whirlwind of

snow with him. At the sight of the worry on all their faces, he teased, "Hey, why all the long faces? Somebody die?"

"We were beginning to think you had," his mother retorted with a grin that matched his own. Reaching him first, Sara McBride ignored the snow that clung to him and hugged him fiercely. At sixty-three, she hardly looked old enough to have four children in their thirties. Oh, there was a definite touch of gray in her brown hair, but she was still as slim as a girl, and in her blue eyes, there was a sparkle of good humor that only the young at heart were blessed with. "You're a little late, Son."

"I called—"

That was the wrong thing to say. Both his sisters pounced on that. "That was an hour and a half ago!" Janey scolded. "Haven't you been listening to the radio? There's a travel advisory for western Colorado. Highway 90 was closed down over forty minutes ago."

"There's been at least a dozen wrecks just in Falls County alone," Merry added. "We were afraid you'd run off into a ditch or something."

"Actually, I wasn't the one who had trouble," he replied. "There was this woman—"

"There always is," Joe drawled, his brown eyes twinkling. "Though how you manage to find one in the middle of a blizzard, God only knows. What's her name this time?"

"Mrs. Nick Kincaid."

That stopped the entire family in its tracks. Frowning, Merry sputtered, "*Our* Nick Kincaid?"

"That's what she said," he said as he shrugged out of his coat.

"But Nick's not married."

"He never has been."

"Apparently she didn't know that," Zeke retorted. "Or

if she did, she was hoping I didn't. Of course, she didn't actually mention Nick's name,'' he added ruefully. ''She just said she was married to the sheriff, and I didn't have to help her because he would be along any moment. I think I scared her.''

''Zeke! You didn't!'' his mother scolded. ''What did you do to the poor girl?''

''Nothing! But I couldn't just drive off and leave her there. She was stuck on a rock right there by the old Murphy place, and I knew if I didn't help her, nobody else was going to come along. Not with the storm intensifying the way it was and the condition the roads were in.''

''So what was she doing out there in the first place?'' Janey asked. ''Who was she?''

Zeke shrugged. ''I haven't got a clue—I'd never seen her before. She said she was visiting a sick aunt.''

''But nobody lives out that way but the Hollisters and old man Jackson, and neither one of them have any family in the area,'' Joe pointed out. ''What'd she look like? And don't tell me you didn't notice because she was all bundled up and it was dark,'' he said before Zeke could even open his mouth. ''A woman would have to be wrapped in a shroud for you not to notice her. So let's have it. Age, weight, physical description.''

Amusement glinting in his eyes, Zeke didn't bother to pretend innocence. ''Pretty, late twenties, early thirties, big green eyes, dark blond hair, five-six, a hundred twenty pounds. She was gutsy, the independent type. She might have been stuck on a rock, but she wasn't sitting around waiting for a man to come along and rescue her. I don't know how long she'd been there when I stopped, but she was already on her knees trying to stuff a branch under one of the tires of her Jeep.''

It was, he knew, a description that could have fitted any

number of women who lived in western Colorado, but
something he said struck a cord with Joe. Surprised, he
said, "That must have been Elizabeth Davis. Was she driving a white Jeep?"

"Yeah. How'd you know?"

"*Independent* doesn't begin to describe the lady. She
rented the Murphy place about four months ago, before she
even moved to town."

"She's no dummy," Merry retorted. "She knew nobody
would rent to her once they found out who she was. And
I think it's a dirty shame. She's done nothing but do her
job, and all she gets for it is grief."

Scowling, Joe opened his mouth to disagree, but that was
as far as he got. "Oh, no you don't," his mother said,
stepping between them. "We're not going to get on the
subject of that darn wolf project again. Not when supper's
already two hours late and drying out on the stove. Girls,
help me dish the food up. Joe, you can fix the tea while
your brother washes up."

She used her mother voice, the one that could, even now,
when they were long past adolescence, make them
straighten up and behave. Grinning, they all saluted
smartly, drawing a laugh from her, and fell to their assigned
tasks.

The meal, as expected, was one of Zeke's favorites.
Smothered steak and gravy, mashed potatoes and homemade biscuits. He groaned at the first bite, savoring familiar
tastes, but as they sat around the old dining room table
while the storm raged outside, it was the company he enjoyed the most. It had always been that way, ever since
he'd left home for college the first time. He could be gone
for months at a time, but he only had to hug his mother,
greet his brother and sisters, and it was as if he had never

left. They would sit together for hours at the table, devouring the apple pie his mother had made as they talked and laughed and caught up on each other's lives.

They shouldn't have been close—not when they were such a diverse group. A Ph.D., a rancher, a prom queen and an old maid. He didn't like labels, especially for the girls, but in a rural community where everybody knew everyone else, there was no avoiding them. But as different as they were, they all had one thing in common. All in their thirties, they'd never had much luck when it came to the opposite sex. Oh, Joe had been married, but it lasted less than a year when the city girl he'd fallen for went back to the bright lights and shopping malls of Denver. Then he himself had made the mistake of losing his head over a pretty medical student when he was working on the last year of his doctorate. She'd had his engagement ring on his finger when he'd caught her in bed with a plastic surgeon. He hadn't loved her enough to forgive her.

The girls had been luckier, he supposed, if you could call it that. Merry could have her pick of dates, but she'd never given her heart. And then there was Janey. She was thirty-six and had, to his knowledge, never dated a man in her life. While other women were looking for Mr. Right, she seemed content to devote herself to her patients at the nursing home, where she was a nurse. It sounded like a lonely existence to him, but at least she'd been spared the pain of a broken heart. That was something he wouldn't wish on anyone.

"Why the frown?" Merry teased, interrupting his musings. "She got home safely."

Blinking, he growled, "Who?"

"Elizabeth Davis. Even if you hadn't come along when you had, she still would have found a way to get off that rock. She's a very resourceful lady."

"And evidently not very popular with the locals." More than willing to be distracted from thoughts of his love life, he settled back in his chair and said bluntly, "Okay, so who is she? An ax murderer? A stripper? What? Why wouldn't anyone want to rent to her once they found out who she was?"

"Because the only reason she's here is to reintroduce wolves into the Liberty Hill National Forest," his brother told him grimly. "She may not use an ax, but in some cattlemen's eyes, she's as close to a murderer as they want to get. She's a wolf biologist."

Surprised, Zeke whistled softly. "Did she work at Yellowstone?"

Joe nodded. "She was part of the recovery team that selected the wolves in Canada, then reintroduced them into the park. The project was so successful that the government decided to try it again here." Finishing the last bite of his pie, he pushed his empty plate away. "As you might imagine, some people haven't exactly greeted her with open arms."

"I heard the people involved in the Yellowstone project received hate mail and even death threats," he said, frowning. "Surely that's not going on around here."

"There has been talk," his mother said somberly. "People are afraid. There haven't been any wolves in this area since the thirties, and no one knows what they'll do. They haven't even been released from their holding pen yet, and the teachers at school are afraid to let the kids outside for recess."

"But that's ridiculous!" Zeke said. "Wolves won't attack people. In most cases, they won't even go after cattle or sheep." He knew. He was a wildlife biologist, and although wolves weren't his particular field of study, he knew enough about them to know that the odds were slim that one would attack anything but elk and coyotes.

"It's the worst-case scenario that's got people all jumpy," Janey said. "Ever since Elizabeth Davis and her team came to town, the wolves are the only thing people are talking about. They don't care what statistics say, they're scared."

"There's a town meeting scheduled for tomorrow night at the VFW hall to discuss the project," Joe told him. "I was hoping you'd go with me and give me your input."

He didn't have to ask him twice. "Are you kidding? I wouldn't miss it. We don't have the protected eco system Yellowstone does, but it's still a damn interesting project. I suppose Elizabeth Davis is going to be there."

He said it casually enough, as if he couldn't care less whether she was or not, but his family knew him too well. Grinning, Merry warned, "Don't waste your time, Romeo."

All innocence, he blinked. "What? I just asked if she was going to be there."

Far from fooled, Joe grinned, "Yeah, right. That was real subtle, little brother. You try that on the lady, and she's going to eat you for lunch. If you want to keep your hide in place—and your ego—you'll steer clear of her."

"She doesn't date, Zeke," Janey told him bluntly. "And it isn't because she hasn't been asked. She just doesn't seem to be interested in anything but her wolves."

Far from discouraged, he only flashed his dimples at her and winked. "That was before she met me. Trust me, Sis, the lady won't know what hit her."

"But—"

Stopping her sister's protest with just a look, Merry smiled broadly at him. "You go, boy. Just let me know when you ask the lady out so I can sell tickets. This is going to be good.''

The VFW hall had been built after World War I and was still the largest building in town. Rented out for parties, occasionally used for political rallies and town meetings, it held two hundred people comfortably but seldom drew more than fifty. Tonight the parking lot was full, and cars had spilled over into the street. It looked as though just about everyone in the county had shown up for the town meeting.

Quickly circling the parking lot one more time and finding nothing, Elizabeth told herself this was what she got for not watching the clock closer. Punctuality wasn't normally a problem for her, but the entire day had been out of sync. Maybe it was because of last night's storm, which had finally blown itself out, and the fact that everyone had been late to work because of the huge drifts that had piled up, but nothing had seemed to go right. The phones were down for a while, she couldn't find paperwork, and to make matters worse, her allergies were acting up. Given her choice, she'd be home in bed right now with the covers drawn over her head and the phone off the hook.

But she had a town meeting to chair, and as much as she wanted to, she couldn't postpone it. It was too important. People had very real concerns, and this was her chance to convince them that as much as they disliked the wolves roaming free in their neck of the woods, they really did have nothing to fear.

Resigned to the fact that she was going to have to park down the street, she pulled out of the parking lot and finally found a spot three blocks away. A glance at her watch reminded her that the meeting had been scheduled to start five minutes ago. Swearing softly, she grabbed her notes, thanked God she'd had the sense to wear her boots, and stepped out into the cold night air.

Harried, her thoughts on the speech she'd been working on all week, she pushed through the VFW hall's double doors and almost bumped into Nick Kincaid, who was standing just inside the foyer. "Oh, I'm sorry," she began. "I—"

Whatever she was going to say next drained right out of her head at the sight of the man standing next to him. Tall and lean, his angular jaw neatly shaved and his jet-black hair fighting a curl, he should have been a stranger to her. They'd only spoken briefly, and then in the middle of a blizzard, when they were both bundled up and barely visible in the dark, blowing snow. But blizzard or no blizzard, she'd have known Zeke McBride on the dark side of the moon. There was just something about the man—the way he held himself, the breadth of his shoulders—that a woman didn't forget.

And he knew her. She saw recognition flare in his deep blue eyes, watched amusement curl the edges of his mouth, and suddenly her bold announcement from last night hung in the air between them as clearly as if she'd just shouted it to the heavens.

My husband's on his way. He's the Falls County sheriff.

Realization hit her then, stunning her. He knew Nick. She only had to look at the two of them, to see the way they'd been talking and laughing when she'd walked up, to know that they were obviously old friends. So last night, when she'd claimed to be married to the sheriff, he'd known all along that she was lying. And he hadn't said a word—*then*. Now, however, was a different matter.

She could see the devilish glint in his eyes, the wicked laughter he made no effort to hide. Any second now he was going to ask Nick about his *wife,* and she'd sink right through the floor. Unless she could beat him to the punch and tell Nick about last night herself.

She opened her mouth to do just that, but before she could say a word, Nick stepped forward with a smile of greeting. "There you are! I was beginning to wonder if something had happened to you. I guess you know you've got a full house tonight."

"Yes. The closest parking place I could find was three blocks away. Nick, there's something I need to tell you—"

"Have you met Merry McBride's brother?" he asked before she could pull him off to a private corner to confess. "I know you're in a hurry to get the meeting started, but you two might want to talk later—you've got a lot in common. Zeke's a wildlife biologist. Zeke, this is Elizabeth—"

"Davis," she said quickly, cursing the heat that climbed into her cheeks as Zeke's grin broadened. Drat the man, he was really enjoying this! "We met last night," she told Nick stiffly. "I had some trouble on the way home and Zeke stopped to help me. The weather was so crazy, though, that we didn't take time to properly introduce ourselves." Shooting him a look that just dared him to expose her, she smoothly extended her hand and gave him a cool smile. "How do you do?"

A gentleman would have followed her lead and graciously let her little white lie die without comment. But she only had to look in Zeke's laughing eyes to suspect that he was no gentleman. She knew it for a certainty when his fingers closed around hers and he teased huskily, "Nice to meet you, Elizabeth Davis. I hear you live all by yourself out at the old Murphy place."

Her heart lurched in her breast, but if he expected her to squirm, he was in for a rude awakening. She didn't rattle so easily. "That's right. I've leased it for the rest of the year."

"Funny, but I thought you were married. I wonder where I got that idea."

Carefully extracting her hand from his, she looked him right in the eye and traded him smile for smile. "I can't imagine. But you shouldn't believe everything you hear."

"I don't. And I try not to embarrass a lady when I can avoid it."

"Oh, really? That's good to hear. I guess the women of Liberty Hill can relax then, can't they?"

Enjoying himself, he grinned. "For now. But one of them owes me—big-time."

Her heart thumping crazily in her breast at the idea of owing Zeke McBride anything, Elizabeth thought he was entirely too sure of himself. Color tingeing her cheeks, she said coolly, "You know what they say about paybacks, but I wouldn't count on collecting anytime soon if I were you. Now, if you gentlemen will excuse me, I've got a town meeting to start. The natives are getting restless."

She fled, leaving the two men staring after her. Confused, Nick looked from her slim form disappearing into the crowd to Zeke, who was grinning broadly. "Would you like to tell me what the hell that was all about? I haven't got a clue."

Chuckling, Zeke slapped him on the back. "Don't ask, old buddy. You don't want to know."

Chapter 2

"Isn't he gorgeous? It's the eyes. Did you notice? They just dance with laughter. And I always did like a man with a great sense of humor. No wonder the women around here could never resist him. He smiles at you, and you just want to melt."

In the process of getting her notes together, Elizabeth glanced up in distraction at her assistant and frowned. "What? What *are* you talking about?"

"Not what," Tina Ellison retorted with a grin. "*Who.* Zeke McBride! I'd heard talk about him, but you know how gossip is. People exaggerate. But look at him! Is that not the best-looking thing you ever saw in your life or what?"

Looking anywhere but at the back of the hall where Zeke stood with Nick Kincaid, Elizabeth refused to admit any such thing. "You'd better not let Peter hear you talking that way. You know how jealous he gets."

Unrepentant, she only laughed. Tina's husband, Peter, didn't have a jealous bone in his body. Totally devoted to her and sappy in love after ten years of marriage, he trusted her completely. And Tina felt the same way about him. "Peter knows he has nothing to worry about. But just because I'm married doesn't mean I'm blind. And that is one fine specimen. Of course, he doesn't have a faithful bone in his body, but he is easy on the eye."

She had a point, but Elizabeth had no intention of admitting that. From what she had seen, Zeke McBride was far too sure of himself already, and she didn't doubt it was because women had been making fools of themselves over him from the time he was old enough to smile up at them from his crib. She didn't intend to join his fan club.

"Why do I have a feeling I don't want to hear this?" she said dryly. "You know how I feel about you gossiping, Tina."

Five years her senior, Tina hadn't been in town any longer than she had—just three months—but she loved to talk. Within a matter of days of moving to Liberty Hill, she knew the skinny on just about everyone in town. "Yeah, but this is good, boss. And I didn't actually snoop around. You know how people talk. All I did was listen."

"But you don't have to repeat it."

"But I'm only telling you," she pointed out reasonably. "And if you don't hear it from me, you will from someone else. Everyone's talking about it. He was engaged to a doctor in Chicago and she caught him with another woman a week before their wedding! Can you imagine? She had this big fancy shindig planned and had to cancel the whole thing at the last minute. Talk about low! The poor girl must have been mortified."

Elizabeth didn't doubt that for a minute. Time and time again as a child, she'd watched her mother suffer the embarrassment of her father's little affairs. He had tried to be discreet, but they'd lived in a small town in Idaho, and there were some things that just couldn't be hidden. Everyone had known when her father had strayed; everyone had talked when her mother invariably took him back. To this day, Elizabeth didn't know how her mother had borne it—she just knew she never intended to follow in her footsteps. She didn't care how good-looking a man was, she wanted nothing to do with him if he was a flirt.

"I imagine she was," Elizabeth said stiffly. "But we're not here to talk about the locals. If we don't get this meeting started, we're going to have a riot on our hands."

The huge crowd packed into the hall was, in fact, already more than a little hostile. Not that Elizabeth was surprised. She was an outsider in charge of a government project to reintroduce wolves into the area for the first time in over sixty years, and the local ranchers didn't have the power to stop her. She was just as concerned about their rights as she was the wolves, but all they could see was she was going to release killers into the midst of their cattle. In their eyes that made her the enemy.

Nothing could have been further from the truth, but as she stepped to the podium to face her detractors, her stomach was a lump of nerves. This was her least favorite part of the job. Still, her smile was cool and self-possessed as she said, "Ladies and gentlemen, we have a lot to cover, so let's get started. For those of you who didn't attend the other meetings, I'm Elizabeth Davis, the project leader for the wolf recovery program, and I'd like to thank you for coming. As most of you know, the wolves are scheduled to be released from their holding pen at Eagle Ridge a week from Friday, and I know you have a lot of questions."

"You're darn right we do!" a gravelly voice called out from somewhere near the back of the room. "And it's about time we got some answers. We want to know what

Uncle Sam's going to do to protect our cattle when you let those killers loose.''

"And don't tell us the bastards won't kill!'' an angry old man on the other side of the room growled as he jumped to his feet to scowl at her. "They killed in the thirties and they'll kill now.''

"Statistics show—''

"To hell with statistics!'' a woman three rows back from the podium cried. "Statistics don't mean squat to a dead calf.''

Hostility vibrated in the air—angry grumblings that buzzed from every corner of the room and came at Elizabeth in waves. Another woman might have been alarmed, but she'd been through this before, when she'd worked with the team that reintroduced wolves into Yellowstone. Then she'd received hate mail and death threats, and more than once she'd come out of her apartment to find all four of her tires slashed. And as much as she'd hated it, she'd understood. People were angry, and anger always stemmed from fear. They were afraid of the wolves, and they had a right to be. There was nothing reassuring about the animals. They were unpredictable, they ran in packs, they killed. And yes, sometimes they preyed on cattle and sheep. But those instances were rare. Very rare. And *that* was what she had to get across to this crowd.

She didn't fool herself into thinking it would be easy. This was the West, and people didn't like to be told what they could and could not do on their own land. When it came to protecting what was theirs, they got downright touchy. Contingency plans for rogue killers meant nothing to them once their animals were dead. In the eyes of most citizens, all wolves were killers and they wanted them gone, if not from the entire West, then at least from their little corner of it.

Holding up her hand to stop the angry mutterings, she said into the tense silence, "I know you might not believe me, but I really do sympathize with your concerns. That's why I scheduled this meeting, so I could bring you up to speed on the release date and discuss the problems any of you are having with that."

Glancing around the room, she met people's hostile gazes head-on. "I'm not going to stand up here and lie to you and tell you that a wolf isn't ever going to look twice at your livestock. But I will tell you that elk—not cattle or sheep—is his dinner of choice. And when he can't have elk, coyotes are easy pickings. So either way, the odds are that you have nothing to worry about when it comes to your livestock."

"Tell that to Matthew Grisham," a thin-faced elderly woman said coldly from the front row. "And Ned Berry and the Lane bunch. I can name you dozens of families that almost went under because those murdering monsters took a liking to the taste of beef and wiped out half their herds. Some of them had to file bankruptcy. Some of them never recovered. A few even sold out and moved to the city and never came back where they belonged. All because of those damn wolves."

"But that's not going to happen this time," Elizabeth assured her. "We're not going to just turn the wolves loose to roam free. They'll be carefully monitored. And at the first sign of trouble, any rogue killers will be shipped out of here."

"Before or after we're all bankrupt?"

She tried to explain that she would never stand by and let the situation get so desperate, but she might as well have saved her breath. Most of the people in the crowd had already decided that the government was comprised of a bunch of liberal tree huggers who cared more about cramming a bunch of ruthless killers down their throats than their rights, and there was nothing Elizabeth could say to persuade them otherwise.

Not that she didn't try. For the next hour, she patiently answered questions—and accusations—and explained the steps of the program over and over again. But when the meeting finally broke up, people were just as resentful as ever.

Resigned to the fact that she was, in all likelihood, never going to win the more hostile citizens over, she smiled ruefully as Peter and Tina joined her at the podium while the rest of the crowd headed for the exits. "Well, that went rather well, don't you think?"

"Oh, yeah," Peter drawled, his grin mocking. "For a public lynching."

"For a moment there, I thought you were toast," Tina told her, her brown eyes dancing behind her glasses. "But you gave 'em what for, boss. I'm proud of you. Let's celebrate. We can pick up a bottle of wine—"

"No celebrating until the project's a success," she reminded her. "And if tonight was any indication of the progress we're making with people, we've still got a long way to go."

She didn't have to tell Tina or Peter how quickly things could turn nasty. They'd been at Yellowstone with her. They'd been refused service at gas stations and restaurants and even been thrown out of their apartment. They'd seen firsthand how people could lash out in fear and hate, and for all their sakes, she hoped people showed more restraint in Colorado.

Reading her mind, Peter said soberly, "It's not as bad as Yellowstone. People might not like us being here and they don't hesitate to speak their minds when they get the chance, but the phone calls are usually at a decent hour, and they're not as vicious as I expected. All and all, the locals are tolerating us, and that's more than a lot of folks did last time.''

''And things will be much better once the wolves are actually released and the ranchers realize they don't have nearly as much to fear as they first thought,'' Tina added. ''They'll come around. It's just going to take some time.''

Elizabeth knew most people were decent—but those weren't the ones she was worried about. It was the fanatics, the survivalists who went a little too far, the antigovernment types who saw all government projects as a threat to their rights, that were as unpredictable as the wolves they claimed to hate. So when she gathered her notes and slipped into her coat, it went without saying that Tina and Peter would walk her to her car, now that the crowd had dispersed and the streets were dark and empty.

Her Jeep was right where she'd left it, under a streetlight, and appeared untouched. Still a block away, she told her friends, ''You don't have to walk me the rest of the way. I'll be fine—''

Whatever she was going to say next died on her tongue as she spied the man leaning against her front fender. His own vehicle was parked across the street from hers, but it was hers he rested against, his black hair glinting in the golden glow from the streetlight, totally unconcerned with the fact that the temperature hovered somewhere around the mid-twenties. He looked up, saw her and smiled, and even from a block away, Elizabeth felt the kick of his dimples. Annoyed, she frowned. Why did the infuriating man have to be so attractive?

Beside her, Tina followed her gaze to her car and groaned softly. ''Be still my heart. If ever a man looked as if he was up to mischief, that one does. Need some help?''

''No, she doesn't,'' Peter answered for her. His smile

indulgent, he took his wife's hand in his and grinned down at her. "Behave yourself. I met Mr. McBride before the meeting started, and I'm sure Elizabeth can handle him just fine by herself. Say good-night, Tina."

Not the least bit repentant, Tina obediently said, "Good night, Tina."

Chuckling, Elizabeth hugged her, then Peter. "Thanks for coming with me tonight, guys. I wouldn't have wanted to face that crowd alone."

A former pro football player with shoulders as broad as a boxcar, Peter hesitated and cast one more look at where Zeke McBride waited at her car. "You will be okay, won't you? Mr. McBride said he stopped and helped you last night when you got stuck in the snow. If you don't want to talk to him—"

"I'll be fine, Peter," she assured him, touched. "I'll see you both in the morning at the office."

"I want to hear all about this!" Tina called softly as her husband dragged her away. "Every little detail."

Elizabeth could have told her right then there would be nothing to tell, but she only waved and turned back toward her car...and Zeke McBride.

Leaning against her fender, his arms folded over his chest and his feet crossed at the ankles, Zeke watched in appreciation as she approached. The lady was, he had to admit, one surprise after another. To look at her, a man could be forgiven for thinking she was a cream puff. Soft. It was the first word that came to mind when she'd walked into the hall tonight and he'd gotten his first good look at her in the light. Soft honey-colored hair, soft skin, soft, tender mouth that invited a man to touch, to kiss, to lose himself in. Then he got a look at that stubborn chin of hers and should have known she could handle whatever life threw at her. She certainly had last night. And tonight.

He still couldn't get over the antagonism that had slapped her right in the face the minute she started the meeting. He'd known Larry Dawson and Jack Jenkins and Thelma St. John and most of the others who had angrily expressed their opinion all of his life, and they weren't the kind of people to condemn someone for doing their job.

Every other woman he knew would have left the meeting in tears, but not Elizabeth Davis. Oh, no. She was made of sterner stuff than that. She'd lifted that stubborn chin of hers and held her own. And when the meeting came to an end, her head was high, her spine straight. She had spunk, and he liked that.

Especially when she had that "don't mess with me, mister" glint in her eye the way she did now.

She was still steamed at him for teasing her in front of Nick. Grinning, he settled more comfortably against her car and waited for the fireworks to fly as she drew near. He didn't have to wait long.

Walking straight to him, she lit into him. "I don't know what you think you were doing in there, Mr. McBride, but you wasted your time. I plan to tell Nick all about my little fib tomorrow."

Making no effort to hide the amusement he knew would infuriate her, he said, "That's good. A wife shouldn't have secrets from her husband."

"He's *not* my husband!" she ground out between her clenched teeth. "I lied. Obviously you already know that, but what else was I supposed to do? It was dark and there was nobody else around, and for all I knew, you were a serial killer. I had to say something to make you go away and leave me alone."

"It was a smart move. You think quick on your feet,"

he said approvingly, and had the satisfaction of seeing her drop her jaw. Chuckling, he nudged her under the chin and gently closed her mouth. "Careful, Mrs. Kincaid, you'll catch flies."

Scowling, she jerked back, her green eyes sparking fire. "You can be the most infuriating man. If you've had your fun, I'd appreciate it if you'd find somewhere else to sit besides my car. It's late and I'd like to go home."

She expected him to give her a hard time, but he was nothing if not accommodating. Pushing to his feet, he took her keys from her before she could guess his intention, unlocked the driver's door for her and pulled it open. Before she could slip into the driver's seat, however, he stopped her with a hand on her arm. "People around here are usually a lot more polite to newcomers," he said seriously. "It's the government that's got people's shorts in a twist, not you. Try not to take it personally."

Elizabeth knew he was right. The more vocal ones in the crowd tonight were all decent people. They were just mad and frustrated and looking for someone to blame. "I know," she sighed. "People are angry and they've got to vent that anger on someone. Unfortunately, that's the downside of the job. I'm the only target in sight."

Just that easily, his grin was back, more wicked than ever. "Poor baby. Feeling used and abused? Why don't we go over to Ed's for some hot-fudge cake? What do you say?"

Just that easily, he asked her out and didn't have a clue how he tempted her. Liberty Hill was barely more than a wide spot in the road, and it had only one restaurant. Ed's Diner, owned and operated by Ed Randolph, a former prison chef who had a mouth-watering way with anything chocolate. Her first week in town, Elizabeth had walked in expecting meat loaf and home cooking on the menu and found instead the best desserts she'd ever had the good fortune to stumble across. Instantly falling in love, she was a regular there now, just like all the other locals.

But her heart thundered just at the thought of going there or anywhere else with Zeke McBride. How could she even consider it? This was a man who, according to his own friends and neighbors, had betrayed his fiancée with another woman a week before their wedding. He was just like her father, and with nothing more than a smile and a teasing line, he'd made her forget that. And that made him far too dangerous for her peace of mind.

Immediately drawing back, she said, stiffly, "I'm sorry, but I can't." And with no more explanation than that, she slipped around him and slid into her car.

Standing in the middle of the road, his hands buried in the pockets of his jacket as he watched her drive away, Zeke stared after her, a bemused grin flirting with his mouth. So his brother was right. She didn't date. He'd just have to see what he could do to change that.

Elizabeth told herself that putting Zeke McBride out of her mind should have been a piece of cake. After all, she had more important things to worry about. In less than two weeks, three months of hard work would culminate in the release of the wolves back into the wild, and it was her job to make sure that went off without a hitch. With a lot of work still left to do before that could happen, she didn't have time to brood over a man.

But every time she turned around over the course of the next few days, it seemed as if she was tripping over Zeke McBride and his wicked, knowing smile. It was enough to drive a sane woman right out of her tree. Frustrated, she tried to convince herself it was no more than she should have expected. Liberty Hill was hardly bigger than a postage stamp, and in a town that small, a person couldn't sneeze without someone across the way saying, "Bless you." If she'd just ignore him, he'd go away.

But she couldn't. She ran into him everywhere: the post office, the gas station, the drugstore. Then, on Sunday, she took a seat in one of the back pews of the Methodist church, moved to pass the collection plate, and there he was, sitting with his family at the far end of the very aisle she sat on, his smile full of the devil—and in church, no less!

Jerking her gaze from his, she snapped her eyes to the front and swallowed a groan. What was he doing here? Zeke McBride was a rogue and a flirt, the kind of man who slept in on Sunday mornings after partying hard Saturday night. He had no business being at the early service with his family, looking for all the world like a choirboy in a suit and tie with his hair slicked back!

Chewing on her bottom lip, she tried to convince herself she'd mistaken someone else for him. But there was no one else in town with those engaging dimples and laughing eyes who seemed to enjoy watching her quite as much as he did. He caught her staring and winked at her, and she wanted to sink right through the floor. Letting her breath out in a huff, she jerked her gaze to the front again and pointedly ignored him. But all through the service, she could feel his eyes on her.

If she hadn't been so irritated, she might have been amused. She suspected that a man with his kind of charm didn't get turned down very often. His ego was bruised, poor baby, and he didn't like it. He thought if he smiled and flirted with her every time fate threw them in each other's path, he'd eventually win her over. He thought wrong.

Granted, the man had a way about him, a self-deprecating sparkle in his eyes that always caught her off guard and had her fighting a smile. But she wasn't looking for a man, didn't want one. Her stay in Liberty Hill was a limited one, and her work was the only thing she was interested in. Still, it took all her concentration not to sneak a peek to her right to see if Zeke was still watching her from the far end of the pew.

All her senses focused on him, she didn't even hear the rest of the service. Suddenly the minister was giving the benediction, the organist jumped into a hymn, and people rose to linger and visit. Normally Elizabeth would have stuck around to do the same. But when she saw Zeke standing in the center aisle at the end of the pew, just daring her to come his way, her heart lurched in her breast, and like a coward, she cut out a side door to the parking lot. As the door swished shut behind her, she would have sworn she heard the infuriating man chuckle.

She won that round, but she wasn't foolish enough to think her luck would hold forever. And it didn't. The very next day she was in the town's only grocery store when Zeke walked in and cornered her in the produce section. Trapped, her heart starting to trip over itself, she could do nothing but stand there as he strolled toward her with a male grace she'd have given anything not to have noticed.

"Well, well," he teased with a broad grin. "If it isn't Liz Davis hanging out with the other hot tomatoes. What's for supper, sweetheart? Spaghetti and meatballs? Great! I'll bring the wine."

She shouldn't have encouraged him, but he had a way of surprising a laugh out of her. "Nice try, Romeo, but the last time I made spaghetti and meatballs, it came out of a can. I don't think you'd like it. And just for the record, it's Elizabeth. There's only one Liz and her last name's Taylor."

"Hey, no problem," he said easily. "You're right. You

don't look a thing like her. But Lizzie? It's got a ring to it. I like it.'' Pleased with himself, he flashed his dimples at her. ''So what time do you want to eat tonight, Lizzie? Don't worry, you won't have to haul out the can opener. I'll cook.''

Not sure if she wanted to laugh or cry, Elizabeth thought he had to be the most incorrigible man she'd ever met. And she had no intention of telling him just how much she abhorred the nickname Lizzie, or she'd be stuck with it for the rest of her stay in Liberty Hill.

Giving him an arch look, she said, ''For me? I don't think so.''

''Why not? You think I can't cook?''

''I'm sure there's no end to your talents, but—''

''You're turning me down,'' he finished for her, grinning. ''Again.''

She couldn't deny it—or stop her lips from twitching. '''Fraid so. Are you horribly offended?''

''I don't know if I'll ever get over the disappointment,'' he said with a straight face. ''Sure you don't want to change your mind? You're passing up the chance of a lifetime. I'm a darn good cook.''

Elizabeth would have sworn he couldn't tempt her, but caught in the warmth of his smile, she was stunned by the sudden need to give in, just this once, and say yes. Her eyes searching his, she wondered wildly if she was losing her mind. The man was a flirt. He had the gift of gab and a talent for making a woman feel as if she was the only female on the planet—until a prettier one came along and distracted him. She knew that, accepted it…and liked him in spite of it.

And that scared her to death.

Shaken—God, how could she have let this happen?— she quickly gathered up her groceries. ''I'm sure you make a mean marinara, but it's been a long day and I wouldn't be very good company. Ask somebody else.'' Brushing past him, she hurried to the checkout stand.

''Elizabeth, wait! Dammit, I didn't mean to upset you. Let's talk about this.''

But she couldn't wait, couldn't take the chance that he would charm her into changing her mind. Abandoning the items she'd meant to purchase, she rushed outside to her Jeep and sped away like the hounds of hell were after her.

Too agitated to think clearly, she couldn't have said where she was going. She just had to get away, to think. She would have sworn she just drove aimlessly, but when she found herself pulling into the parking lot that over-looked the holding pen at Eagle Ridge, she wasn't really surprised. She could spend hours there just watching her wolves.

They weren't hers, of course. She could keep them penned up for the rest of their lives, and they would never be anything but wild. But she had handpicked all twelve of them from the wilds of Canada, had them checked to make sure they were free of disease, then organized the complicated process of transferring them to Colorado. And wild or not, somewhere along the way, she had come to think of them as hers.

She loved them all, but two in particular tugged at her heartstrings. Napoleon and Queenie. The alpha male and female of the group, they were officially assigned numbers for names, but right from the beginning, their strong, regal personalities had demanded names, and Elizabeth hadn't been able to resist.

Gray wolves, they were both big and strong and hadn't liked each other any more than they had her at first. They'd nipped and growled and snarled, warily circling each other like two adversaries in a boxing match. They both bitterly resented their captivity, more so than the rest of the wolves, and never stopped looking for a way out. To this day, they still tried to dig their way out on a regular basis.

But in the process of trying to escape, something magical happened right before Elizabeth's eyes. Dislike turned to grudging acceptance, then, gradually, to a reluctant trust. And with trust, everything changed. Like two teenagers falling in love, they played and nuzzled each other and even grabbed the other's snout in a clear sign of affection. And when they slept, they slept closer and closer together, until they finally curled up next to each other as though they'd been doing it all their lives.

But while they had accepted each other, they still had not accepted her or any of their other captors, and for that, Elizabeth was grateful. They would soon be released into the wild again, and if the pack was to survive, the wolves had to be suspicious of humans. That didn't mean, however, that Napoleon and Queenie hadn't learned to communicate with her. Waiting at the front of the pen, almost as if they'd known she was coming, they didn't cower from her as the rest of the pack did. Instead, they glared at her with unblinking disdain and just dared her to come anywhere near them.

She didn't, of course, not without sedating them first, and that was done only when an animal appeared to have a health problem and needed to be examined. But, Lord, they were something to see. Scowling at her as if she was the cause of all his problems, Napoleon looked right at her and howled mournfully. A split second later, Queenie joined in, then the rest of the wolves, lifting their snouts to the sky in an eerie serenade.

From her years of study, Elizabeth knew that wolves would come running from miles away for a good howling, but it wasn't often that she was witness to such a spontaneous songfest. Delighted, she laughed. "I know you want out of there," she told Napoleon when the howling ended as quickly as it had begun. "I'm just as anxious for you to run free as you are. But you're going to have to be patient and give it till the end of the week. Then you and Queenie can start your life together."

In actuality, though, they had already done that. Wolves mated for life, and Napoleon and Queenie were clearly devoted to each other. Pregnant and due to den within weeks of her release, Queenie would soon give birth to the first wolf pups born in that area of Colorado in generations. In the days and weeks to come, when their pups were born and the two of them worked together to ensure the growth and survival of the family unit, the bond between them would grow even stronger.

And Elizabeth envied them that. They were just animals, but they could teach humans a thing or two about loving. Why couldn't she find a man who was looking for that kind of commitment?

Because you keeping running into ones like Zeke McBride and your father, a voice retorted in her head. They're charming and funny and endearing...and they wouldn't know the meaning of commitment if they tripped over it. If you forget that, even for a second, you're going to get hurt just like your mother.

That, she assured herself grimly as she headed home later, wasn't going to happen. She wasn't her mother. She wouldn't make the mistakes her mother had. She loved her dearly, but she wasn't weak like her. As much as Zeke had tempted her earlier, she wouldn't let herself fall for a man who was a flirt. That could only lead to heartache, and that was something she was determined to avoid.

Considering that, she should have been able to dismiss Zeke from her thoughts with a mental snap of her fingers.

But when she opened a can of soup and heated it for supper, she could hear him teasing her about hauling out the can opener. All too easily, she could see that grin of his as he tried to wheedle her into letting him cook for her. And despite herself, she couldn't hold back a smile.

And it didn't stop there. Throughout the rest of the evening, he slipped in and out of her thoughts at will, teasing her, distracting her and making a general pest of himself. In self-defense, she turned to her work. She had a progress report on the wolves to write for her boss, but when she sat down at her computer, she couldn't seem to think of anything but Zeke. By the time she organized her jumbled thoughts and finally got the thing written, it was going on midnight, and she was as disgusted with herself as she was with him.

She would not, she promised herself, take the infuriating man to bed with her! There were limits to just how much she would let him bother her, and he had just reached it. Before she'd spend the night dreaming of him, she'd stay up all night reading a murder mystery!

But when she finally crawled into bed, she'd hardly punched her pillow into a comfortable position when the phone rang, and all thoughts of Zeke flew right out of her head. Her heart pounding, she froze, dread welling in her throat. She didn't try to fool herself into thinking the caller on the other end of the line was a friend. Like Tina and Peter, she'd gotten her share of nuisance calls in the early evening, but occasionally, over the course of the past week, there'd been others that she hadn't told them about, ones that were vile and filthy and upsetting.

Every time she got one, she thought about calling Nick and reporting it, but she'd been through this all before, and she knew from past experience that it wouldn't do any good. The calls were short and nearly impossible to trace, and were made by a number of callers. If she called in the sheriff, word would get out that she was scared, and that was just what her detractors wanted. And she'd be damned if she'd give them the satisfaction.

Still, she considered letting the answering machine take the call. But no one ever left an incriminating message on tape. Instead, they kept calling back throughout the night until she finally answered in person. Resigned, she reached for the phone.

"Hello?"

"Well, if it isn't the wolf lady herself," a cold, ugly voice sneered in her ear. "Bitch! Why aren't you up on Eagle Ridge with those killers of yours? You're just like them, you know. You're nothing but a…"

His language abruptly turned even more obscene, and Elizabeth stopped listening. When she'd first moved to town and started getting hostile calls, she'd tried to reason with the callers and make them understand that they really had nothing to fear. But she'd quickly learned she was just wasting her breath. People didn't want to be educated about wolves or hear how they could benefit the area. All they knew was that the wolves were a threat to them and they wanted them gone—and her along with them.

She didn't want to antagonize people, but giving up on the project wasn't something she was willing to do. So she let the callers have their say even though she didn't listen to it, assured them she would consider their opinion when policies were set, then hung up, dismissing them from her thoughts as quickly as she could.

This caller, however, was particularly vile and not so easily ignored. When he threatened her personally, she recoiled in distaste. She didn't, she told herself, get paid enough to tolerate this kind of verbal abuse. Not even bothering to defend herself, she started to hang up. Then he threatened the wolves.

"Everybody knows where you're hiding them," he told her slyly. "Right up there on Eagle Ridge in that fancy cyclone fence corral you built with taxpayers' money. You ever stand up there in the trees and look down on them?" he taunted. "They look just like ducks in a barrel. And everybody knows just how easy it is to pick off ducks in a barrel. You don't even need a scope."

Elizabeth's heart stopped dead in her chest. *Ignore him!* a voice cried in her head. *He doesn't mean it. He'd never have the guts to shoot them—he's just a coward who gets off hiding behind a phone line and making threats. Don't even give him the satisfaction of an answer. He's just pushing your buttons.*

She knew that, but she couldn't slam the phone down as she wanted to. Not when her wolves might be in jeopardy. "If you harm so much as a hair on their heads, I swear I'll make sure you spend the next twenty years behind bars," she said fiercely. "Stay away from my wolves!"

"Too late," he said mockingly, and hung up.

For what seemed like an eternity, Elizabeth just lay there, the dial tone echoing softly in her ear. With horrifying ease, she could see someone standing on the ridge that overlooked the holding pen, using the trapped wolves one by one for target practice.

"No!"

She didn't remember rolling out of bed or grabbing her clothes, but within moments, she was racing in her car toward Eagle Ridge, breaking every speed limit she came to without even checking her speed. Terrified of what she would find when she got there, she prayed like she had never prayed in her life. And over and over again, the prayer was always the same. "God, please don't let me be too late!"

Chapter 3

Half expecting the wolves to be lying in pools of their own blood, she raced into the holding pen's parking area and braked to a screeching halt, not even bothering to cut the engine before she burst from the car with her flashlight clutched in her hand. An icy wind slapped her in the face, but she never even noticed. All her attention was focused on the holding pen and the wolves.

Her heart slamming against her ribs, afraid of what she would find, she unconsciously held her breath as she swept the beam of her flashlight over the pen. She wouldn't have been surprised to find the wolves injured or even dead, but at first glance they appeared perfectly fine. They weren't used to seeing her at night, but they still greeted her with their usual mournful howling.

Her knees turning to jelly at the sight of them, Elizabeth laughed weakly. "Good evening to you, too. I guess I came charging out here to the rescue for nothing. You guys look just fine."

Then she noticed Napoleon. He hadn't come forward as he usually did to greet her, but instead paced agitatedly inside the pen's western perimeter, his attention divided between her and something off in the trees outside the pen. Concerned, she turned her flashlight into the trees. "What is it, boy? What's wrong?"

Nothing moved in the night. Frowning, she swept the powerful beam of her flashlight back and forth among the lodgepole pines to the west of where the holding pen sat in the middle of the small mountain meadow. Then, just when she was convinced that she was imagining the wolf's agitation, she caught sight of something lying on the ground at the edge of the clearing. Bathed in shadows, it was impossible to tell what it was in the darkness, but the goose bumps that suddenly raced over Elizabeth's skin told her whatever it was, she wasn't going to like it.

In the two and a half months that she'd been making nearly daily visits to the holding pen, the place had become as familiar to her as the lines on the palms of her hands. She'd been there at all hours of the day and night, and despite the animosity she'd had to deal with from the locals, she'd never been afraid.

But as she started around the west side of the pen armed with nothing but a flashlight, she became aware for the first time of just how isolated the pen was. Set back from the highway and surrounded by trees, it was out of sight of the road and miles from the nearest neighbor. It was that very isolation that had made the meadow the perfect site for the holding pen, but that was hardly reassuring now. All she could think of was that if she had to scream for help, no one would hear her.

Too late she realized that she never should have come out there alone, especially at that hour of the night. She wasn't one of those paranoid women who was afraid of her own shadow—she didn't scare easily. But right then her gut was telling her that there was something sinister on the edge of the woods, and all her instincts were urging her to run for the car and get the hell out of there. But by then, she was less than twenty feet away from the shadowy object lying on the ground on the edge of the clearing, and even as she started to turn away, it came into focus and she realized what it was. Something dead.

Alarmed, she rushed forward, afraid that one of the wolves had somehow gotten out of the pen and been shot by whoever had called her. But as she drew closer, it quickly became apparent that the animal wasn't a wolf, but a coyote. And it hadn't been shot. There was no blood, nothing from outward appearances to show what had killed it. It just looked as though it had fallen where it stood.

Then she saw the meat.

The coyote had collapsed on top of it, half concealing it from view, but from what she could see, it appeared to be a large slab of beef. Swallowing thickly, Elizabeth's blood ran cold at the sight of it. She didn't have to have it analyzed by a lab to know that it was laced with poison.

Just that quickly, she was furious. And scared for Napoleon and the others. This was just a warning, a threat left by someone with a sick mind. Whoever the bastard was, he wanted her to know that he could have killed every one of her wolves tonight if he'd wanted to simply by throwing the poisoned meat over the fence. And next time, he just might.

No! she raged silently. It wasn't going to happen. If the bastard thought she would stand around wringing her hands and let him get away with that, he could think again. Nobody terrorized her or her wolves.

The light of battle shining in her green eyes, she stormed back to her car and retrieved her cell phone from her purse.

Punching in the number of the sheriff's office, she said, "Nick, this is Elizabeth Davis. We've got a problem."

The kitchen in Zeke's mother's house hadn't changed for as long as he could remember. Big and open, with pane-glassed cabinets and an old commercial stove that had cooked thousands of meals for family and ranch hands alike, it was full of sunlight and the smells of breakfast in the morning. Sitting at the old scarred table that had been in the family longer than anyone could remember, Zeke took his first sip of coffee of the day and savored it with a groan of appreciation.

It was barely six o'clock and his mother was already cooking breakfast. Joe and Merry were out in the barn checking on an ailing mare, and Janey was upstairs getting ready for work at the nursing home in town. It would be at least another hour or longer before the sun even thought about putting in an appearance, but the day had already started. And he didn't even have his eyes open yet.

When the phone rang, his mother answered it without missing a beat as she turned pancakes on the grill. Recognizing the caller, she smiled broadly. "Well, good morning, Steve. And how are you today?"

Setting his mug down with a thud at the mention of his boss's name, Zeke frantically motioned that he wasn't there. "Tell him I went fishing or to an auction. Anything!"

Her blue eyes sparkling with laughter, his mother nodded, only to give him up without a whimper of protest. "Yes, he's here," she said. "And scowling at me like a three-year-old. You're not going to call him back to work, are you? He just got here."

"Tell him to call somebody else," Zeke said loudly enough that his friend and boss had to catch it. "I'm on vacation."

His mother, listening to the other man, grinned and held out the phone. "He says you're right where he needs you to be. If he's lying, he'll sell you his '65 Mustang."

Still suspicious, Zeke hesitated. The Mustang was one of the few things that Steve Haily didn't joke about. He'd always claimed that he'd sell his soul before he'd sell that car, and Zeke didn't doubt it for a minute. He loved the damn thing—even if it was turquoise.

Frowning, he took the receiver from his mother and braced for a trick. "This better be good, Haily. I'm not due to punch in again for another week and a half."

"Did I ask you to punch in?" the other man asked with a feigned innocence Zeke saw right through. "I just thought you might want to look into something for me while you're in that neck of the woods and get another two weeks vacation for it since you'd officially be on the job. But hey, if you're not interested, I just may take this one myself. The big boys in Washington are damn sensitive about this wolf project they've got going down there—"

In the process of reaching for his coffee, Zeke almost spilled it. "Wolf project?" he repeated sharply, now wide awake. "Are you talking about Elizabeth Davis?"

"Yeah," he said, surprised. "You know the lady?"

"Yeah. I sat in on a town meeting last week to bring the locals up to speed on the project. Things got kind of heated. Has something happened to her?"

"Not yet," his boss said grimly, "but I don't like the sound of what's going on down there. Apparently she's been getting nuisance calls ever since she moved to town to set up the project, but she's been handling that all right— until last night. Someone threatened the wolves, then left some poisoned meat outside the wolves' holding pen to make a point. The lady herself went out there around midnight and found the meat next to a dead coyote."

Zeke swore. Little fool! What the hell did she think she was doing, traipsing around the woods at that hour of the night by herself? She should have called Nick, dammit, and let him check out the situation for her. She knew how people felt about the project—they'd certainly made no secret of it the other night at the town meeting. It was a powder keg, just waiting to explode. All it needed was a nut to light the match, and somebody was going to get hurt. Last night it could have been her.

His gut clenching at the thought, he didn't have to think twice about whether he wanted to give up his vacation to take a case someone else could have handled. That decision was made the second Steve mentioned Elizabeth's name. "I'll start checking it out first thing this morning," he promised.

"We're going to have to install more squirrel equipment in the trees at the edge of the clearing," Elizabeth told Peter and Tina grimly the next morning.

Her eyes burning from too little sleep, she'd spent what was left of the night at the holding pen after Nick inspected the area and announced that whoever had been there was now gone. He'd tried to convince her to go home, and she'd promised she would after he left, but she hadn't been able to bring herself to leave. So she'd sat in her car, run the heater and made plans. And the first thing she'd decided was that security had to be increased at the holding pen.

Peter agreed. "I'll get on it right away."

The team's security expert, he was in charge of the secret squirrel equipment that monitored activity around the perimeter of the holding pen. If anything so much as moved within fifteen feet of the pen, an alarm sounded on the beepers they all carried with them. Which was why no alarms had sounded last night. The poisoned meat that Nick had confiscated and sent to the lab in Colorado Springs had been planted thirty feet from the compound's west boundary.

"I hate to be the one to bring up the topic, but what about money?" Tina asked bluntly. "We're working on a shoestring as it is...which is why we didn't wire the trees around the meadow in the first place," she reminded them. "Who's going to pay for this?"

"I'll find a way to deal with it," Elizabeth promised. "The whole purpose of the project is to release the wolves back into the wild. That's not going to happen if we can't keep them safe until their release date."

The phone rang then, drawing a groan from her. Despite the fact that Liberty Hill was so small it didn't even have its own newspaper, the word had somehow already gotten out about the threat against the wolves the previous night, and calls about the episode had been coming in ever since she walked in the door ten minutes ago. Not surprisingly, reaction was mixed. Some expressed horror over the attempted poisoning, while still others called to warn her that this was no more than she should have expected when she brought those killing monsters into the county in the first place.

"Go ahead and draw up an estimate of what this is going to cost us," she told Peter as she reached for the phone. "I'll call Irene just as soon as you have the numbers."

But her boss was already on the other end of the line, calling to get the particulars about last night. "It sounds like you had quite an evening," Irene Johnson said dryly. "I guess I don't have to ask where you spent the night. Did you get any sleep at all?"

Tired, her body aching from sitting up all night, Elizabeth had to laugh. No one knew her like Irene. "Not much, but I couldn't take a chance that whoever left that meat would come back during the night and finish his dirty work.''

''Of course not,'' the other woman agreed. ''I'd have done the same thing. I'll put in a requisition for security cameras.''

Not surprised that their minds were on the same track, she told her about the numbers Peter was already working on. ''I'll fax them to you as soon as he's finished. How *did* you hear about this, anyway? I didn't tell anyone but the sheriff, and I've been getting calls from all over the county ever since I got in this morning.''

''Evidently, the good sheriff has been concerned about the situation for some time. He notified poison control and the state police, and that started the ball rolling. The powers that be in Washington have decided to send you some help.''

''Help?'' she echoed, frowning. ''You mean with security?''

''Not exactly. He's a Ph.D.—''

''A *what?*''

''I know what you're thinking,'' the older woman said quickly, ''but it's not as bad as it sounds. Wolves aren't exactly his specialty, but he is a wildlife biologist, so it's not like he's one of those crazy scientists who never steps out of the lab.''

''But I don't need help with the wolves, Irene,'' Elizabeth said in frustration. ''*I've* got that under control. It's the threats against them that I'm worried about. Their release date is only days away. If whoever called me last night carries through on his threats, they could all be dead by then!''

''Not if Fish and Wildlife has anything to say about it,'' Irene retorted. ''That's why they've called in this McBride fellow—''

Sure she must have heard her wrong, Elizabeth stiffened. "McBride!" she said sharply. "Did you say McBride?"

"Yeah. Zeke McBride. Why? Have you heard of him? He grew up in the area, which is one of the reasons the powers that be wanted him on the job. He not only knows the terrain, but the people. And he's good. Damn good, from what I've heard. He has a degree in criminology and is one of Fish and Wildlife's best troubleshooters. Not your average egghead, huh?"

At that moment the main door to the office opened and Elizabeth looked up from her conversation just in time to see Zeke walk in. "Speak of the devil," she told her boss quietly. "Einstein himself just walked in. I'll call you back."

He started toward her as she hung up, and she was forced to admit that a woman would have to be stone-cold dead and in the ground a week not to appreciate a tall drink of water like Zeke McBride. And as much as she hated to admit it, she was far from dead where he was concerned.

She'd thought about him last night, during the long hours between three and four in the morning when her defenses were down and she couldn't control her own thoughts. His smile, the mischief in his eyes, the way her heart just seemed to roll over whenever she turned around and he was there. And it shook her. She didn't want to like him, didn't want to think about him, didn't want him in her world. And now she had to work with him? She didn't think so! There had to be another solution.

Agitated, aware of Tina's and Peter's interested eyes, she pushed to her feet and said, "We can talk in the back room."

Without another word she headed for the small room where the security monitoring system was set up, and turned on him the second the door shut behind them. "I can't work with you. We'd be at each other's throats inside an hour.''

Far from perturbed—and apparently not the least bit surprised that she knew why he was there—he grinned. ''She wants me. Yes!''

She would *not,* she promised herself, laugh. The man was already full of himself as it was. But her lips still kept struggling with the need to curl into a smile as she said dryly, ''Somebody has a hearing problem here, and it's not me. I said 'I can't work with you,' McBride. Not 'I want you.' There's a difference.''

''Oh, no, there's not,'' he argued, his eyes teasing. ''You can't work with me because *you want me.*''

''I do not!''

''I understand, sweetheart,'' he soothed. ''But if we're going to work together, there's something you should know. I don't play around on the job. I know you're disappointed, but there's a time and a place for a thing like that, and you're just going to have to control yourself.''

He was so outrageous that Elizabeth couldn't help but strangle on a laugh. Drat the man! Why did she keep letting him do this to her? ''*I'm* not the one who's got a problem with self-control,'' she finally told him when she could manage to do so with a straight face. ''And even if I were, it's not an issue, since we're not going to be working together.''

Far from discouraged, he only grinned. ''One of these days we'll see about that self-control of yours, but you're right. It's not an issue. Control or no control, we're working together. The suits in Washington want me in on this, so it looks like we're stuck with each other.''

She wanted to argue, to cry out that this couldn't be happening, but she'd worked for the government bureaucracy long enough to know that when orders came down from on high, they were followed to the letter if you planned to keep your job. Like it or not, he'd been called in on the case, and there was nothing she could do about it.

Frustrated, she tried to take consolation in the fact that it wouldn't be forever. It wasn't as if he was going to be involved in the project itself. His sole purpose was to catch the sicko who'd left that threatening meat for her wolves, which meant he would be working with Nick, not her. *That* she could tolerate, if it meant keeping her wolves safe.

"All right," she said, sounding resigned. "You made your point. We have to work together—but on a limited basis. If we're going to do that successfully, I suggest that we both act as professional as possible. That means you don't call me sweetheart."

"Whatever you say, Lizzie, darlin'," he retorted, then chuckled when she groaned. His grin quickly faded, though, when he brought up the subject of last night. "Tell me about what happened. I already talked to Nick, but I'd like to hear your version of the story."

They returned to the main office then, and she told him everything from the moment she'd gotten the phone call last night, leaving nothing out. Jotting down notes, Zeke didn't know if he wanted to shake her or lock her up in one of Nick's jail cells to keep her safe when he learned that she'd spent the night at the holding pen. Crazy woman, didn't she know what a chance she'd taken?

Dead serious now, he said, "Tell me again about the phone call. Close your eyes and replay it in your head. Is there a possibility that you've heard this guy's voice before?"

Startled, her eyes flew open. "Oh, I don't think so!"

"Don't be so quick to dismiss the idea," he told her solemnly. "This is a small community. In the three months you've been here, you've probably talked to just about everyone in a fifty-mile radius without even realizing it. Think about it. At one time or another, everyone goes to the post office, the grocery store, church. And then there's the town meeting the other night. Quite a few jackasses stood up and raked you over the coals. Could the caller have been one of them?''

''Oh, surely not!'' she replied. ''The whole town was there, including the sheriff. What kind of nut would publicly criticize me, then threaten to kill one of the wolves? He had to know that would automatically make him a suspect.''

''If he was playing with a full deck, yes,'' he agreed. ''But at this point we have no evidence that this man is completely sane, so there's no way to say what he's capable of.''

''Are you saying he'll carry through on his threats?''

She sounded so horrified that he wished he could assure her that wasn't going to happen, but he couldn't. ''He left poisoned meat for you to find,'' he said flatly. ''Frankly, I wouldn't put anything past him.''

She paled at that, but he had to give her credit, she didn't cower from the truth. ''Then we'll just have to make sure he doesn't get the chance.''

Closing her eyes, Elizabeth concentrated on the conversation that had sent her racing out to Eagle Ridge last night, but she couldn't for the life of her remember so much as a single inflection that sounded familiar. ''I'm sorry,'' she finally said with a shake of her head, ''but if I've ever spoken with this man before, I have no memory of it. His voice was sort of flat, without much of an accent. And cold. Very cold.''

''But you'd know it if you heard it again on the street?''

''I'd know it on the other side of the moon,'' she retorted. ''Don't worry—if I hear it again, you'll know it. The whole town'll probably hear me screaming for the sheriff.''

Satisfied, he nodded. ''Good. In the meantime, we're not going to stand around with our hands in our pockets and wait for this jerk to give himself away. Get your coat. I need you to go with me out to Eagle Ridge and walk me through what you found there last night.''

There was nothing the least bit flirtatious in his remark. Once he'd started questioning her about last night, he'd been totally focused on the investigation. Still, Elizabeth hadn't forgotten that this was the same man who had teasingly asked her out every time he'd seen her over the course of the past few days.

Hesitating, she eyed him suspiciously. ''This is just business, isn't it, McBride?''

''Of course. What else would it be?''

Another woman might have fallen for that wounded choirboy look, but Elizabeth knew better. She'd seen it too many times on her father's face to be taken in. ''Then you won't mind if we go in separate cars, will you?'' she asked innocently. ''Just so we can each leave when we need to?''

She had him, and they both knew it. There was absolutely no reason why they had to drive out to Eagle Ridge together. Giving in graciously, he grinned, scoring her the point. ''You're quick, Lizzie. I like that.''

Fighting a grin of her own, she tried not to be charmed. It wasn't easy. ''You'd be wise not to forget it,'' she warned as she pulled her purse from the bottom drawer of her desk, then grabbed her coat. ''C'mon. Let's go.''

More than happy to trail after her, even if it was in a separate car, Zeke followed, grinning all the way. It wasn't a date, but a man had to take his victories where he could find them.

* * *

Unhappy with all the activity around their pen within the last twelve hours, the wolves, with Napoleon in the lead, greeted Elizabeth with a symphony of mournful howling that was truly something to hear. Impressed, Zeke waited for the eerie serenade to end before arching a brow at her. "Do they always do that?"

"Not to that extent, no," she said. "But they're still agitated from last night."

Nick had called someone to dispose of the dead coyote and marked the spot where the poisoned meat had been left with yellow spray paint, but the scent of death still lingered on the air. Restless, their hackles raised in warning, the wolves nervously prowled the inner perimeter of their pen, their gazes cold and steady as they watched their visitors suspiciously.

Moving to the yellow *X* Nick had left on the rocky ground, Zeke studied it and the surrounding area thoughtfully, but there was little to see. Whoever had threatened the wolves was no fool. He'd chosen the perfect night to strike out at the wolves. The wind had kicked up last night, blowing snow and covering tracks. With a windchill near zero, he hadn't had to worry about anyone being out and about near Eagle Ridge. He'd had the place all to himself.

Still, Zeke scoured the entire area for clues, but without much success. The wind had swept the landscape clean, leaving behind an unbroken expanse of snow that was free of tracks in every direction. If Zeke hadn't known better, he'd have sworn another human being hadn't been anywhere near the holding pen for at least a week.

Returning to where Elizabeth waited for him by her Jeep, he said, "The place is clean, but I pretty much expected that."

"So what happens next?"

His hands stuffed into the pockets of his down jacket, he said, "Once I get the lab report back on the meat and know what kind of poison it was laced with, I start tracking down the suppliers in the area."

"And how long will that take?"

"To get the lab results back? A week, less if we're lucky. I know," he said when she gasped in dismay. "That gives our boy a lot of time to cause trouble, but I've got other leads I can follow while I'm waiting on the lab. According to Nick, a lot of antigovernment thugs have moved into the county over the last couple of years, and more than a few of them were flapping their gums at the town meeting the other night. As soon as I get back to town, Nick and I are going to make some house calls and check out their whereabouts last night. In the meantime, you've got some decisions to make."

Surprised, she blinked. "About what?"

He nodded to the holding pen and the wolves who watched them warily. "The wolves. With the way things are heating up, I don't think you're going to be able to keep them safe much longer. This area's too isolated, and once word gets out about the poison, it's only going to give the rest of the nutcases out there ideas. The next person might not be content with just scaring you and riling them up. He could bring a gun with him."

Following his gaze to the holding pen and the tree-covered hills that rose around the meadow on all sides, Elizabeth felt her heart sink. Anyone who actually wanted to harm the wolves didn't have to come anywhere near them. With a high-powered rifle, they could hide in the hills overlooking the pen and, just as last night's caller had warned, pick the animals off like fish in a barrel.

Sick at the thought, she looked up at Zeke with eyes that were dark with worry. "So what do you suggest?"

"Release them early," he retorted promptly. "Today. Trust me, they'll be a lot safer on their own, running wild, than they will be in that pen. Unless, of course, they're in quarantine or something. They're not, are they?"

"Oh, no," she said. "They're disease free. They went through a battery of tests before they were even brought into the country. We've just kept them penned to make sure they were fully acclimated to the area before we opened the gates. After all the time and money that's been spent on this project, we didn't want them running back to Canada the first chance they got."

"They're scheduled to be released on Friday, anyway, aren't they? Is a few days going to make that much difference?"

"Not to the wolves. The locals are another matter. I already announced the release date. They're not going to be happy about moving it up, even if it is only a couple of days."

"They'll get over it," he assured her. "So you can release them. Today."

It wasn't a question, but a statement, one she had no argument for. He was right. The time had come to open the gate. The wolves were already fitted with radio collars that would transmit their every move in the wild. All she had to do was make a call to the office, notify Tina and Peter that the release had been moved up so the monitors tracking their movements would be watched, then open the gate and step back.

It should have been simple. Feeling a pang in the region of her heart, she reminded herself that she'd always known this day would come. She just hadn't expected to feel like an overprotective mother sending her firstborn out into the big, bad world without a quarter to call home in case he got into trouble.

When she hesitated, Zeke stared down at her quizzically. "Lizzie? What do you want to do? It's your call."

Caught up in her thoughts, she didn't even think to protest the use of the nickname. In the end there was no choice, and she knew it. From the moment the wolves were first captured in Canada months ago, she and an entire team of people from Canada to Colorado had been working toward this day, the day of their release. Nothing was more important than that. If she was sad because she would probably never again be able to get close to Queenie and Napoleon, that was her problem, one she had no business bringing to the job.

Forcing a smile, she said, "I've got to call the office."

Five minutes later, from the protection of the trees a thousand yards away, Elizabeth stood next to Zeke and watched the wolves eye the open gate to their prison with blatant suspicion. Not surprisingly, after three months of captivity, they didn't trust anything that altered the parameters of what had grudgingly become their home.

"The Yellowstone wolves wouldn't go anywhere near the open gate of their pen for two days when it was finally time to release them," she said huskily. Her gaze on Napoleon and Queenie, she never noticed that Zeke's attention was focused solely on her. "I think they associated the gate with their captors and wouldn't go anywhere near it. We eventually had to cut a hole in the fence at the back of the pen and bring in some roadkill before they could be tempted to leave the compound."

"You won't have to do that here," he said confidently. "The alpha male's too bold. What'd you name him?"

Caught off guard, Elizabeth jerked her eyes from the wolves up to his. "I never said I named him." She'd been careful not to. Officially, he was Number Eight, nothing more.

"You didn't have to," he retorted. "You can't take your eyes off him or his mate."

She expected to find censure in his gaze—he was, after all, a Ph.D. and knew the value of maintaining objectivity in any kind of field work—but there was nothing there but amused understanding. And just that easily, she knew that he understood how difficult releasing the wolves was for her, because he'd been where she was.

"So what'd you name him?" he prompted again. "King? Duke? How about Bubba?"

She had to laugh at that. "Does he look like a Bubba to you?"

Grinning, he shrugged. "He does have a certain swagger to him."

"That's pride," she corrected him. "And his name's Napoleon."

"Then his bride is...?"

"Queenie," she said softly. "It seemed to fit her better than Josephine."

Turning his attention back to the wolves, Zeke had to admit that the names did indeed fit. In a pack of twelve animals, Elizabeth's favorites stood out like the rulers they were. Napoleon, in particular, had a real attitude, and after glaring at the open gate for nearly five minutes, he obviously decided he'd had enough of being intimidated. His hackles up, he dared to take first one step, then several, toward the opening. Encouraged when nothing happened, he lifted his head and scented the air. A split second later, before even his mate suspected what he was going to do, he streaked through the open gate.

"Good boy!" Elizabeth whispered huskily. "I knew you could do it!"

Left behind, Queenie barked sharply in protest, but she didn't have to fear Napoleon would leave without her.

Stopping well outside the gate, he turned to face her, then barked and yipped and danced in front of her, urging her to follow him. Cautious because of the unborn pups she carried, she was agitated and clearly wanted to follow him, but she had to work up her nerve. Another ten minutes passed while she hesitated, then she raced to join her mate.

Fascinated, Zeke had never seen anything quite like it in all his years of studying wildlife. The two wolves greeted each other as if they'd been apart for days instead of minutes, then by unspoken agreement, they turned away from the pen and bounded across the snow to the western edge of the clearing. The rest of the pack, not liking the thought of being left behind, soon found the courage to follow, and within minutes, they'd all disappeared into the trees. For the first time since long before Zeke was born, wolves ran free in southwestern Colorado.

It was, he knew, something he would remember for the rest of his life. Long after the wolves had disappeared from view, he and Elizabeth just stood there as silence fell softly around them. When he finally took his eyes from the spot where he'd last seen Queenie and Napoleon in the trees, he glanced down at Elizabeth and wasn't surprised to see quiet tears trailing down her face. But then she looked up at him and smiled, and he felt the tug of that soft, beautiful smile all the way to his toes.

"I thought you'd be sad," he said, surprised.

"I am," she said simply. "But it was the right thing to do. Now they're where they belong."

Like magnets her eyes were drawn back to the spot in the forest, but he couldn't look at anything but Elizabeth. Intrigued, fascinated, he couldn't figure her out. Who was this woman? he wondered, confused. She could stand in front of the whole town and not even blink at the insults that were thrown at her from all sides, yet she cried like a baby at the thought of never again seeing the wolves she'd unofficially adopted as her own. Anyone with eyes could see that she loved them, but that hadn't stopped her from doing the right thing and releasing them.

Damn, he liked her! More than was smart. If she'd been any other woman, he would have reached for her then, but he was already off balance as it was. He had a feeling if he kissed the lady, it'd be a long time before he'd want to come up for air. And neither one of them was ready for that…yet.

So he resisted the temptation by doing what he did best where she was concerned—he ruffled her feathers. Reaching into his pocket, he handed her his handkerchief and grinned down at her. "Dry your eyes, Lizzie, darlin'. A man's ego takes a real beating when a woman cries on the first date."

Just that quickly, her delicately arched brows snapped into a scowl. "This isn't a date, McBride."

On more solid footing, he teased, "Well, damn! And here I thought I was going to get to kiss you."

"McBride!"

"Don't get your knickers in a twist," he chuckled. "You're safe with me—for now. But later, you'd better watch out!" Giving her a wink, he started down through the trees toward their parked cars. "See you later, honey. I've got work to do."

He thought he heard her strangle back a curse, then she yelled after him, "I'm not your honey!"

Waving a hand in acknowledgment, he laughed all the way to town.

Chapter 4

When Zeke drove through the entrance of the ranch late the following afternoon, he was tired and disgusted and wanted nothing more than a hot bath and a cold beer, not necessarily in that order. The last day and a half had, to put it bluntly, been hell. Armed with the list of suspects that Nick had drawn up for him, he'd driven all over the county on roads that a mountain goat wouldn't step foot on, shaking loose what felt like every bone in his body. And in the process, he'd done nothing but run into one dead end after another. He'd finally found the men he was looking for, but if any of the antigovernment wackos he'd questioned knew anything about the poisoned meat left at Eagle Ridge, they weren't talking. And every damn one of them had an alibi for Wednesday night.

Back to square one, he'd had no choice but to report back to Nick that he'd struck out, then call it quits for the day. He wasn't, however, beaten. Whoever had made that threatening phone call to Elizabeth was out there somewhere, so close he could smell his rotten hide. And he was going to find him. Even if he had to turn over every rock in Colorado to do it.

His mind on the investigation, he pulled into his regular parking spot at Joe's house and cut the engine. Ever since his brother had built his own place, he'd been baching there whenever he came home for a visit, and this time was no different. He was halfway to the front door when he noticed Merry's red Explorer parked out front.

Surprised, he walked inside the house to find her dressed in a green wool dress and heels, all decked out for a party and, as usual, looking absolutely stunning. She might have been his sister, but it was easy to see why she'd been prom queen in both high school and college. Given the chance, she could have put Grace Kelly in the shade.

Whistling softly, he raised a brow at her. "Who's the lucky guy?"

"You," she said, her sapphire eyes dancing impishly. "There's a singles' dance at the VFW hall tonight, and I need you to take me."

"Oh, no!" Throwing up his hands, he made the sign of the cross with his two index fingers. "Back off, sister. I steer clear of lonely ladies looking for a husband."

"Oh, c'mon, Zeke, don't be that way," she wheedled. "It won't be like that. Yes, it's for singles, but everyone goes. It'll be fun."

"So go. You don't need me tagging along."

"But I don't have a date. Well, I did," she said, wrinkling her nose prettily, "but he got sick and had to cancel. And I hate going to this kind of thing by myself."

"Why? People are supposed to go alone—it's for singles! Anyway, it's not like you'd be walking into a roomful of strangers. You'll probably know everybody there."

She rolled her eyes at that. "Men! You don't understand

anything. That doesn't mean I want to walk in alone. And I have to go. Laura's on the organizing committee, and if I don't show up, my name'll be mud.''

He should have known Laura Ralston was involved in this. Merry's best friend since grade school, she was her partner in crime in just about everything. ''What about Joe?'' he suggested, even as he knew he was losing the argument. ''Why don't you ask him?''

''Are you talking about *our* brother, Joe?'' she retorted mockingly. ''The one who swore off women the day he and Belinda divorced? The one who won't even go to church if he thinks he's going to have to sit next to a single woman? That Joe?''

She did, he had to admit with a grin, have a point. ''All right, forget Joe. What about Janey?''

Even as he asked, he knew Janey was nearly as bad as Joe when it came to socializing. Quieter than the rest of them and more reserved, she preferred small gatherings or, better yet, one on one. She hadn't been to a dance since high school, and if he remembered correctly, only once then.

''Forget that,'' he said before she could say anything. ''This doesn't sound like her kind of thing at all. She'd be miserable.''

Which meant there was no one else but him to go with Merry. Resigned, he groaned. ''What time does this shindig start?''

''Seven.'' Laughing, she gave him a quick hug, then drew back to tease, ''Don't look so down in the mouth. It's not like I'm asking you to take me to a funeral or something. It'll be fun. At least three of your old girlfriends will be there. Oh, and Elizabeth's coming.''

He would have sworn he didn't so much as flicker an eyelash in response, but Merry knew him too well. Something in his eyes gave him away, and she grinned in triumph. ''Aha! That got your attention! Go change, big brother,'' she chuckled, pushing him toward the stairs. ''We've got a party to go to.''

Given a choice, Elizabeth would rather have had a root canal than spend an evening at a singles' dance. She hated the awkwardness of it, hated the idea of small talk and phony smiles and dancing with men who held her too close while they pushed her around the dance floor like a broom. But when Merry called her earlier that day and asked her to come, she never gave a thought to refusing. She couldn't. The word had gotten out that she'd freed the wolves ahead of schedule, and even though it was only by a few days, people were outraged that she'd dared to take such a step without warning them first. She'd tried to explain why the early release had been necessary, but few of the people who called her office to complain had been willing to listen.

Damage control was drastically needed, but there weren't that many opportunities to meet and talk with people at any kind of a social gathering in Liberty Hill. Then Merry called, and she'd known better than to look a gift horse in the mouth. She'd put on one of her favorite dresses—a red, princess-style jersey that always made her feel like a million bucks—plastered on a smile, and here she was.

Too late she realized that a dance was hardly the place to try to win over her enemies with any kind of meaningful conversation. Onstage, a country-western band belted out the latest Garth Brooks hit, and she could hardly hear herself think. Even if she could have made herself heard, no one seemed interested in anything but having fun.

Couples whirled around the dance floor, and those who didn't have partners sized each other up from across the room. Several cowboys started toward her, eyeing her as if

she was the cherry on top of their hot-fudge sundae, and
suddenly she wished she'd worn anything but her red dress.
She knew she looked great in it, but it felt too tight, too
low, too revealing. The last thing she wanted to do was
draw attention to herself as a woman. That wasn't why she
was here.

Hot color spilling into her cheeks, she turned away and
gave serious thought to leaving. She wasn't going to ac-
complish anything here tonight anyway, and if she went
back to the office, she could check the radio blips coming
from the wolves' collars and track their progress as they
explored the mountains and valleys of their new home.

The decision made, she started toward the main entrance,
but she'd hardly taken two steps when the door opened and
Zeke walked in with Merry. In the time it took to stop in
her tracks, her heart was knocking crazily in her breast.

Dressed in pressed jeans, a white long-sleeved shirt, and
a Western-cut jacket that was similar to what most of the
other men wore, he was hardly dressed to draw attention
to himself. But she wasn't the only one caught flat-footed
by his entrance. Women all over the room looked up when
he came in, and not surprisingly, a good many of them
knew him. Within seconds the bolder ones were rushing
toward him with delighted smiles on their faces.

Stepping out of the way so she wouldn't get trampled
by the stampede, Elizabeth wouldn't have been surprised if
they were all old lovers. He was a man who would leave
broken hearts behind him everywhere he went. Not that she
cared, she assured herself with a scowl as a busty blond
wrapped herself around Zeke like an octopus. If he wanted
to stroll down memory lane with every old girlfriend he'd
ever flirted with, it was nothing to her. She was here to do
a job, nothing else.

Turning away from the sight of him hugging a redhead

who had on a dress that was at least two sizes too small for her, she started to head for the refreshment table, but she never made it that far. Standing directly in front of her was one of the two cowboys that had been ogling her earlier. If she remembered correctly, he was a hired hand at the Double Bar J out west of town and was as harmless as a baby donkey.

"You sure look pretty in that dress, Ms. Davis," he said with a crooked grin. "I don't know if you remember me, but I'm Alvin Newton. People call me Fig, though. You know…Fig Newton. Get it?"

Elizabeth smiled…and wondered what it must be like to go through life being called by the name of a cookie. "Yes, I get it…Fig."

"It's not so bad," he said, noticing how she hesitated to use his nickname. "Just think what would have happened if my last name would have been Chip. I'd have had to go around answering to Chocolate."

"You do have a point," she laughed.

Pleased, he grinned. "Would you like to dance? I promise not to step on your toes."

If he could get her halfway around the room without annihilating her poor feet, Elizabeth would be surprised, but she didn't have the heart to turn him down. "As long as you don't pull anything fancy on me, I'd love to. The two-step is about all I know."

"Me, too," he admitted, and gingerly took her into his arms.

From across the room, Zeke watched Elizabeth trade partners for the third time in nearly as many minutes and told himself the lady would dance with him before the evening was over. He was a patient man. He could wait his turn.

It should have been easy. He saw friends—men and women—he hadn't talked to in years, and there was a lot of catching up to do. But even though he was gracious to his old girlfriends and talked ranching with the guys, the only person he was interested in was Elizabeth. And she never once even looked his way.

She knew he was there, of course. There weren't that many people there that she couldn't have noticed him, but the lady seemed to be going out of her way to avoid him. Another time he might have been amused. But not tonight. Not when every long, tall cowboy in the county was sidling up to her, then sweeping her off in his arms on the dance floor. *He* wanted to dance with her, dammit! Oh, he could have asked other women—more than a few looked longingly at the dance floor as they reminisced with him about old times—but he didn't take the hint. If he danced, it would only be with Elizabeth. He was just waiting for her to look his way, and he'd ask her.

But he could have been on another planet for all the notice she gave him. Amused, he was determined to wait her out. But then she stepped into the arms of a cowboy he'd never seen before. Tall and solid, with an arrogant air that Zeke immediately took exception to, the man pulled her closer than he should and got far too familiar with his hands.

Stiffening, Zeke's first instinct was to rush right over there and belt the jerk. But Elizabeth was a lady who could take care of herself, and even as he watched, she eased back in the cowboy's arms and said something that had him returning his hands to where they belonged.

After such a reprimand, a gentleman would have behaved himself, but it quickly became apparent that the idiot who shuffled her around the floor was dumber than a fence post.

Ignoring her frowns and admonitions, he took advantage of every turn in the dance to let his hands wander.

Scowling, Zeke tried to stand back and let her handle the situation, but his patience only lasted so long. And when the jerk guided her to a dark corner of the dance floor and she tried to push out of his arms without success, Zeke had seen enough. Excusing himself in mid-sentence from the woman who had once been his eighth-grade sweetheart, he headed straight for Elizabeth.

Tapping the cowboy hard on the shoulder—and just barely resisting the urge to flatten him—he growled, "I believe the lady's promised me this dance."

When Elizabeth turned to him with blazing eyes, he thought she was going to rake him over the coals for interfering. Then she said coolly, "Zeke's right. I did say I'd dance the next one with him." And he realized he wasn't the one she was angry with. If looks could kill, the cowboy would have drawn his last breath right there in the middle of the dance floor.

And he was too dumb to know it, Zeke thought in amazement when the big lug just stood there, refusing to release her. What did he think he was going to do? Force her to circle the floor with him again? Like hell!

He opened his mouth to tell him not to even think about going there, but apparently the jerk wasn't quite as thick-skinned as Zeke had first thought. Scowling, he let Elizabeth go, but he wasn't happy about it. Grumbling, he stalked off to the bar just as the band switched to a slow, romantic ballad.

Grinning, Zeke opened his arms to her. "It sounds like they're playing our song. Shall we dance?"

It was a line he'd probably used a thousand times, one that a smart woman wouldn't have fallen for. But caught in the warmth of his gaze as the music swirled around them like something out of a dream, Elizabeth couldn't find the strength to resist him. Not when he had eyes only for her and made her feel like the prettiest girl at the ball. It was just one dance. What harm could it do? Without a word she went into his arms.

She'd spent the past hour dancing with one cowboy after another and could say with all honesty that not a single one had moved her to anything but indifference—except for the last one, of course, who had infuriated her with his arrogance and roaming hands. But when Zeke took her into his arms, the last thing she felt was indifference.

Startled, she tried to tell herself her imagination was just playing tricks on her. A woman's bones didn't melt because a man held her close; her heart didn't stumble in her breast because his hand closed around hers. If her pulse seemed to be pounding and she was more than a little light-headed, it was just because someone had turned up the heat in the building and she needed some air.

Then she looked into Zeke's eyes and knew he was feeling the same thing she was, and her heart jumped into her throat. What was happening here? "Zeke…"

"Let's just dance," he said gruffly, and eased her gracefully into a slow, enticing two-step around the dance floor.

If she lived to be a hundred, she didn't think she would ever forget that one dance in his arms. Time ground to a halt. All around them couples swayed to the music, yet she saw nothing but Zeke, heard nothing but the hammering of her heart, felt nothing but the strength of his arms around her, cradling her close, keeping her safe. It was wonderful, exhilarating, terrifying.

She wanted to run for her life…and never let him go. And that's when she knew she was in trouble. What was she doing? Had she lost her mind? This was a man who was just like her father, a tease and a flirt who flitted from woman to woman and didn't give his heart to any of them. And she loved being in his arms.

How had this happened? When? She didn't want to be attracted to him, didn't want to like him one way or the other. But he made her laugh, made her feel, whether she wanted to or not, and it shook her to the depth of her being. What had he done to her?

Shaken, in desperate need of some time to herself to think, she eased out of his arms the second the song ended. The band immediately launched into a country rock number, but neither of them noticed. Over the blare of the music, she would have sworn he could hear the thumping of her heart. "Thank you for the dance," she murmured.

"My pleasure," he replied huskily. "Anytime you want to do it again, just give me a holler."

One word, that's all she had to say and she could step back into his arms. It would be so easy. Too easy. And that was what scared her. She could get used to this man's touch.

Wanting to bolt, she forced a smile that didn't come easily for her. "Actually, I think I've had enough dancing for one night, but thanks for the offer. I'm going to call it a night. It's been a long day and I have to be in the office early in the morning."

With a shaky good-night, she turned away and headed for the coatroom to retrieve her coat, then forced herself to walk, not run, to the nearest exit. And with every step, she felt the touch of his eyes on her. Tempted to look back, she didn't dare.

He'd danced only one dance with her. Just one, dammit. Considering the crowd that packed the VFW, no one should have noticed. But the second he and Merry headed home, she started in on him. Little sisters, he thought with a groan. They saw everything.

"I must say, I'm impressed," she said as she settled into her seat with a broad grin. "The lady isn't the fluffy, brainless type you usually go after."

"I didn't *go after* anyone."

"Sure you did," she retorted, chuckling. "You turned those baby blues of yours on her and expected her to fall into your arms. And all you got was one dance." Delighted, she laughed. "I always knew there was something about Elizabeth Davis I liked. She's going to make a great addition to the family. Mom'll love her."

"Whoa, girl!" he said, shocked. "It was one dance, for God's sake! Who said anything about bringing her into the family?"

"Nobody. But I know what I saw." Pleased with herself, she snuggled down into her coat and started humming the wedding march.

His lips twitching, Zeke gave serious thought to killing her. "Don't start planning the reception yet," he growled. "It's not going to happen."

Not if he had anything to say about it, he added to himself as he continued to Joe's place after dropping Merry off at the small house she'd built next to her clinic. He'd already tried the engagement thing and still had the scars on his heart to prove it. God, what a sap he'd been! He'd thought he was a pretty damn good judge of character, but Rachel had proven him wrong. She'd swept into his life like a tornado, convinced him she loved him and lived for the day she could be his wife. Then just days before they were to be married, he'd found her in bed with another man.

That was two years ago, and although he'd learned to let go of the hurt, bitterness still burned in his gut like old battery acid. Rachel, horrified that she'd been caught, had claimed it meant nothing, that she'd just missed him because he was halfway across the country and she'd foolishly turned to someone else out of loneliness. He was the man she loved. The man she wanted to spend the rest of her life with.

Yeah, right! If that was her definition of love, then he'd wanted no part of it. Or her. He'd walked away from her without a backward glance, canceled all the wedding plans and promised himself then that he would never again make the mistake of letting a woman get close enough to him to hurt him.

Oh, he still liked women. He enjoyed everything about them…the scent and feel and mystery of them…and the day he didn't, he'd be six feet under. But that was all there was ever going to be to it—just liking.

Given that, he should have fallen asleep later, without giving a second thought to any of the women he'd charmed and flirted with at the dance. But when he crawled into bed in the guest room in Joe's house and turned out the light, it wasn't any of the old girlfriends who had swarmed him earlier in the evening that kept him awake. It was the scent and feel and mystery of one woman in particular. Elizabeth. He couldn't close his eyes without remembering the way she'd felt in his arms. It was, he thought grimly, going to be a long night.

The following Monday, Zeke got the lab report on the poisoned meat that had been left outside the wolves' holding pen. It was laced with a pesticide that, while not uncommon, wasn't normally used in that area of the country because it was too difficult to obtain. Anyone buying it had to not only have training in the use of pesticides, they

couldn't purchase it without signing for it because it was
so lethal.

Spending the morning on the phone at the desk Nick had
cleared out for him at the sheriff's office, Zeke called every
source of supply within a hundred-mile radius, without
much success. Only four people had bought the pesticide
within the past six months, and none of them lived anywhere near Liberty Hill.

Still, he wasn't taking any chances. He made a quick trip
up toward Aspen and Glenwood Springs and talked to all
four in person. None of them claimed to know much about
the wolf project, which wasn't surprising, considering how
far they lived from Liberty Hill. Upfront and honest, they
answered his questions without reservation, and Zeke had
no reason to suspect any of them of lying.

Returning to Liberty Hill, he could only conclude that
the pesticide had, in all likelihood, been stolen. There was
no way of tracing it unless the theft had been reported,
which, he discovered after talking to Nick when he got back
to town, it hadn't. So once again, he was back to square
one, without a single lead to follow up.

Disgusted, he should have faxed the lab report to Elizabeth. But when he called her office to get her fax number,
her line was busy. When he tried two more times and got
the same busy signal, he hung up and sat back in his chair
to frown consideringly at the report. Getting it to her wasn't
a high priority since there was nothing in it that she could
use to protect her wolves, but he hadn't seen the lady in
three days, ever since the dance. And in a town the size of
Liberty Hill, where you couldn't cross the street without
running into half the population, that was pretty amazing.

She was avoiding him. All because of a simple little
dance that he was sure she hadn't forgotten any more than
he had. A smart man would have kept to his side of town,

let her have hers, and accepted that it was for the best. But he'd never had any patience with playing it safe. Pushing to his feet, he picked up the lab report, grabbed his coat and headed for the door. Maybe it was time he dropped in on the lady for a little visit.

Resisting the urge to slam the phone back down on its base, Elizabeth gritted her teeth and with a civility that cost her dearly, thanked the rancher on the other end of the line for calling. But when she hung up, it was all she could do not to throw something. The last three days had been the worst of her life. And the best. After all the planning and hard work, not to mention the opposition, the wolves were finally running free, and she was so thrilled, she wanted to laugh out loud with joy. Just as she had promised over and over again, they were doing what wolves did best, feeding on elk and giving the coyote population fits. Not one single cow or sheep had been harmed. In fact, from all reports, the wolves hadn't even spared the local livestock a glance. Their food of choice was elk, and that was all they were interested in.

She'd expected the ranchers in the area to be thrilled. After all, none of their fears had come true. Granted, the wolves had only been on the prowl for three days, and there was always the possibility that things could change. But that wasn't likely to happen. With a healthy population of elk to feed on, there was no reason for the wolves to go on a wild killing spree of livestock.

But no one seemed to care that the wolves had lived up to their advance billing. It was their early release that still had some people in a snit. Despite all her efforts at damage control, they called, they stopped by the office to register their dissatisfaction in person, they came up to her in the grocery store. She couldn't even go home to escape. The phone was usually ringing when she stepped inside her front door, and it didn't stop until she unplugged it at bedtime.

She was, she told herself, a reasonable person. She knew people were upset because they felt as if the government was shoving the project down their throats whether they wanted it or not, and it was that, not the early release of the wolves, that they had a beef with. So when they called her names to her face and shunned her on the street as if she was some sort of home wrecker, she hung on to her temper and tried to act as if it didn't matter. But her patience was wearing thin, and if one more person came into her office and tried to read her the riot act, she wasn't going to be responsible for her actions!

The bell over the front door rang just then, and with a muttered curse, she looked up, braced for another confrontation. But the man who walked in had a crooked grin on his face, not a scowl, and she couldn't for the life of her hold back the smile that formed on her lips. Then she remembered a dance that left her hot and breathless and, after three days, still haunted her dreams. In a heartbeat, her smile switched back to a scowl.

"What do you want, McBride?"

Wriggling his brows, he leered at her playfully. "I'm not sure you want to know, Lizzie, darlin'."

Amused in spite of herself, she struggled to hold on to her frown. "State your business, McBride. I'm busy. This is the first time all morning that the phone hasn't rung, and I've got work to do."

"I heard you were still getting flak over the early release," he said, sobering. "Any calls I should know about?"

She knew what he was asking—whether she'd heard from the creep who'd left the poisoned meat outside the holding pen—and shook her head. "No. It's just the usual, nothing vicious like the other night. So how's the investigation coming? Have you found anything?"

Dropping into the chair in front of her desk, he said in disgust, "Not yet. He's a clever bastard—I'll give him that. But he's not as smart as he thinks he is. The wolves are free, and nothing he did could stop it. That's got to eat at his craw. You didn't knuckle under to his threats, and he's not going to accept that lying down."

"You think he'll come after me?" she asked, surprised. "But why? The wolves are free."

"Exactly. And you're the one who opened the gate. If he's looking for someone to blame, you're it. So just be careful, okay? We don't know what this nut's capable of."

She appreciated the warning, but she'd been taking precautions ever since she first moved to Liberty Hill. From her past experience at Yellowstone, she knew better than to relax her guard just because the wolves were now free to go wherever they liked.

Nodding at the oversize envelope in his hand, she said, "What's that?"

"The lab report. I brought you a copy, not that there's much in it that can help us," he added. "Our boy used strychnine, but God only knows where he got his hands on it. It's not used much—it's too lethal—and the government requires strict records on everyone who purchases it. I checked out everyone who bought it within the past six months, and they all turned out lily-white."

"Could it have been stolen?"

"If it was, there were no reports of the theft."

"Then maybe it was bought more than six months ago. Or up in Denver. Is there a possibility that whoever laced that meat with the stuff could have already had it on hand?

Does it go bad if it's not used within a certain time period?''

"I'll check it out," he promised, "but I don't think so." Holding out the report to her, he said, "This is your copy to keep. I figured you needed it for your files."

"Yes, I do. Thanks."

She leaned forward to take it from him and, in the process, inadvertently brushed his fingers with hers. That's all it was, just an innocent touch that didn't last a split second, but instantly the heat that had flared between them on the dance floor three days ago was back stronger than ever. And this time, there was no pretending it didn't exist. The warmth of it was right there in both their eyes.

"This isn't going to go away, you know."

She felt a blush stealing into her cheeks and knew it was too much to hope that he hadn't noticed. "I don't know what you're talking about," she said stiffly.

"Yes, you do," he said bluntly. "There's this crazy chemistry between us. And don't tell me you don't feel it, too, because I know better. Go out with me."

He'd asked her a half dozen times before, always teasingly, but this time there was no spark of mischief dancing in his eyes, no grin flirting with that sensuous mouth of his. He was dead serious. He really wanted her to go out with him.

Her mouth dry and her heart thumping, Elizabeth shook her head. "I don't think that would be a very good idea."

"Why not? Because you're as fascinated with me as I am with you?"

Her cheeks hot with embarrassment, she narrowed her eyes at him dangerously. "Don't go there, McBride."

She might as well have saved her breath. "It threw me for a loop, too," he said honestly. "I don't have to tell you that you're an incredibly attractive woman. But I'm only here for a vacation, and I was supposed to spend it working with my brother on the ranch, riding fence and getting ready for spring. Instead, when I'm not trying to figure out who the hell is threatening your wolves, I'm thinking about ways to talk you into going out with me. Every time you turn me down, it only encourages me to ask you again. If you really want me to stop, say yes.''

It was the most convoluted reason Elizabeth had ever heard for going out with a man. ''Let me get this straight. I'm supposed to go out with you so you'll quit asking me? Is that what you're saying?''

''Pretty much,'' he retorted. ''Think about it. We've worked together some, but that's it. Given the chance to spend some time with each other in a social setting that doesn't involve work, we may discover that we don't even like each other. In that case, whatever chemistry there is between us will die a swift death, and we can forget that we ever looked twice at each other.''

If any other man had suggested such a thing, she might have been willing to concede he had a point. But this was Zeke McBride, and she wasn't quite sure she trusted him to behave himself. ''Why do I have the feeling you're setting me up?''

''Me? C'mon, Lizzie, you know me better than that. It just seemed like the logical solution, but if you don't want to go out, hey, that's okay.'' He shrugged, as if he couldn't care less one way or another. ''We can just go on the way we are.''

It would have served him right if she'd called his bluff. But she couldn't sleep for thinking about the man as it was now. She spent her nights dreaming of him, her days hoping to catch a glimpse of him. And it had to end. He was driving her crazy! If going out with him would put an end to this ridiculous fascination she had for him, then it was worth a shot.

"All right," she said, giving in abruptly. "How about dinner Thursday evening? We can go to the diner."

Since it was the only restaurant in town, that was a given. Grinning broadly, he said, "Wear something sexy."

"To the *diner?*"

"Hey, this could be our one and only date. Let's do it up right. I'll pick you up at seven at your place."

Already going through her closet for the most conservative outfit she had, she nodded, her eyes twinkling. "Seven it is."

Chapter 5

Spring was still weeks away, but over the course of the next few days as she, Tina and Peter tracked the wolves through the mountains and valleys and forests surrounding Liberty Hill, Elizabeth could have sworn she smelled the changing of the season on the air itself. There was a freshness, a sense of expectancy that made even the grayest day brighter. Then a late-winter thaw set in, the temperature started to rise, and the steady drip of snow melting from the eaves was like music to her ears. She found herself smiling for no reason and looking and listening for other signs of spring…sandhill cranes gracefully skimming the treetops, the haunting call of Canada geese, the happy bubble of the creek in the meadow behind her house as a winter's worth of ice thawed.

Then, just as quickly as the snow had begun to melt, the weather changed overnight the day before her Thursday-night date with Zeke. A fresh storm blew in from the north, bringing with it a wet, heavy curtain of snow that fell all night long. The next morning, old man winter was once again firmly entrenched in southwestern Colorado.

The winds were gale force, the conditions almost white-out, so for most of the morning, Elizabeth and her team had no choice but to hole up in her office and keep track of the wolves by monitoring the radio beeps that emanated from their collars. It was Elizabeth's least favorite way to track the animals, but with roads closed all over the county, she had to wait for the storm to blow itself out before she could head out in her Jeep to observe the wolves in person. By noon the sun was peeking through the clouds, the wind had died, and the snowplows were out, going to work on the roads. An hour later, armed with her camera and binoculars, Elizabeth ventured out with Tina in search of the wolves.

As expected, she found three members of the pack down in the valley below Eagle Ridge. The younger animals in the group hadn't strayed very far from the holding pen once they were released, choosing to spend their time feeding off a large herd of elk that made their home in the area. On most days, they could be seen slipping in and out of the trees, stalking their prey.

However, Elizabeth really longed to see Queenie and Napoleon. The most adventuresome of the pack, they had roamed up and down the Hawk River Valley, sometimes ranging as far away as forty miles in their exploration of their new home. Merry McBride, acting as the project veterinarian, had gone up with Tina in the chopper earlier in the week and caught sight of them, but Elizabeth hadn't seen the pair since they were released over a week ago.

There was a good chance that today would be her lucky day. Peter had picked up their radio signals north of Eagle Ridge. After a week of nearly constant travel, Queenie and Napoleon had finally come full circle.

"Let's pull into the overlook and see what we can see," Elizabeth told Tina as the road leveled off at the top of the ridge. "They were heading south when we left the office. If they didn't make any turnoffs, they should be making their way up Beaver Creek right now."

The highway that cut through Eagle Ridge was the main pass to towns farther north and one of the first roads plowed in the county. Still, driving conditions were far from ideal. Concentrating on the snow-covered road, Tina nodded. "I'll try, but we might have trouble getting in if the plows didn't leave the entrance clear. Sometimes they don't, especially after a storm."

The parking lot for the overlook came into view then, and luckily the entrance was open, but just barely. The drifts were nearly as high as the Jeep, and the snowplow had only cleared out enough space to turn around. Carefully maneuvering through the snow, Tina had to park well back from the actual overlook itself. They would have to walk through fifty yards of heavy drifts just to reach the observation area.

Staring balefully at the unbroken expanse of snow that awaited them, Tina said, "In my next lifetime, I think I'll study spiders in the Sahara. How much coffee did we bring?"

"Not enough," Elizabeth chuckled, and reached for the handle to her door.

The wind might have died down below in the valley, but there was always a strong draft along the ridge, and the second Elizabeth stepped outside, an icy gust swirled around her, engulfing her. The windchill wasn't any lower than it normally was, but after a few days of springlike temperatures, the cold seemed to cut straight through her clothes to her bare skin. And they hadn't even stepped into the knee-deep snow yet.

Muttering curses all the while, her eyes tearing from the cold wind, Tina joined her at the front of the Jeep. "Tomorrow morning, remind me to put in for a transfer to Las Vegas."

Grinning, Elizabeth said, "The only wolves there walk on two legs. I don't think Peter would be thrilled at the idea of you studying that particular breed of animal."

That put a sparkle in her eyes. "No," she agreed, "but think of the skimpy lingerie I could wear to bed even in the winter without getting cold. He'd love that!"

Laughing, they stepped into the snow.

Decked out in winter gear, they were winded by the time they made it to the overlook, but the view was worth it. Spread out before them, Hawk River Valley was postcard beautiful in the late-winter sunshine. Curving and meandering its way through the middle of the long, narrow valley, Beaver Creek was a thin ribbon of steel-blue. During the summer, when the wild grasses were thick and green, the valley drew all manner of wildlife, but today, with the snow deep and the creek all but covered with ice, it was quiet and still and deserted. No animal tracks marred the clean, virginal sweep of snow; nothing moved among the dark stand of fir and pines that bordered the valley on all sides. Untouched by man or animal, it could have stood just the same a thousand years ago.

Appearances were deceptive, however, and Elizabeth knew better than to take the scene below at face value without putting a glass to it. Reaching for the binoculars that hung around her neck, she started at the north end of the valley and began a slow sweep to the south. At her side, Tina did the same.

"Something's moving just below the ridge in that stand of aspens at the end of the valley," Tina said softly a few minutes later. "See it? It could be coyotes—"

"No, the legs are too long," Elizabeth said, glassing the same area. "And the color's wrong, though it's hard to tell in the shadow of the trees. They look gray—they are! Look, there's Napoleon now. And Queenie. Don't they look gorgeous?"

They were, in fact, beautiful. While they were in the holding pen, she'd observed them every day for nearly three months and thought she knew everything there was to know about them. They'd always been regal and majestic—hence their names—but since their release from captivity, they'd grown in size and stature and were truly magnificent in the wild. They'd explored their new world and claimed it as theirs, and you could see their confidence in every stride. Without an ounce of fear or hesitation, they came down through the trees and bounded out into the meadow, kicking up fresh powder, their powerful bodies stretched out lean and low as they ran with a joy that couldn't be contained.

Sudden tears welling in her eyes and throat, Elizabeth didn't know if she wanted to laugh or cry. *This* was why she'd fought so hard to convince people to accept the project, why she suffered through the name-calling and threats and championed the wolves when they were attacked on all sides. If people could just see them like this, running free, surely they would see why they belonged here.

Dropping her binoculars so they could dangle around her neck, Tina blinked back a few tears of her own and laughed self-consciously. "They get to you, don't they? It's just that they look like two kids who were just let out of school."

They did appear to be having a ball. Like streaks of lightning, they raced the length of the valley as if they didn't have a care in the world and disappeared into the trees again, where they were quickly lost to view. God only knew where they'd turn up next.

Amazed, Elizabeth could only shake her head in wonder. "You'd think they'd be slowing down after the distance they've covered in the last few days. It's forty miles to Wild Bear Canyon, and they made it up there and back in a week after spending three months in captivity. And Queenie's pregnant!"

"I know, but she's certainly not letting it slow her down. She'll breed strong pups."

Elizabeth agreed. Napoleon couldn't have found himself a better mate. "She should den in a couple of weeks," she said as they made their way back to the Jeep. "We'll have to keep a close eye on her. Those pups'll be the first generation of wolves born in this valley in decades, and we don't want anything to happen to them."

Normally, Elizabeth would have spent the rest of the daylight hours tracking the other wolves in the area, but the afternoon was slipping away, and she had her dinner date with Zeke to get ready for. The nerves she'd been trying to ignore all day tingled just at the thought of it.

Heading back to town, Tina glanced over at her and began to grin. "Uh-oh, I know that look. You're thinking about your hot date tonight."

"It's not a hot date…"

"So you keep saying," her friend said, chuckling. "It's just dinner. A chance for you and Zeke McBride to sit down together for an hour and discover you have absolutely nothing in common. Though why you'd want to do that is beyond me! Have you looked at the man? Really looked at him?"

Of course she had! That was the problem. She couldn't stop looking! "I never said he wasn't attractive. I'm just not interested in him."

"Why, for heaven's sake? Every single woman in this town, not to mention a few of the married ones, would give their eyeteeth if he'd just wink at them, but you're the only one he looks at. Go! Enjoy yourself. You're going to have a great time.''

Elizabeth didn't doubt that. Zeke was the type of man who knew how to cater to a woman, how to make her feel special and beautiful, and that was what she was afraid of. She'd always dated the serious types in the past, the studious ones, who were as different from men like her father and Zeke as donkeys were from peacocks. A man who wasn't quite sure of himself she could handle. One who was charming and sure of himself was a whole other kettle of fish.

She should, she realized too late, never have agreed to this madness, but she'd given her word and it was too late to back out now. And how bad could it be, after all? It was just dinner, and in a public place, at that. It wasn't as if he was going to jump her bones or anything in front of a diner full of people. He would flirt with her, of course—she didn't think he could breathe without doing that—and make her laugh, and in the end, remind her of her father and why she couldn't let herself be taken in by a pair of dancing eyes and a quick line. Which was the only reason why she was going out with him in the first place.

Satisfied that she finally had everything worked out in her head, she actually found herself looking forward to the evening as she drove home after work to change for her date. Finding something suitable to wear should have been easy. Ed's Diner was hardly the kind of place you dressed up for, and her first inclination was to reach for black jeans and a red sweater. But Zeke had said to wear something sexy—which she had no intention of doing—and the sweater definitely fit that description. Hastily, she put the outfit back and reached for a black wool dress instead.

She didn't wear it often, but as she studied its long lines, she couldn't help but smile. It showed about as much skin as a nun's habit. It was perfect. She'd hardly pulled it on, stepped into black pumps and slipped around her neck the diamond drop necklace her parents had given her for getting her Masters, when the doorbell rang.

Up until then she'd convinced herself she could get through the evening without feeling a thing. But at the first sound of the doorbell, her heart immediately began to pound. What, she wondered wildly, had she set herself up for? Her hands not quite steady, she swept back her hair on one side and secured it with a plain gold clip, then quickly touched up her lipstick. Ready or not, it was time for her date.

Zeke thought he had the evening planned right down to the last detail. Then Elizabeth opened her front door to him and everything changed. He'd expected her to wear something prim and sedate that covered her from her throat to her ankles, something that warned him not to get any ideas about anything other than dinner, and at first glance, her black dress certainly did that.

It was that second look, the double take that turned his mouth to dust.

Black wool never looked so seductive. Rich and soft, it lovingly draped every sweet curve of her breasts, then hugged her small waist before flaring over her hips, to fall in seductive folds to three inches below her knees. Just looking made him want to touch.

He didn't, of course. He didn't dare risk losing a hand. But, Lord, she was something. Slender and delicate, with an unconscious seductiveness that Grace Kelly would have envied, she could have easily brought him and every other man he knew to his knees.

"I know you said sexy, McBride, but you're just going to have to make do with this."

Make do? he thought, stunned. *Didn't she realize...*

Even before he could finish the thought, he saw by the glint of mischief in her eyes that she'd thought she pulled a fast one on him. She didn't have a clue just how close she'd come to knocking him out of his shoes!

"Yeah," he said on a strangled laugh. "I think I can manage to suffer through. If you're ready, we should be going. I've got reservations."

Amused, she arched her brow at that. "At the diner?"

"If you want Ed to make one of his special desserts, you've got to put your order in ahead of time. Where's your coat?"

She retrieved it from the old-fashioned hall tree just inside the foyer, and he quickly helped her with it. To his relief, she was bundled up to her ears in coat, gloves and scarf within a matter of seconds and shouldn't have looked the least bit appealing. Zeke had never wanted to kiss a woman more.

"You've lost it, old man," he grumbled to himself after he helped her into his car, then hurried around to the driver's side. "Just stepped right over the edge. The lady already thinks you're the biggest flirt this side of the Mississippi. You even *think* about touching her and this really will be your one and only date. Get a grip, for God's sake!"

It should have been easy. He wasn't some young kid who didn't know how to control himself. But when he slid behind the wheel and started toward town, the scent of her perfume drifted to him, teasing his senses and scrambling his brain. Later, he knew he carried on an intelligent conversation during the drive, but he couldn't have said about what. She was all he could think about. It was the sweetest kind of torture.

When they reached town, he wasn't surprised to find both sides of the street in front of Ed's Diner crowded with cars. Not just famous for his fancy desserts, Ed made a mean pot of chili every Thursday, and that always drew a crowd. On a really cold night like tonight, it wasn't uncommon for customers to wait for as long as thirty minutes for a table.

There was only one parking place available in the whole block, and that was a reserved spot in front of Myrtle Henderson's antique store. For as long as Zeke could remember, she'd run off anyone who dared to park in that spot who wasn't a true customer—it didn't matter if her shop was open or not. So over the years, the locals had gotten in the habit of leaving that spot open for Myrtle. Without batting an eye, Zeke pulled into it and cut the motor.

At his side, Elizabeth eyed him in amusement. "I wasn't in town a week when I heard about Myrtle and this parking place. You like to live dangerously, don't you?"

Grinning, he didn't deny it. "Myrtle has a soft spot for me. What can I say? Old ladies just love me."

Her lips twitching, she shook her head at him. "You're shameless."

"Are you just now noticing that? It's one of my more endearing qualities."

Winking at her, he pushed open his door and came around the Suburban to open her door for her and help her to the sidewalk. Elizabeth automatically turned toward the diner, but she'd only taken a single step when he stopped her simply by touching her arm. "This way," he told her, and tried to urge her toward the front door of the closed antique store.

Confused, she looked up at him surprised. "I thought we were going to the diner for dinner."

"We are," he assured her. "But the crowd's packing the front, and there's a back entrance through Myrtle's place."

Not budging so much as an inch, Elizabeth looked pointedly at the closed sign strategically placed in the plate-glass window of the antique store. "Myrtle's is closed."

"She gave me a key."

He dug it out of his pocket and held it up for her to see. Elizabeth stood right where she was on the sidewalk. "You're up to something, McBride."

"Moi?"

"Don't give me that wounded look. I'm on to you."

Playfully he slapped a hand on his chest. "Be still my heart. Quick, let's find a bed!"

She didn't mean to laugh, but she just couldn't seem to help herself. "Dammit, I'm trying to be serious here—"

"But that's not what tonight's about," he told her quietly. "It's just fun. That's all. Just dinner and a few laughs. Nothing serious or tense, nothing that you have to worry about or be on guard over. Because nothing's going to happen that you don't want to. I guarantee it."

Her eyes searching his, Elizabeth looked for the spark of teasing devilment that was almost always there in his eyes, but he was dead serious.

Trust me. He didn't say the words, but she heard them, nonetheless. And she was stunned by how badly she wanted to do just that. She didn't trust that easily, especially when it came to men with quick smiles and an even quicker line. He could hurt her, and he'd probably never even realize it. Charming men never did.

If she'd been wise, she'd have returned to his truck right then and insisted he take her home. But when her feet finally moved, it was toward the front door of the antique shop. "I'm counting on you being a man of your word, McBride. Don't disappoint me."

"Not in this lifetime, Lizzie, darlin'," he assured her. "Just relax and put yourself in my hands."

"Said the spider to the fly," she snorted.

Grinning, he unlocked the door to the shop, then motioned for her to precede him inside. Hesitating, she frowned up at him one more time, wondering what she had foolishly agreed to, but his face gave nothing away. Her curiosity getting the best of her, she stepped inside.

Over the course of the past three months, Elizabeth had been in Myrtle's shop several times, and it never failed to fascinate her. Piled to the ceiling with everything from old washtubs and beer signs to beautiful oak sideboards and rare Turkish rugs, it was the kind of place she could browse in for hours. There was absolutely no rhyme or reason to the way Myrtle displayed items, no method to her madness. And that was what made the shop so much fun. Packed full of trash and treasures, you never knew what you were going to find as you wandered through the crowded aisles.

She'd never seen it quite like this, however. A light shone somewhere near the rear of the building, but the rest of the shop was bathed in deep, mysterious shadows. Feeling eyes on her, she glanced up and gasped at the sight of a stuffed owl staring down at her from its perch on a mammoth walnut cabinet.

Behind her, Zeke chuckled and shut the shop door behind him. "Don't let Henry rattle you. He's not going anywhere. He's been stuck up there in that same spot for as long as I can remember. C'mon. We're going back here." Stepping around her, he took her hand and led her through the maze of antiques toward the rear of the shop.

With his fingers warm and strong around hers, Elizabeth hardly noticed her surroundings for the thundering of her heart. A voice in her head furiously tried to remind her that the whole purpose of going out with Zeke was to prove to herself that they had nothing in common. Instead, all she could think of was that nothing had ever felt better than her hand in his.

Bemused, she blindly followed him around an old upright piano piled high with dusty, out-of-date books, past a display of kitchen utensils that had gone out of style at the turn of the century, through an archway of wooden chairs that looked as though it was going to tumble in on itself any second. She assumed he was leading her to the door that connected Myrtle's shop with the diner next door…until he pulled her around a gorgeous Duncan Phyfe china cabinet that blocked the view of the rear of the shop.

Stunned, she stared at the scene spread out before her, unable to believe her eyes. The light that she'd assumed had been left on for security purposes was, in fact, candles. Dozens of them. Short ones, fat ones, tapers, in every kind of candleholder she could imagine, from priceless crystal to simple elegant brass. And there, right in the middle of them and the wonderful chaos that was Myrtle's shop, furniture had been cleared away to create an alcove that was just big enough for a small round table. Covered in antique lace, it was set simply for two, with Blue Willow china and a small bowl of yellow roses. In the incongruous setting, Elizabeth had never seen anything more elegant—or romantic—in her life.

And it scared her to death. This wasn't the safe, public meal she had envisioned, but something far more dangerous, far more appealing. And that's when she knew she was in trouble. Because she would have liked nothing better than to share a meal with Zeke McBride, alone, in that magical setting.

"This isn't what we agreed to," she reminded him huskily. "You said the diner—"

"No, I said we would go someplace public," he said

quickly, triumphantly. ''Myrtle's is public—it just happens to be closed at the moment.'' When she narrowed her eyes at that, he actually had the gall to laugh at her. ''C'mon, sweetheart, admit it. I got you. You wanted public, I gave it to you. You didn't say a thing about other people being around.''

He had her and they both knew it. And she only had herself to blame. She should have known that a flirt like Zeke would find a way to get a woman alone. ''You think you're pretty tricky, don't you, McBride?''

Grinning, he didn't deny it. ''You're damn straight. And I'm cute, too,'' he added outrageously, his blue eyes laughing. ''Go ahead. You can admit it. I know you've noticed.''

She had, darn it, but she wasn't about to admit that to him. ''How did you manage all this?''

''Did I happen to mention that Myrtle's one of my mother's best friends?''

It figured. ''I should make you take me right home. You know that, don't you?''

''But you won't,'' he said confidently. ''Because you know you're going to have fun.''

She might have argued about that, but just at that moment he reached over and set the needle of an old phonograph on a record, setting the strains of the ''Tennessee Waltz'' drifting through the shop. It was one of her favorites. How had he known?

Her pulse racing, she looked up at him helplessly. ''Zeke—''

The music must have been a signal because the door between Myrtle's place and the diner opened, and a waiter swept through, balancing a tray of food on one hand. Pulling out a chair for her at the table, Zeke arched a brow at her. ''Shall we eat?''

He would have taken her home if she'd stood her ground

and insisted. But that seemed petty. He had gone to a lot of trouble. And as much as she hated to admit it, she wanted to stay. Without a word, she slipped into the chair he held for her.

Considering that it was Thursday night and people were lined up at the diner for Ed's special, she expected a hot, spicy bowl of red chili. But when Zeke was seated and the waiter served them, the tossed salad, chicken cordon bleu, and baby asparagus he set before them was a far cry from chili.

Chuckling at her reaction, Zeke said, "Did I forget to mention that Ed's a romantic?"

Elizabeth couldn't have been more surprised if he'd told her the man watched old Fred Astaire and Ginger Rogers movies. She ate breakfast just about every morning at the diner, and over the course of the last few months, she and Ed had discussed everything from the stock market to Armageddon. He was rough and hard edged, and she liked him, but not once had he ever let on that he was an old softie when it came to matters of the heart.

"Not mentioning things seems to be a habit with most people around these parts," she said dryly. "What else haven't you told me, McBride?"

"You get that on the second date, darlin'," he promised, flashing his dimples at her. "Try to be patient."

"And you think there's going to be one?" she asked archly.

"Hey, you're here, aren't you? After turning me down at least a gazillion times. So, yeah, I think there'll be a second one. Why wouldn't there be?" Teasing, he threw his arms wide. "What's not to like?"

What, indeed? That was why she was there, to discover reasons not to like the darn man, but, Lord, he made it difficult. Fascination—that was what he made her feel.

There was no other way to describe it. She tried to convince herself it was just their surroundings—any woman would have been hard-pressed not to be seduced by the champagne and music and romantic setting, not to mention the most delectable meal she had ever eaten—but she'd never lied to herself and she couldn't start now. It was the man. *He* was what fascinated her.

The knowledge rattled her. She didn't want to be captivated by him, was determined not to be charmed. But he'd slipped past her guard, and she didn't know how it happened. She wasn't used to being the focus of a man's unrelenting flirting, and she was sure she wouldn't be able to enjoy the meal at all. But once she'd agreed to stay, he let up on the teasing remarks and drew her into conversations about everything from politics and religion to John Wayne movies and psychic predictions. Before she knew it, she was telling him about her childhood, her family, her hopes and dreams.

Suddenly realizing that she'd been going on forever about herself, she blushed. "I didn't mean to ramble on. How did we get on my childhood, anyway?"

"We were talking about fishing and you mentioned going ice fishing with your father once. You must have been a daddy's girl."

Her smile slipped slightly. "Yeah, I guess I was. Once."

He didn't ask her what happened, but she could see the questions in his eyes, and without quite intending to, she told him far more about herself than she'd intended to. "When I was little, I used to worship the ground he walked on. He had this wonderful knack for making me feel special. Like I was the prettiest little girl in the whole world. Then as I got older, I realized that there were a lot of special 'girls' in my father's life." Shrugging, she said, "It wasn't all that difficult to attract his attention. All you had to do was be female.''

She said that simply enough, without an ounce of emotion, as if she had long since accepted her father's shortcomings, but Zeke heard the words she didn't say, saw the hurt that she quickly suppressed. And suddenly the puzzle pieces that were Elizabeth Davis fell into place. Her old man had played around on her mother. And judging from the pain she couldn't hide, he'd done it more than once.

Oh, she didn't quite say that, but it explained a hell of a lot. Like why the lady kept coming up with reasons not to go out with him when he knew she was as attracted to him as he was to her. She thought he was like her father.

He supposed she was justified. She didn't know him, and considering her background, he could see why she would be leery of him. From the moment they'd first met, he'd done nothing but tease and flirt with her and try to get her to go out with him. That didn't mean, however, that he went around panting after anything in skirts. Yes, he liked women—he readily admitted it. But there was no crime in that. He was a healthy, single man, free to date and see whoever he wanted, whenever he wanted. He had his standards, though. He never dated more than one woman at a time—only a fool did that. And he believed in commitment.

Unlike Elizabeth, he'd been lucky enough to have parents who were totally devoted to each other and their marriage vows. They'd had twenty-five years together before his father died of a heart attack at the age of fifty, and in all that time, neither his mother or father had ever even dreamed of looking at someone else.

That was what he wanted one day. So no, he wasn't like Elizabeth's father. He was too much his father's son. When he finally found a woman he could love and trust enough to make a commitment to, he would never put that love in

jeopardy by doing something stupid like flirting with another woman.

But Elizabeth didn't know that. She would when she got
to know him better.

The waiter appeared to whisk their empty plates away
and ask them about dessert. But the only sweet Zeke was
interested in was the woman across the table from him.
"We'll wait," he told the waiter, and rose to his feet to
change the record on the phonograph. Instantly the smooth
voice of Frank Sinatra, backed by a full string section,
drifted through the shop.

Turning back to Elizabeth, he held out his hand. "May
I have this dance?"

Chapter 6

Hesitating, she stared at the hard, male hand he held out to her and felt her heart literally skip a beat at the thought of going into his arms. She shouldn't. The music was too romantic, the setting far too intimate, her senses too attuned to Zeke's every move. If she let him touch her now, she didn't know if she'd be able to control her heart's foolish, traitorous response to him.

She should have thanked him for the meal, the conversation, an evening she wouldn't soon forget, then politely asked him to take her home. Because, as much as she found herself liking him, it didn't change who he was. But even though she tried, she couldn't say the words. This was, she knew, the last time she would go out with him, the last time she would have a chance to feel his arms around her. How could she deny herself that?

The decision made, she ignored the voice of reason grumbling in her head and placed her hand in his. With an easy tug, he pulled her from her chair and into his arms.

If Elizabeth lived to be a hundred, she didn't think she would ever forget what followed. She should have felt awkward. They were in a closed antique store, for heaven's sake, dancing on what was just about the only clear floor space in the entire building, and it was hardly big enough to turn around in. Dusty pieces of furniture encircled them like silent spectators while candle flames danced on their wicks. If anyone had chanced to look through the shop's large plate-glass window and spied them swaying in each other's arms, they would have been the talk of the town.

It couldn't have been more magical.

Feeling as if she had stepped into a fantasy, Elizabeth couldn't have said if they danced one song or a dozen. Time ceased to have meaning, and she couldn't find the strength to care. There was just the music and the candles and the feel of Zeke's arms around her. Nothing else mattered.

Caught up in the wonder of it, she never noticed when their steps slowed, then stopped altogether. The music changed, and she realized that their dance had come to an end. So this was it, the end of the fairy tale, time to turn in the glass slippers and go home. Disappointed, she said huskily, "Thank you for the dance."

She started to draw back, but his arms tightened ever so slightly, and when she looked up in surprise, his blue eyes were dark with a heat that stole the air right out of her lungs. Her heart lurching crazily in her breast, she went still.

Later she couldn't have said how long they stood there just so, their gazes tangled and the air between them crackling with anticipation. She would have sworn neither of them moved, but suddenly his mouth was only a heartbeat away from hers, his moist breath warm against her lips, so close she could almost taste him.

Startled, her throat desert dry, she swallowed thickly and tried to hang on to her common sense. "I...I think I should be going."

"In a minute," he promised, his voice as rough as ground glass. "I haven't kissed you yet."

"Zeke—"

His name was the only protest she could manage, the only one he allowed her. His mouth skimmed hers lightly, ever so softly, and she felt the punch of it all the way down to her toes. Stunned, she could do nothing but stare at him.

If she hadn't looked at him quite that way, with such surprise in those beautiful green eyes of hers, Zeke might have found the strength to let her go. But he'd felt that lick of heat, too, like the kiss of a bolt of lightning that came out of nowhere, and he was just as shaken as she. He was an experienced man; he knew about the wallop chemistry could pack. But from a chaste, innocent brush of mouth against mouth? The last time that had happened, he was sixteen and thought he had died and gone to the moon when Becky Sutter let him kiss her under the mistletoe. What was going on here?

Right then and there he should have pulled back. But he had her in his arms, and he couldn't bring himself to let her go. Not yet, not without another taste. Giving in to the need, he brushed her lips again, and found her just as tempting as before. And a man could, he reasoned, only resist temptation so long. Throwing caution to the wind, he covered her mouth with his and, quite simply, devoured her.

He wouldn't have been surprised if she'd punched him one. He certainly wouldn't have blamed her. He'd finagled her into going out with him by using the ruse that the only way to get past their unreasonable attractiveness for each other was to prove that they didn't like each other. Yeah, right about now, he was really convincing the lady that he couldn't stand her, he thought cynically. If he drew her any closer, she'd be right inside his skin. And all he could think of was that he wanted more. A hell of a lot more.

Her head spinning, fire burning low in her belly, Elizabeth clung to him, the pounding of her heart loud and fast in her ears. She shouldn't do this. Couldn't. She wouldn't be another conquest for Zeke McBride, wouldn't be another brainless bimbo who fell for his cocky smile and the wicked twinkle in his eye. She was smarter than that. Wasn't she?

It was the doubt that stunned her, that had her pulling back to look up at him in pained, shocked confusion. She thought she knew herself, thought she knew how she would react to something as innocent as a kiss. After all, she wasn't the sort of woman who let her emotions rule her head. No, sirree, Bob. Her hormones only jumped into overdrive when she gave them permission, and not until then. At least they always had before.

Too late, she realized the entire evening had been nothing but one mistake after another. She never should have agreed to stay once she saw the romantic setting he'd arranged for them, never should have danced with him, never, ever, should have let him kiss her. She would never be able to look him in the eye again without remembering the taste of his mouth on hers. Dear God, what had she done?

Her heart pounding frantically, she jerked back. "I have to leave. Now!"

"Lizzy, wait! Honey, let's talk about this—"

"No! There's nothing to talk about." They'd talked enough already. Talking had gotten her into this whole mess in the first place. She knew just how dangerous a flirting man could be, and still she'd let him charm her. Well, no more! She was going home, and from now on, she was steering clear of Zeke McBride.

Whirling away from him, she looked frantically for her coat and purse, but she couldn't remember where she'd put them, and in the shadows that engulfed the shop, everything just blended in. Frustrated, she never realized just how close she was to cracking until she heard a sob hitch in her throat. Horrified, she stiffened. She would not cry, dammit!

She heard Zeke swear behind her, and then his fingers were closing gently around her shoulder. "Sweetheart—"

Whatever he would have said next was lost with the jingling of the bell on the front door to Myrtle's shop. Surprised, they both turned in time to see Nick step inside.

It was obvious that he knew he'd walked in at a bad moment. The tension was so thick Elizabeth could feel it in the air, and she knew her cheeks were fiery, her hair tousled from Zeke's fingers. Five minutes earlier, and Nick would have caught them in each other's arms, kissing as if there was no tomorrow.

Not a dense man, he had to know what he'd interrupted. The evidence was all around them—the remnants of their meal, the candles, the love song that drifted throughout the shop, setting an intimate, romantic mood. To his credit, though, he didn't even blink. From his expression, you'd have thought that walking in on couples using Myrtle's shop for a trysting place was an everyday occurrence. Not the least bit embarrassed, he headed straight for them.

"Sorry to interrupt," he said by way of a greeting. "When I saw Zeke's truck out front, I stopped in at the diner, and Ed told me I'd find you two in here."

"No problem," Zeke said shortly, instantly alert. "*Is* there a problem?"

He nodded. "Tina Ellison's been trying to get Elizabeth on her cell phone."

Alarmed, Elizabeth went pale. "I left it at home. What's wrong? Has there been another threat against the wolves?"

His lean face more serious than she'd ever seen it, he hesitated, then broke the news as gently as possible. "We're not sure yet, but you need to get back to your office. That wolf you're so crazy about, the alpha male—"

"Number Eight? Napoleon?" At his nod, she pressed suddenly trembling fingers to her mouth. "Oh, God, something's happened to him, hasn't it? What? Dammit, Nick, tell me!"

"His radio collar's been emitting a mortality code for the past twenty minutes. Tina tried calling Ed's, but it's chili night, and the place is a madhouse. Someone took the phone off the hook, so she tried getting you on your cell phone instead. When that didn't work, she called me. She thinks he may be dead."

The words hit her like a knife to the heart, draining every last ounce of blood from her cheeks. No! Not Napoleon! He was too big, too strong, too cunning. Of all the wolves that had been selected for the project, he was the one that everyone agreed was destined to not only survive, but thrive. She'd just seen him that afternoon, running through the Hawk River Valley without a care in the world. He loved his freedom, loved his new home. He couldn't be dead. There had to be a mistake.

"No," she said hoarsely, refusing to even consider the possibility. "He's not dead. He can't be." Turning away, she looked around distractedly for her purse. "Dammit, where's my purse? I've got to get to the office."

"Here," Zeke said quietly, and took it and her coat from the old hall tree where he'd hung them earlier. Holding her coat out, he helped her into it, then reached for his own. "Let me blow these candles out and lock up, and we can go."

"You don't have to—"

He gave her a look that had the words dying on her

tongue. Even if he hadn't been assigned to investigate who was threatening the wolves, there was no way he'd have let her handle this alone. Not after the evening they'd just shared and a kiss that still had his blood humming. "I'm going," he said flatly.

She didn't argue, but hurriedly helped him blow the candles out instead. Within seconds, Myrtle's shop was dark and locked and they were racing down the street in Zeke's truck with the sheriff right behind them.

The minute Elizabeth walked through the front door of her office, Tina and Peter were both there to greet her, their grave expressions telling her more clearly than words just how serious the situation was. "Thank God!" Tina exclaimed, hugging her. "We've been frantic. Napoleon—"

"I know. Nick told me." She cut to the heart of the matter. "Has there been any change?"

Peter shook his head. "No, nothing. I picked up the radio signal over twenty minutes ago, and it's remained steady ever since."

"Maybe his collar malfunctioned," Tina said hopefully. "It's been known to happen."

"But only in the rarest incidents," her husband said with a warning frown, not wanting to give Elizabeth false hope. "These collars are state-of-the-art and designed to hold up in all kinds of conditions. They don't emit the code unless the animal hasn't moved for five hours. We all know that doesn't happen with wolves unless they're dead."

"In laboratory tests of the collar, sudden fluctuation of temperatures also produced the code," Elizabeth retorted. "And the weather the past few days has been crazy—up, then down, and all over the place. That's a much-more-logical explanation than that he's dead."

Even to her own ears, she sounded more than a little desperate. Wincing, she struggled for control and clung to the thought that it was too early to jump to conclusions. "What about Queenie? Where is she?" she asked Peter as she threw off her coat and moved to the electronic radar screen to show the pregnant wolf's position. "They've been together constantly since their release. I can't believe that she would run off and leave him unless something was seriously wrong, and maybe not even then. They're devoted to each other."

"No, she's there, nearby," Peter said, pointing out the blinking dot on the screen that was Queenie. "But it's hard to say if she's okay. She hasn't moved around a lot since Napoleon's collar started emanating the code. So we don't know if she's hurt or we miscalculated the due date of her pups and she's in labor or she just refuses to leave him."

Quietly listening to the conversation up until then, Nick said, "You could just all be missing the obvious, folks. Maybe the wolf just figured a way to wriggle out of the damn collar and it's just lying in the snow up there at Eagle Ridge sending out that darn code."

"You know how rugged the terrain is around here," Zeke told Elizabeth. "And Napoleon and Queenie have been all over the place. He could have snagged it on a rock or broken tree limb or even a fence post. Or maybe he just found a way to slip the damn thing off over his head."

She wanted desperately to believe him, but she wasn't a woman who deluded herself. Reluctantly she shook her head. "I wish I could say that was possible, but I just don't see how. These aren't your average two-bit dog collars that can be bought at some pet store. Each wolf was sedated, then personally measured for a custom fit. The collars don't buckle—they're secured in place with bolts and designed to hold up to the most trying conditions. There's no way Napoleon could have slipped it over his head, even if he did get it caught on something. And no one could have removed it without taking a chance that he'd take their hand off. Unless they sedated him."

Or he was dead.

No one said the words, but they hung there in the air nonetheless—a grim, very real possibility. The stark reality of that could have brought Elizabeth to her knees if she'd let it, but she couldn't give in to her emotions, not when she didn't know anything for sure yet. Only when she saw Napoleon's body would she cry. Until then she had to operate on the premise that there was another explanation. With time, she would figure out what it was. In the meantime, she had work to do.

Turning back to the monitoring system, she asked Peter, "Where's the signal come from?"

"One mile northwest of Eagle Ridge," he said promptly. "It's impossible to pinpoint the exact location from here, but it's somewhere in that vicinity."

Zeke's gaze sharpened at that. "That's just over the hill from the holding pen."

Elizabeth watched him exchange a look with Nick and knew what both men were thinking. Whoever had planted the poisoned meat outside the holding pen last week could have very well come back and finished the job.

"Tina and I saw him and Queenie running through the valley about one this afternoon," she told them. "They were headed south and disappeared into the trees."

"So if it takes five hours of stillness before the mortality code kicks in," Nick said, "then something must have happened to Napoleon right after you saw him. The snow's pretty bad up on the ridge after last night's storm. Did you see any other vehicles?"

She shook her head. "No, but I was glassing the valley with my binoculars and not paying too much attention to who was going by on the road behind me. This was the first time I'd seen Napoleon and Queenie since their release, and I was too busy checking them out to notice much else.'' Glancing from one man to the other, she said, ''You think that bastard who called me that night the poisoned meat was left at the holding pen killed him, don't you?''

She would have forgiven Zeke if he'd lied to her then and let her go on hoping that this was all some horrible mistake, but he didn't. His square, rugged face grave, he nodded. ''Yeah, I do. I know you don't want to hear that, but you don't have the luxury of burying your head in the sand right now. If he's dead, then whoever killed him is feeling pretty damn cocky right now. And Queenie is somewhere nearby. There's nothing to stop him from going after her next.''

''The hell he will!'' All her protective instincts crying out in outrage at the thought, she snapped into action. ''We can't do anything tonight, but in the morning we're going to search every inch of Eagle Ridge until we find both wolves. Tina, get on the phone and call Fish and Wildlife in Aspen and Gunnison and see if they can loan us some of their people. We'll need everyone here at dawn.''

All business, she turned to Nick. ''Can you lend us some of your deputies? That's rugged country. We're going to need all the help we can get.''

He nodded. ''I'll have them here.''

''And I'll get some of the men from the ranch,'' Zeke added. ''Would you like me to call Merry? You may need a vet.''

She didn't want to think that would be necessary, but he was right. ''Thanks,'' she said huskily. ''I appreciate that. I hope we don't need her, but it's better to play safe.''

''I'll call her right now,'' he said, and helped himself to the phone at the nearest desk.

Tina and the sheriff did the same thing, and Elizabeth

was left with the unenviable job of calling her boss at home in Denver and relaying the latest turn of events. Just last week she'd called her about the wolves' release, and they'd celebrated the first step of what they'd both expected to be a very successful project. At the time, Elizabeth had never dreamed she'd be calling her back so soon to report the possible death of one of the wolves. Especially Napoleon. He was the pride and joy of the entire project. She wasn't looking forward to it.

Punching in her number, she waited for the other woman to come on the line, then said grimly, "Irene? This is Elizabeth. I'm sorry to call you at home, but I've got some bad news."

Once arrangements were made for the morning search and everyone had been notified, there was nothing else that could be done until dawn. Nick got a call about a domestic dispute and left, promising to be back before sunup, while Tina made arrangements for her and Peter to spend the rest of the night at the office just in case there was a change in the radio signals. No one really thought that was going to happen, but they—like Elizabeth—couldn't give up hope.

"I'll call you if there's the slightest change," Tina assured her when Elizabeth lingered, hating to go home. "You should try to get some sleep. Tomorrow's going to be a long day."

And a difficult one. Elizabeth didn't kid herself into thinking that finding either Napoleon or Queenie would be easy, even with the help of electronic tracking devices. The area they would be searching was primitive and rugged and covered in two feet of new snow. Unless they got lucky early, there was a possibility they would have to cover hundreds of acres, and every step could be treacherous. Only a fool would go into something like that with too little sleep.

"All right," she sighed. "But if there's anything you think I need to know, you call me immediately."

"Even if it's three in the morning," Peter promised gruffly. "You've done everything you can tonight, boss. Try to get some sleep."

She wouldn't, not when worry was burning a hole in her stomach, but that was something she kept to herself. "You, too," she said huskily. "I'll be back around six unless you need me earlier."

She retrieved her coat and purse and turned to find Zeke still seated at the desk where he'd called and enlisted people for the morning search, now patiently waiting for her. For the first time in what seemed like hours, she remembered their date and a kiss that never should have happened.

Pushing to his feet, he lifted a brow at her. "Ready to go?"

Her heart started to knock against her ribs at the thought of riding all the way out to her place with him. "I hate to ask you to take me all the way home when you live in the opposite direction," she blurted out. "I can take Tina's car, since she and Peter aren't going anywhere—"

"We had a date," he cut in softly. "I picked you up—I take you home. Here, let me help you with that."

Always the gentleman, he took her coat and helped her shrug into it, guiding the soft black wool all the way up her arms to her shoulders. It was, Elizabeth knew, an instinctive courtesy on his part, one that he would have performed for Myrtle or Tina or any other female between the ages of two and a hundred and five. But when his fingers brushed her neck as he straightened her collar for her, there was nothing innocent about her response to the gesture. Her pulse scattered, her breath feathered out of her lungs, and just that easily, her body remembered every time he'd touched her tonight.

Don't go there, she told herself quickly. *You're too vulnerable now, too shaky. You start thinking about what the man can do to you with just a touch and you're going to be in serious trouble.*

Stiffening, she stepped away from him because if she didn't now, she might not be able to later. But, Lord, it was hard when all she could think about was how she wanted to just sink into his arms!

"We should be going," she said hoarsely, and hurried toward the door. "It's getting late."

With his long legs, he had no trouble keeping up with her, and a half second before she reached the office's outer door, he stepped around her to push it open and hold it so she could precede him outside. Even to a dense man, it was obvious that she was all but running from him, and if there was one thing she knew about Zeke McBride, it was that he was in no way, shape or form, dense. But if he noticed that she was once again skittish where he was concerned, he made no comment. Instead, he followed her outside and fell into step with her as they crossed the parking lot to his truck.

The night was cold and still, alight with stardust and a low-slung crescent moon on the horizon. It was the kind of night that lovers loved, when they could snuggle before a crackling fire and share slow, hot kisses that blocked out the world. If she let herself, she could see it now, feel it, the stroke of sure, hard hands on her, the lingering kisses, the groans and sighs of passion and pleasure with a man that took her outside of herself. A man like Zeke, who knew how to make a woman feel—

Suddenly realizing where her thoughts had wandered, she gasped, mortified, thankful for the darkness that concealed her hot cheeks. Just as they reached his truck he glanced down at her in puzzlement. "You okay?"

No! she wanted to cry. She would never be okay again. And it was all because of him. Because he'd given her a taste of something she hadn't allowed herself to want before, hadn't allowed herself to even dream of, and she'd liked the woman that she was when she was with him. Because he'd kissed her and made her want things she couldn't have, not with a man like him. Not with a man like her father.

"I'm just tired," she choked, looking anywhere but at him. "It's been a long day."

Staring down at her in the darkness, his eyes searching her pale face, Zeke knew that something more than that was troubling her, but he let it slide. This wasn't the time to push her into telling him what was going on inside her head, not when she had the ordeal of tomorrow hovering over her like a thunderhead.

And there was no question in his mind that it was going to be a hell of an ordeal. She appeared to have accepted the fact that there was a good chance that Napoleon was dead, but Zeke knew better. Her head might have accepted the logic of the argument that there was no other likely explanation for the sudden cessation of movement in an animal that was the most active in the pack, but her heart was telling her something else entirely. She loved that damn wolf, and she wouldn't give up on him. Even now she was fighting the truth with every breath of her being, holding out hope against all odds, praying for a miracle.

As the head of the project, she never should have allowed herself to get that emotionally involved with an animal she was going to have to eventually release back into the wild. It just wasn't the professional thing to do. But if there was one thing Zeke was learning about the lady, it was that she couldn't hold back when it came to her emotions. She just didn't have it in her.

And dammit, he liked that about her. She cared. But he didn't have a clue if she realized how vulnerable that made her. She'd left herself wide open to hurt, and there wasn't a damn thing he could do to protect her from that. Except be there for her when the pain came crashing down on her.

And he would be there, he vowed silently. Tomorrow he wasn't letting her out of his sight.

When Elizabeth first moved to Liberty Hill and had looked around for a house to rent for the duration of her stay, she'd wanted something small and secluded, the farther she could get from neighbors, the better. It wasn't that she was unsociable—she wasn't. But when she'd worked on the Yellowstone project, she'd learned that after dealing with hostile locals all day, the last thing she wanted to do was to come home and contend with angry neighbors who lived close enough to throw rocks. Not that anyone tried to hurt her. But she'd felt like an unwanted intruder in people's lives, and had promised herself when she was assigned to the Liberty Hill project that she wouldn't make the same mistake twice. So she'd found a small house fifteen miles from town and well off the road. She'd wanted isolation and she'd gotten it, and she'd never regretted it.

But now, as Zeke pulled into the long drive that led to her house, she noticed just how cut off she was from the rest of the world. There were no houses close by, no lights. And with trees surrounding the house on all sides, it was completely invisible from the main road. Up until now, that had been a plus. Now she wasn't so sure.

Zeke was obviously thinking the same thing. Frowning as they emerged from the tree-lined drive into the small clearing that surrounded the old wooden house, he frowned at the single porch light that did little to dispel the darkness that engulfed the place. "You might think about having a security light put in out here," he said as he braked to a stop in front of the porch steps and cut the engine. "It's damn dark out here."

"The landlord promised to have one installed when I signed the lease. That was three months ago. Every time I call about it, he claims it's being installed next week."

"Figures," Zeke snorted. "Ralph Murphy always was tight-fisted. His ex-wife Bertha used to say he wouldn't give a plugged nickel to a beggar on the street if he thought he could find a way to use it. Call the hardware store yourself and tell them to install one and charge it to his account."

"And get myself thrown out on the streets? I don't think so."

His grin flashed in the darkness. "You gotta be kidding. You think he'd throw you out? Darlin', this house was sitting empty for three years before you came along—renters aren't easy to come by in this neck of the woods. There's no way Ralph is going to throw you out and lose the rent you're paying him. He may be tight, but he's not stupid."

He had a point. "And all this time, I've been stumbling around in the dark!" she said, chuckling. "I'll call first thing in the morning—"

Too late, she remembered that she would be combing Eagle Ridge for Napoleon long before the hardware store even opened, and her smile faded. "I'll have to get to it when I can. But thanks for the advice." Blindly she stared at her poorly lit porch. "I guess I should be going in."

"The search starts early," he agreed. "You'll need all the sleep you can get."

She wouldn't sleep, probably wouldn't be able to close

her eyes, but that was hardly something she could say when she knew already that he was going to be one of the main causes of her sleeplessness. At this point, it was useless to deny it. She watched him push open his door, then come around to open hers for her, and her heart did a slow, dizzy roll in her chest. Too late, she realized that she should have thanked him for the evening and rushed inside while she still could. Now he was going to walk her to her door and probably kiss her good-night, and that just might be her downfall. Because she wanted that—wanted him, God help her—and she was horribly afraid she wasn't going to be able to resist him.

The walk to the front door seemed the longest of her life. With every step her heart thundered in response, but she needn't have worried. Instead of kissing her, he took her keys from her, unlocked the door for her, then preceded her inside.

"Hey, what're you doing?"

"Don't worry," he said, chuckling, searching for and finding the light switch just inside the door. "I'm not staying the night. I just want to look around and make sure everything's okay." And without waiting for her permission, he made his way through her house, turning on lights as he went, testing the locks on her windows and back door, looking in every closet and even under her bed for an intruder.

He didn't find anyone, of course. Elizabeth hadn't expected him to. Even when the hate mail and phone calls had been at their worst, no one had ever actually stepped foot on her property. But then again, no one had actually dared to harm one of the wolves, either. Until, possibly, today.

Sobering at the thought, she trailed him back into the living room, once it was obvious no one was there. "I'll be fine, Zeke,'' she assured him when he appeared anything but satisfied that she was safe. ''The phone's right by my bed and so is my shotgun. I won't hesitate to use either one of them if someone tries to break in.''

Surprised, he grinned. ''You know how to use a shotgun?''

''My father gave it to me when I got my first apartment,'' she told him. ''I'm not much of a marksman, but you don't have to be with a shotgun. You just point it in the right direction and pull the trigger. You're bound to hit something.''

She'd never had to aim it at another human being and couldn't say for certain that she would actually pull the trigger, even if she was afraid for her life, but any man with brains in his head would surely know to be leery of a terrified woman with a gun in her hands. ''So you see? You don't have to worry about me. I'm perfectly safe here.''

He wasn't convinced—she could still see the worry darkening his eyes—but short of insisting on staying the night, there wasn't a heck of a lot more he could do. ''If you're scared or lonely or you just can't sleep, I want you to call me at Joe's. I can be here in twenty minutes.''

He spied a notepad on the table next to the couch and quickly scribbled down his brother's number. ''If it's an emergency, call Nick first—he can get here quicker. Dammit, Elizabeth, are you sure you don't want me to stay? I can sleep on the couch if that's what you want—''

If he stayed, he wouldn't sleep anywhere but in her bed and they both knew it. And she wasn't anywhere near ready for that. ''It's the wolves that are in danger, not me,'' she said. ''So will you relax? I'll be fine.''

''You call me if you're scared?''

''If a tree limb so much as scrapes the eave,'' she assured

him with a crooked, teasing smile. "I never would have figured you for such a worrier."

"I don't like the idea of you being way out here by yourself when there's a nutcase out there killing your wolves," he said simply. "But if you're sure you'll be okay, I guess I'd better be going. Try to get some sleep."

He kissed her before she could even think about objecting, brushing a soft, lingering kiss to her cheek. Then, before she was ready to let him leave, he was striding out the door and she was alone. He didn't look back, which was, she decided, a good thing. Because long after his truck rumbled down the drive to the highway, she still stood there, her hand pressed to her cheek, holding in the warmth of his kiss.

Chapter 7

Just as she'd suspected, Elizabeth didn't sleep. When her dreams weren't haunted with images of Napoleon's lifeless body lying dead in a ravine somewhere, she found herself replaying, again and again, the moments she'd spent in Zeke's arms at Myrtle's shop. Restless, aching, she tossed and turned and crawled all over the bed. By the time her alarm went off at five-thirty, she was thoroughly exhausted.

With her eyes squeezed shut, she slapped at the alarm until it abruptly ceased its irritating buzzing, every muscle in her body protesting at the thought of getting up. Just another couple of hours, she told herself with a groan. That was all she needed. Just two hours for her mind to shut down and off so she could sleep. Maybe then she could face the search for Napoleon without feeling as if she was about to come apart at the seams.

But she didn't have a couple of hours, didn't, actually have much time to spare at all. The search began in a little over an hour, and as much as she dreaded it, she had to be there. If she had to scour every hollow and crevice of Eagle Ridge, she would find him and deal with whatever had happened to him.

Her eyes gritty, she rolled out of bed and headed for the bathroom and a hot shower. It didn't help much, but by the time she was dressed and had downed a cup of the strongest coffee she could brew, she was at least starting to feel human again.

Then she gathered her things and stepped outside onto her front porch, only to stop dead in her tracks at the sight that met her eyes.

Fog. Damp and cold and thick, it had silently slipped in over the mountains like a thief in the night and settled in, reducing visibility to practically nothing and swallowing everything in sight. Twenty yards away, her car sat in the drive, but she could just barely make it out.

If she'd had any tears in her, she could have cried then. She knew about fog in the mountains, knew how it could cling to the peaks and valleys, cutting people off from the rest of the world for God only knew how long before it finally lifted. And somewhere out in that mess was Napoleon. How was she ever going to find him now?

She should, she realized, call the search off until conditions improved. Hiking the Eagle Ridge area was difficult enough on the best of days. Traipsing all over it when you couldn't see two feet in front of your face was downright dangerous. Even someone who knew the area well could get turned around in a blinding fog and walk off the side of a cliff if they weren't very, very careful.

And danger aside, what was the point? With the fog hiding whole mountains from view, she could walk within yards of Napoleon and never even know it.

But even as she acknowledged the logic of that, she knew that as long as there was a slim hope that Napoleon might still somehow be alive, the search would begin at dawn, as scheduled.

Thankful she could finally *do* something, she headed for the office. The drive, usually one she could make with her eyes almost closed, was a test of nerves. The fog moved like a living thing, swirling in front of her, blocking her view, then floating off again at the most unexpected moments, making it impossible for her to relax her guard for so much as an instant. Afraid to pick up too much speed in the clear spots, only to suddenly slam into another blinding wall of fog, she crawled all the way into town. And the drive that usually took her only fifteen minutes took well over a half hour.

Her eyes trained straight ahead, straining to see, she sighed in relief as she rounded the last curve of the windy road that led into Liberty Hill. The town should have been spread out before her. Not surprisingly, she could only make out the vague, shadowy outline of a building here and there in the fog. Inching her way down Main Street, she felt as if she'd stumbled into an old episode of *Twilight Zone* by mistake. The bank was gone, the sheriff's office, the square, all lost in the mist.

Later, she never knew how she found her office. With all the landmarks wiped out by the fog, she couldn't judge distances. Then suddenly the fog parted and there it was. With a sigh of relief, she turned into the parking lot and wouldn't have been surprised to find it empty. Instead, it was nearly full.

Stunned, she blinked at the vehicles that were nearly concealed by the fog. She'd known Tina and Peter would be there, of course, and had expected Zeke and Nick and his three deputies, but that was it. With the weather so raw and nasty, she hadn't dared let herself hope for more.

But as she made her way to the entrance of her office

and stepped inside, she was stunned to discover that she had vastly underestimated the citizens of Liberty Hill. In a single glance, she picked out the entire McBride family except for Zeke's mother, Sara, the Hoffsteaders and Jenkinses and Carsons, all local ranchers who had money and power and were the movers and shakers of Falls County. All of them had put in appearances at the town meeting, and without exception, they'd watched with stoic faces while other people berated the program and never said a word.

Elizabeth had always thought she was good at reading people's faces, and she'd have sworn that the elite of Liberty Hill wanted nothing so much as for her to be gone, and her wolves with her. But here they were, out at dawn on a miserable morning that wasn't fit for a duck, offering a show of support that floored her.

At a loss for words, she said huskily, "I can't believe you're all here. I—I'm stunned."

Martha Hoffsteader, a crusty rancher's wife who had her husband and six sons wrapped around her little finger, sniffed and said, "We might not be crazy about wolves running around our neck of the woods, but that doesn't mean we're going to stand by and let someone get away with killing one, either, just for the sheer pleasure of it. We don't cotton to that around here."

The others seconded her. "That's right. You need help, so here we are."

"We'll go over every inch of Eagle Ridge with you if that's what it takes to find that wolf of yours. We're ready when you are."

For the first time since Elizabeth had heard of Napoleon's disappearance, the sting of tears burned her eyes and welled in her throat, and she thought she was going to lose it right there. Something of her distress must have shown in her face, because suddenly Zeke was stepping forward to draw the attention away from her. "Okay, everyone, the radio signal from the wolf's collar is still coming from Eagle Ridge, so we're going to head up there and concentrate on searching the east side of the highway. It's too dangerous in this weather for all of us to drive up there, so we're going to carpool. Everyone with Suburbans and vans raise your hands."

Thankful for the chance to regain control, Elizabeth turned away and had just drawn a steadying breath when Zeke's sisters joined her. Hastily, she wiped at the foolish tears that threatened to spill over her lashes. "I'm sorry," she choked. "I didn't mean to fall apart on everyone. I just never expected this kind of support."

"People might not always agree on government policies around here," Janey told her, "but they don't like meanness."

"That's right," Merry said. "When the word got out that Napoleon could be in trouble, people got on the phone and started calling around, spreading the news and volunteering to join in the search. Once this fog lifts, you watch—half the town will turn up at Eagle Ridge."

Elizabeth prayed she knew what she was talking about. Because it could take half the citizens of Liberty Hill, not to mention a heck of a lot of luck, to find Napoleon. The terrain east of the highway that cut through Eagle Ridge was some of the roughest in the state. Harsh and unforgiving, it was scarred with deep ravines and rocky gorges that offered a wounded animal literally hundreds of places to hide. And most of those places were inaccessible to man. They could search for days, weeks, in the wild country, and never find anything.

Between them, Zeke and Nick lined up six drivers to relay the searchers up to the top of the ridge, and within minutes, it was time to leave. Before everyone could begin the mass exodus toward the parking lot, however, Elizabeth stepped forward to thank them again for coming and to give some last-minute words of caution.

"Napoleon's mate is still in the area," she said. "So if you spot her or Napoleon, please contact me, Tina or Peter. We don't know if Napoleon is dead or injured, and so don't approach him yourself. And please be careful in the fog. We don't want anyone walking off the side of a cliff."

That seemed to strike more than a few people funny, but it wasn't until Zeke joined her that she realized why. "Just about anyone who grew up in this area has spent time traipsing around Eagle Ridge," he told her. "It's one of the best hunting areas around. Most of these people could walk it blindfolded and never take a misstep."

It was the first time he'd spoken to her since last night, the first time he'd allowed himself to get within touching distance. She looked tired, which didn't surprise him. She'd probably spent what was left of the night after he'd brought her home worrying herself sick about Napoleon. He, on the other hand, had spent the hours between midnight and five in the morning, when his alarm went off, staring at the ceiling and thinking about nothing but her and the way she'd felt in his arms. And the taste of her on his tongue, he silently added, swallowing a groan. Lord, the woman was intoxicating! Just one kiss, and he'd wanted to sink right into her and never come up for air.

A man could lose his head with a woman like that—with a *need* like that. If he wasn't careful, she'd get under his skin and then he really would be in a hell of a mess. But what the devil was he supposed to do? Walk away from her when he couldn't sleep for thinking about her? Like hell!

It wasn't as if he couldn't handle her, he reasoned. If she

made his heart slam against his ribs with just a smile, it was just chemistry. It had to be. Because if it wasn't that, then what else could it be? The possible answer to that flitted through his mind and should have sent him running for cover, but a man had his pride. Motioning for her to precede him, he growled, ''C'mon, you're riding with me.''

Most of the locals might have known every wart and wrinkle of the terrain on the ridge, but Elizabeth didn't, and it was for that reason that Zeke planned not to let her out of his sight. It should have been simple. All he had to do was stick close, which was becoming a habit with him, anyway.

But the visibility on the ridge wasn't any better than it had been in town, and keeping an eye on her didn't turn out to be as easy as he'd expected. As everyone spread out among the trees and carefully made their way toward the area where the radio signal from Napoleon's collar was coming from, the fog ebbed and flowed around them. Rocky outcroppings and whole trees disappeared in the mist in a blink of an eye, only to reappear again within a matter of moments.

Still, Zeke would have sworn he knew right where Elizabeth was. Then he stepped around a mammoth pine that appeared from out of nowhere in the fog, and when he looked to his right, to the spot where she'd been only minutes before, she was nowhere in sight.

''Damn!'' Swearing, he looked wildly around, but he was surrounded by the thick, blinding mist. Just that easily she'd disappeared. ''Lizzie? Dammit, where are you?''

''Here.''

She sounded close enough to touch, but when he rushed to the spot where he'd last seen her and called out again, her voice was fainter, even farther away. There was, he told himself, no reason to be alarmed. The fog was just playing tricks on him. Sounds carried strangely in the mist, and in all likelihood, she was no more than twenty or thirty feet away. All she had to do was stand still and he'd find her.

"Don't move!" he yelled. "Just stay where you are and keep talking. I'm coming."

"What? I...can't hear... Where...you?"

He would have sworn she was off to his left, but her disjointed words came back to him in fragments from the opposite direction—right where the rocky ledge of the ridge dropped off without warning to the valley hundreds of feet below.

"Stop!" he cried out hoarsely, his blood turning to ice as he started to run. "You're headed straight for the cliff!"

Surrounded by the mist, Elizabeth thought she heard Zeke yell out something, but he was so far away, she couldn't tell what it was. And when she called back to him, he never answered her. A thick, eerie silence engulfed her, and if she hadn't known better, she would have sworn she was completely cut off from the rest of the world. Nothing moved, not even the wind in the top of the trees. Nothing but the fog that swirled around her, brushing against her, teasing her, touching her face and hair with icy fingers. Chilled to the bone, she shivered, hugging herself. She'd never felt so alone in all her life.

"Now don't get spooky on me, Elizabeth," she told herself firmly, taking comfort in the sound of her own voice. "There's absolutely nothing to be afraid of. There must be thirty people within a stone's throw of you, even if you can't see them. All you have to do is yell if you get in trouble and someone will come running."

Just then, voices carried to her through the fog from off to her right, reassuring her, and with a shaky laugh she let out the breath she hadn't even realized she was holding.

"Idiot," she muttered. "Keep this up and someone's going to hear you talking to yourself and think you've snapped."

Reminding herself why she was there, she returned her attention to the search. Her own discomfort forgotten, she moved slowly through the fog, looking for tracks in the snow, blood, signs of a scuffle, anything that would indicate that Napoleon might have been there. Only when she was sure that he hadn't did she move on.

Concentrating on the ground directly in front of her, she couldn't have said later when she first felt the touch of eyes on her. There was a slight itching at the back of her neck, an awareness that nagged gently at her as the fog parted like waves around her. Hardly aware of it, she glanced up absently, then returned her gaze to the snow-covered ground. She took a step, then another, but something still pulled at her, stronger now, and with a sigh of irritation, she stopped in her tracks and once again looked up.

The fog swirled around her, and for just a second, Elizabeth thought she caught sight of footsteps in the snow just off to the left ahead of her. It was nothing to be alarmed about—with people all over the ridge unable to see where others were searching, it wasn't surprising that they crossed each other's paths from time to time—but suddenly her heart was thundering, and for no explicable reason she was afraid.

"Quit being paranoid," she whispered. "There's nothing to be afraid of. If there's someone out there, it's just one of the volunteers who got separated from the others the same way you did. He's probably as scared as you are right now, thinking he's stumbled across one of the wolves. At least call out a hello so he'll know he's not in danger of being mauled or anything."

Her throat as dry as dust, she called out hoarsely, "Hello? Who's out there?"

Silence was her only answer. Cold, hostile, malevolent silence. She could almost feel the touch of angry eyes on her, the wickedness that came roiling toward her in waves out of the shrouds of mist.

I've seen you parading around town, thinking you're so damn smart and no one can touch you or those damn wolves of yours. Well, think again, bitch. I can come after you anytime I want, and you won't even know it until it's too late. One second you'll think you're safe, and the next I'll be right there in your face, making you wish you'd never been born. Think about it.

Just that easily, the phone conversation she'd had with the monster who had left the poisoned meat at the holding pen came back to her in vivid recall, the cold flat words slapping at her, and the last of the blood drained from cheeks that were already pale with fear. At the time, she hadn't taken the threats made against her seriously. It was the wolves that people hated, not her. But what if she'd been wrong? What if he hadn't been content to just carry through on his threat to shoot Napoleon? He could come after her.

Had he already? she wondered, staring wide-eyed at the fog that surrounded her on all sides. Had he seen this morning's search as a chance to get close to her without anyone being suspicious? Conditions couldn't have been more perfect. No one knew who he was, what he looked like, and no one would question his motive for being there. He could blend in with the rest of the searchers, the rest of his neighbors, then wait to slip up on her in the fog.

Was he the one who was waiting just beyond her sight, silently trailing her in the mist, hunting *her* this time, instead of Napoleon? she thought, chilled. The fog would make it so easy for him. All he had to do was lie back, wait until he was sure no one else was near, then rush her when she was least expecting it. He could push her off a cliff into a ravine, make it look as if she'd lost her way in the fog and tripped and broken her neck, and no one would be the wiser. By the time her body was found, he'd have slipped away in the fog and everyone would think she'd just had an unfortunate accident.

The fog shifted around her, and for just a second she thought she heard the crunch of a footstep on the snow off to her left. Alarmed, she took a quick step to the right, and then another, a scream already struggling to rise in her throat. Oh, God, it was him!

Panicking, she whirled to run, only to slam into a hard male chest. In the time it took to gasp, he had her. Terror closed around her. A scream broke free from her throat and she never even knew it. Blind to everything but the need to get away, she slapped and scratched like a wild woman, fighting against the hands that tried to hold her. But he was quick and clever. Grunting when she kicked blindly out and connected with his shin, he grabbed her wrists before she knew what he was about, crossed them in front of her, and spun her away from him. A split second later he had her pinned against him, her back pressed tightly to his chest, effectively trapped. Still she struggled, sobbing.

"Dammit, Lizzie, stop! It's me!"

Her breathing ragged, the roar of her blood loud in her ears, it was a full ten seconds before Zeke's words penetrated. When they did, she literally wilted. "Zeke! Thank God!"

It was only then that he dared to ease his grip on her wrists and turn her to face him. At the sight of the fear still glazing her eyes, his frown changed to a scowl even as his hands moved to gently cup her face. "Sweetheart, what is it? Who the hell put that look in your eye?"

Just that easily, tears welled and spilled over her lashes.

With a strangled sob, she threw herself into his arms. "I don't know! I couldn't see him. He was just...there...in the mist. Watching me."

Even to her own ears it sounded like she'd gotten spooked in the fog and let her imagination run away with her. But she hadn't, dammit! She knew what she'd felt, and it was vicious!

Drawing back, she said desperately, "He really was there! I could *feel* his eyes on me, feel the hatred. I know it sounds crazy, but—"

"No, it doesn't." It didn't sound anything of the kind. When the damn fog had cut her off from him, a fear he couldn't explain had sunk its claws in him, and he'd known something was horribly wrong. Afraid he'd lost her, he'd found himself tearing through the trees like a madman, cursing the fog that hid her from him, and making all sorts of promises to God if He'd just help him find her.

"You think it's him, don't you?" he said grimly, looking past her to the thickening gray mist that cut them off from the rest of the searchers. "The bastard who planted the poisoned meat near the holding pen? The one who called you that night? You think he's out there somewhere, masquerading as one of the volunteers, and waiting for a chance to kill you?"

It was a plan that only a lunatic would think had a ghost of a chance of working. Her eyes meeting his unflinchingly, Elizabeth nodded. "He said he could come after me anytime he wanted. If you think about it, why wouldn't he make a move in front of half the town? He feels justified in what he's doing—he's protecting his rights, his way of life, the way of the West against an outsider. In his eyes, he's John Wayne and I'm the bad guy. He can sleep nights, knowing he saved Liberty Hill from the wolves and the 'bitch' who was cramming them down everyone's throat."

It did, in a twisted kind of way, make sense. It also scared the hell out of Zeke. Because a psychopath who had convinced himself he was the protector of truth, justice and the American way was capable of anything.

"Then he just blew the only shot he's going to get today," he said grimly, "because I'm not letting you out of my sight the rest of the time we're on this damn ridge. Especially in this fog. I was afraid you were going to run right off the cliff."

"Because I was scared?" she said, surprised. "Zeke, I always knew where the cliff was. There was never any chance of me walking off it. I made sure to keep it to my left from the moment we first started searching. Even when I was terrified, I knew which direction *not* to run."

She was serious, Zeke thought, stunned. She really thought she'd been running *away* from the cliff. Just thinking about it took ten years off his life.

"Sweetheart," he said roughly, "I don't know how to tell you this, but you were headed right for the cliff when I stepped into your path. Another thirty seconds and the ground would have literally disappeared beneath your feet."

Her eyes flew past him to the gray wall of fog at his back. "That's impossible! I was running for the trees—"

"No, you weren't." Gently taking her hand, he turned and carefully led her close enough to the edge of the escarpment so that she could see where the rock ledge just dropped away. She took one look and blanched.

"It's easy to get turned around up here," he said quietly, stepping back now that he'd made his point. "Especially when you're not that familiar with the area and you can't see more than two feet in front of you." Promising himself that whoever put that look of fear in her eyes was going to pay, he took her hand and turned away from the escarpment. "C'mon. If Napoleon's up here, I'm sure he's not this close to the cliff."

The fog lifted slowly, in fits and starts, stubbornly clinging to hollows and crevices before finally disappearing altogether by the middle of the afternoon. With no mist to hide behind, Elizabeth found herself studying the other searchers with a suspicion that hadn't been there before, looking for some sign of the fury she'd felt earlier in the morning. But if whoever had been watching her with such hatred was still there, he hid his hostility well. There were no angry glares, no venomous looks directed her way. Still, she didn't take any chances but made sure that she was never more than a few steps from Zeke at all times.

With the lifting of the fog, locating Napoleon should have been easy. They had the radio equipment to pinpoint his general direction and thirty or more people to scour the countryside. He had to be there somewhere. But just as Elizabeth thought they had to be closing in on him, his radio signal went dead.

"No!" she cried when she listened to the monitoring equipment herself and picked up nothing but a steady drone of static instead of the fast beep of the mortality code that signaled the wolf was in trouble. "It can't just go dead!"

"Maybe the battery gave out," Nick suggested.

"It shouldn't have. It's designed to last forty-eight hours once the mortality code kicks in, and we just picked up the code last night."

"What about Queenie?" Zeke asked. "Is she still in the area?"

Peter switched the equipment to the frequency of the other wolf's collar and immediately picked up the slow, regular beep that indicated all was well. "She's okay," he said with a smile of relief. "But she's not as close as she was earlier in the day. She probably got spooked by all the volunteers and moved a couple of miles farther west.''

The other searchers, seeing that something was wrong, straggled in in groups of twos and threes. ''Did you say *west?*'' a woman in the crowd called out sharply. ''That's Wild Horse Canyon, isn't it?'' When some of the others nodded, she shook her head. ''That's pretty rough territory, and it'll be dark soon. I don't know about the rest of you, but I don't believe I want to be wandering around that canyon once the light starts to go. It's too dangerous.''

''I thought we were looking for the big fella, anyway,'' someone else added. ''He's the one supposed to be in trouble. We start chasing after one of the others, we could go halfway to Wyoming before we ever catch up with it.''

Heads nodded, and others grumbled, and as much as Elizabeth hated to admit it, they all had a point. She and her team could track down Queenie if she continued to migrate west. Napoleon was the one they needed help finding, but that wasn't going to happen today. Not without a radio signal to guide them, and not after a long day of searching. People were wet and tired and miserable, and even as they stood there, the sun sank lower in the sky.

''You're right,'' she said, accepting the inevitable. ''Napoleon is our main concern right now, and as most of you have already heard, his radio collar has gone dead. Without that to guide us, there's not much point in continuing the search today.''

''What about tomorrow?'' Martha Hoffsteader piped up. ''If you need us to show up here again tomorrow, just say the word and we'll be here.''

Smiling for the first time in what felt like hours, Elizabeth could have hugged her. ''That's very generous of you, Mrs. Hoffsteader, but right now I don't know what's going to happen tomorrow. I have to meet with my staff and decide where to go from here. But I do appreciate the offer and all the time you all put in today. We may not have found Napoleon, but thanks to all of you, we know where he's not.''

Moving through the crowd, she personally shook everyone's hand and thanked them for helping. And every time a man's hand closed around hers, she hated the suspicions that flitted through her mind. Was this the one? The one who had threatened her? The one who had probably killed Napoleon? The one who would do the same to her if she gave him a chance? Could he actually look her in the eye and smile like an old friend when he was really plotting to murder her? What kind of monster was he?

Zeke was obviously wondering the same thing because he was one step behind her all the way, eyeing every man who touched her. Oh, he was subtle about it—she had to give him that. He knew everyone there and took a moment to chat and ask about family. But when the gathering broke up and everyone divided into groups to carpool back to town, he didn't immediately head for his Suburban but stood at Elizabeth's side and studied each of the men through narrowed eyes.

Everyone who had met at the office that morning was still there, present and accounted for. Which meant she very well could have shaken the hand of the man who wanted her dead. Just thinking about it made her sick to her stomach. ''Well? What do you think?'' she said, arching a brow at Zeke. ''You know these people. You grew up with them. Which one would threaten murder just because they don't like the government telling them what to do?''

Staring after the departing crowd, Zeke knew the answer should have been easy. She was right—he knew everyone there, knew their politics, knew who cheated on their wives and their income tax. Granted, he hadn't lived in Liberty

Hill for years, but people's basic nature didn't change. A man without scruples didn't usually develop them later in life—he just learned to hide the fact that he didn't have any.

And that was what had him worried. Most of the men who had participated in the search were, as far as he knew, honest, God-fearing men who wouldn't dream of threatening a woman under any circumstances. But how much of that was an act? When push came to shove and Elizabeth's life was on the line, who could she really trust?

"I can speak for myself and my brother and Nick," he said flatly. "After that, I don't know. I wouldn't turn my back on any of them."

Huddling in her jacket, her eyes stark, she said wryly, "Well, that narrows it down, I guess."

It was, he silently admitted, a sorry state of affairs. And the situation only got worse when they got back to town. Because there in the parking lot at her office were television news crews, complete with satellite dishes and relay equipment, from all over the state. Zeke took one look at them and started to swear. Who leaked the news to the press?

Muttering curses, he was out of his truck before he'd hardly thrown the transmission into Park, his only thought that Elizabeth didn't need this now, not after the day she'd had. But before he could get to her, she was surrounded.

"Ms. Davis, did you find the dead wolf?"

"How was he killed? Do you have any idea who the killer is?"

"According to reports from the Department of Fish and Wildlife, you released the wolves early because of opposition you were getting from the locals. Considering what's happened, do you think that was wise, Ms. Davis? Is there a possibility that Wolf Number Eight would be alive today if you hadn't botched things by rushing the release date?"

Like a swarm of locusts pressing in on her, threatening to devour her, the reporters shoved microphones in her face and threw questions at her from all sides, hardly giving her time to reply to one question before they were throwing another at her. Lost in the shuffle, she almost went down.

Snarling, Zeke started to fight his way through the mob, but before he could push his way to Elizabeth, she reached the front steps of her office. Instead of bolting inside as he'd expected, however, she took the first two steps, then turned to face the crowd with a quiet dignity that immediately silenced the jerks still shouting questions at her.

"If you'll just be patient, I'll answer all your questions," she said stiffly. "But one at a time, please. No one can hear anything when you're all shouting."

"What about the wolf? The big male that's missing. Somebody said you named him Napoleon. Is he dead or alive?"

The question hit her like a dart, right in the heart. She didn't so much as flinch, and the pain in her eyes was quickly concealed, but as she explained about Napoleon's radio collar and the mortality code, Zeke knew she was hurting. And there wasn't a damn thing he could do about it. This was her project; she was the head honcho, and as such, it was her responsibility to deal with the press. As much as he wanted to, he couldn't step in and draw the fire from her.

He knew that, accepted it. But that didn't make it any easier for him to stand there and watch her try to hang on to her composure as she was forced to admit that yes, Napoleon was, in all likelihood, dead. Damn the bastards, couldn't they see what they were doing to her! Why was it so important for them to hear her say the words?

More than once over the course of the twenty-minute impromptu news conference, he seriously considered stepping in, anyway, and stopping the whole thing. She was white as a sheet, obviously exhausted, and so close to fighting tears, her eyes were glistening. His jaw grinding on an oath, Zeke told himself he was letting her answer one more question. That was it. If he overstepped his bounds, that was just too damn bad.

But before another question could be shouted out, she decided on her own that she'd reached the end of her rope. "That's all I can tell you tonight," she said abruptly in a voice that was hoarse with strain. "I will release more information as events warrant. Now if you'll excuse me, it's been a long day." And before anyone could dare to ask another question, she pushed through the crowd to her Jeep, climbed in and drove off.

For all of ten seconds, Zeke gave serious thought to going after her. After all that she'd been through, she'd held up remarkably well, but sooner or later it was going to hit her that Napoleon really was dead. And when it did, she had no business being alone. He wanted to be there for her, dammit, to help her through this. But a couple of dances and a kiss didn't give him the right to go home with her. Swearing, he had no choice but to let her leave.

Chapter 8

The second Elizabeth saw the package waiting for her on her front porch, she knew it wasn't good. There was nothing sinister about it—wrapped in brown paper, it was small, not much bigger than a paperback book, and appeared harmless—but anyone who wanted to give her a gift would have given it to her personally, not left it for her on her porch like a thief in the night. She took one look at it and wanted to turn and run.

No, it definitely wasn't good, she thought grimly, scowling at it warily from six feet away. Not if the churning in the pit of her stomach was anything to go by. Dammit, she didn't need this tonight! It had been a miserable day; she was tired and cold, and all she wanted to do was soak in a steaming tub, down a cup of soup and go to bed and forget the world.

Leave it, a voice whispered in her head. *There's no law that says you have to deal with it now. Just step over it and go in the house. Whatever it is, it can wait until tomorrow.*

Tempted, she almost did just that. But just knowing it was there on the porch, waiting for her the minute she opened her front door in the morning, would, she knew, nag at her all night. If she wanted to get any sleep at all, she'd do better to take care of the problem now, rather than later.

And she didn't for a second doubt that whatever was in the package was a problem. Why else would it be wrapped in brown paper, with not so much as her name or a return address to indicate who it was from? No, this had trouble written all over it, and her fingers trembled just at the thought of opening it.

Approaching it cautiously, as if it was a bomb that would go off any second, she gingerly picked it up. It was light and couldn't have weighed much more than a pound. She almost carried it inside to open it, then thought better of it. No, whatever it was, she wasn't taking it into her house, not yet. Not until she knew what it was.

Her heart thumping wildly in her breast, she tore away the paper to reveal a small box. With trembling fingers, she lifted the lid…and found herself staring down at a mangled, blood-stained radio collar.

"Oh, God!"

Later, she never remembered snatching her hands back as if she'd been burned and dropping the collar, box and all, to the porch floor. A sob lodging in her throat, she stared down at it and desperately tried to convince herself it couldn't be Napoleon's. But his identification tag, still etched with #8 on it, was attached to the collar just as it had been when it was first locked around his neck months ago in Canada when he was captured. Specifically designed for this particular project and virtually unseen by the public, the tags couldn't possibly be duplicated. It had to be Napoleon's.

Which meant he was dead.

She'd known in her heart that he had to be, but still she'd fought the truth, demanding proof, and now she had it right there in front of her. He was dead. He had to be. Even though the collar had obviously been cut off with some kind of wire cutters, there was no way anyone could get it off his neck without killing him first. He would never have stood for it.

She waited for the anger to hit her then, the grief, but all she felt was a numbness that left her cold all the way to her soul. Shivering, she started to pick up the collar and box, only to remember that killing one of the wolves in the project was a federal offense. A crime had been committed, and Zeke and Nick would need to examine all evidence. The less she touched it, the better.

Leaving the items where they lay, she unlocked her front door and immediately went to the phone in the kitchen. Before she could reach for it, however, her gaze locked on her answering machine and the red blinking light that indicated she had a message.

She shouldn't have listened to it. She knew who it was from, knew that he had called to taunt her about Napoleon's death. The bastard really got off playing mind games, and if she replayed the tape, she would only be participating in her own torture. Zeke and Nick were handling the investigation—they could listen to it.

But the monster had already killed one wolf. What if he found a way to go after the others? Her heart stopping at the thought, she reached over and hit the play button.

"I told you one of them would die," the caller said in the same cold, flat voice that had haunted her dreams. "You just didn't think it would be the big guy, did you?

How does it feel knowing he's dead because of you? Because you wouldn't listen? You're the one who shot him, who sent that bullet ripping through his heart. You should have been there, should have seen the way he dropped right in his tracks. It was no more than the killing bastard deserved.''

With sick, vicious enjoyment, he proceeded to give her a step-by-step accounting of how he not only killed Napoleon, but gutted and dismembered him, then scattered what was left of him for the coyotes. Bile rising in her throat, Elizabeth could do nothing but stand there, frozen, as the vile words washed over her.

''This is your last warning,'' he told her icily. ''You either cancel the program and get those damn killers of yours out of Liberty Hill, or you'll be the one left for the coyotes next time. And if you don't think I can do it, you're stupider than I think you are, lady. I could have pushed you off that cliff today. Oh, yeah, I was there. But you knew that, didn't you? That's why you stuck like glue to your lover boy all afternoon. But he can't always be there for you, so you think about that the next time you're alone. I'll be out there, waiting. Who knows? I could be watching you right now. And when I'm ready, I'll put a bullet through your heart just like I did that pet wolf of yours.''

It was his night to cook, and Zeke was in no mood for anything that took time. He was tired and hungry and just wanted something hot. So he threw some hot dogs in a pot of water to boil, opened up a can of chili and had dinner ready in fifteen minutes flat.

Joe took one look at it and said, ''I wonder what Mom's having.''

''Tuna casserole,'' Zeke retorted with a grin, knowing he despised it. ''Your favorite.''

Without a word, Joe forked a hot dog onto his plate. When the phone rang, he didn't even look up as he reached for the chili.

"That's for you."

His stomach grumbling and his mouth already watering, Zeke scowled at him. "Oh, no, it's not. This is your house, remember? I'm just a guest. You get it."

"A guest my ass," Joe snorted, grinning. "And let you grab my hot dog when I'm not looking? Not on your life. There's only six of them, and you can down those without even swallowing."

That he could. But so could Joe—and he'd do it in a heartbeat if he got the chance. As kids, their mother had never had to worry about what to do with leftovers—there weren't any. They'd always had ravenous appetites and had competed to see who would get the last bite. Now they fell back into the game as easily as if they were still eight and nine. The phone rang again, and they both just sat there, eyeing each other speculatively and waiting the other out.

The answering machine would eventually get it, but neither of them was going to let that happen and spoil the game. "You sure you don't want to answer it?" Zeke asked finally, craftily. "It could be a woman."

"Oh, I don't doubt that," Joe retorted, amused. "Half the female population of Falls County has been calling here ever since you got back. But it's you they're calling for, not me."

"Well, maybe if you showed a little interest instead of holing up here like a crusty old bachelor—"

"Oh, no you don't. Don't even think about going there. A smart man only has to get burned once to know to stay away from the fire. The last thing I want is a woman. Unless you can say the same thing, the phone's for you."

He had him there and he knew it. Because there was one

particular woman he wanted, more each day, and he couldn't deny it. Joe took one look at his face and reached over and snitched the last of the hot dogs from the pan.

"Hey!"

"Phone's ringing," he said with a grin. "Better get it."

Neatly outmaneuvered, Zeke conceded defeat. But when he rose to answer the phone, he took his plate with him. "Hello?"

"McBride?"

At the sound of Elizabeth's voice, he nearly dropped his hot dog. "What's wrong?" he asked immediately, knowing there had to be some emergency for her to call. She'd danced in his arms, kissed him until he didn't know what planet he was on, but she'd never, ever called him. "Are those damn reporters bothering you again? Did they follow you home?"

"No. But Napoleon's collar was on my front porch when I got home, and there was a message on my answering machine." Calmly and succinctly, she gave him a quick rundown of the threat left on her machine. "I think you'd better come over here."

Zeke didn't need to hear more. She sounded fine, but he wasn't fooled. He knew her now, knew how much that damn wolf meant to her and how hard she'd fought to cling to the hope that he was somehow still alive. Now that hope was gone, and she was not only hurting, but had every right to be scared out of her mind.

"I'll be right there," he growled. "Lock the door and turn on all the outside lights so you can see if anyone approaches the house. I'm on my way."

Slamming down the phone, he turned to find Joe rising to his feet, his food forgotten. "That was Elizabeth, wasn't it? What's wrong?"

Grabbing his coat, Zeke quickly slipped it on. "Napoleon's killer has been there and left his collar. She thinks he's gone, but he left a threatening message on her answering machine. Call Nick and tell him to get out there right now.''

She lived thirty minutes away. He made it in fifteen. It was the longest fifteen minutes of his life. Racing up the private drive to her house, he prayed that the bastard hadn't come back, that he hadn't been there all along, hiding in a bedroom, while she was making the call. Because if he had, she could be dead by now.

His heart rolling over in his chest at the thought, he saw that she'd turned the outside lights on just as he'd told her to. Jerking open his car door, he hit the ground running.

''Elizabeth? It's me! Open up!''

Over the thunder of his heart, he heard the scrape of the dead bolt, then she jerked open the door and he could see that she was unharmed. Pale as a ghost, her green eyes dark with pain, but unhurt. ''Are you all right?'' he asked hoarsely.

Without a word she stepped into his arms.

He could have held her just like that forever. He knew this feeling might keep him up nights, but for now all he cared about was that she was safe. His heart beating at twice its normal rhythm, he was still standing in her doorway with her wrapped close when Nick came racing up in his patrol car, lights whirling and siren blazing. Reluctantly Zeke let Elizabeth ease out of his arms.

His lean, angular face carved in harsh lines, Nick strode up to the porch. ''What happened? Joe said Napoleon's collar was found?''

Elizabeth nodded to the spot where she'd dropped the collar. ''Over there,'' she said huskily. ''It was wrapped up in brown paper and waiting for me on the porch when I got home. Once I realized what it was, I didn't touch it again.''

Hugging herself, she watched from six feet away as the two men examined the collar, as well as the box and brown paper that it had been wrapped in. Careful not to touch anything with their hands, they used tweezers to lift everything to a nearby wicker table, where they thoroughly searched each piece. And all the while, the message Napoleon's killer had left on her answering machine played in Elizabeth's head.

''He beat the hell out of the thing trying to silence the radio signal,'' Zeke said as Nick slipped the collar into an evidence bag.

''He used a sledgehammer,'' Elizabeth said flatly. ''The same one he used to pound Napoleon's brains out.''

Both men's heads snapped toward her at that. Swearing under his breath, Zeke said, ''You didn't tell me that.''

''I couldn't,'' she said simply. ''It was too vile.''

Confused, Nick frowned. ''You *talked* to the bastard?''

''He left a message on my answering machine.'' Just thinking about it turned her stomach. ''He took great satisfaction in telling me how he mutilated Napoleon's body. He's going to do the same thing to me if I don't leave town and take the rest of the wolves with me.''

Nick quickly bagged the rest of the evidence, then headed for the front door. ''I think I'd better hear this.''

Elizabeth would have given anything not to listen to it again, but she deliberately forced herself to. Someone out there intended to kill her. She needed to know every vicious, unspeakable act he was capable of.

She couldn't, however, hear that familiar ugly voice again without her blood running cold. Agitated, she put a pot of coffee on to brew, then restlessly moved around the kitchen, setting out cream and sugar and the thick, diner-style mugs she loved to drink coffee out of. And all the while the tape droned on, the foul, sinister words that were already indelibly etched on her brain every bit as horrible as she remembered. By the time it finished playing, both men were cursing.

A muscle clenching in his jaw, Zeke swore. "So the bastard thinks he's going to hurt her, does he? Like hell! I'm warning you right now, Nick, if he even tries to mess with her, I'll take him down personally."

"You won't get any argument out of me," his friend retorted, his brown eyes black with anger. "He's a smug son of a bitch, I'll give him that. And he's really starting to irritate me. Dammit, who the hell is he? This isn't your average antigovernment fanatic looking to blame somebody because he can't secede from the union and make his own country. This jerk's twisted. He's not just making idle threats. He really wants to hurt her."

Glancing over to where Elizabeth puttered with spoons and napkins at the table, he gave her a hard look. "Was he out on the ridge today, Elizabeth? He said you knew he was there. Did you?"

"I don't know. At the time, I thought he was, but the fog was so thick, it was hard to be sure of anything." Her fingers not quite steady, she stared unseeingly at the spoons she'd lined up. "I got separated from everyone else, and suddenly I could feel someone watching me. I couldn't see anything, but there was this…rage…"

She shivered at the memory of it and reached to pour herself a cup of coffee. But as she wrapped her fingers around the mug, its heat did nothing to warm the cold that chilled her inside. "I thought I heard someone take a step toward me. I was scared. I turned to run and ran right into Zeke."

"She was so upset, she was headed right for the damn cliff when I caught her," he growled.

"And neither one of you said anything?" Nick said incredulously. "Dammit, we could have caught him right there!"

"How?" Elizabeth asked simply. "I was fairly sure it wasn't my imagination, but I had no proof. No one touched me, no one threatened me. I didn't *see* anything. What was I supposed to say? 'I can feel one of the searchers watching me...he wants to kill me'?"

Even to her own ears, it sounded ludicrous. If she'd so much as hinted at such a thing, she would have not only sounded paranoid, she would have offended everyone who had, out of the goodness of their hearts, turned up at the crack of dawn on a miserable morning to search for Napoleon.

"The problem is, we can't even be sure it was one of the searchers," Zeke told him. "Everyone in the county knew about this morning's search. Anyone who wanted to could have driven up there, blended in with the searchers and used the fog and trees for cover to get close to Elizabeth. If he'd have wanted to kill her then, he could have...as long as the fog held."

"Once it lifted, he knew he'd blown his chance for the day and decided to terrorize her with the collar instead," Nick said, putting the pieces of the puzzle together in disgust. "He smashed it, then came straight here to plant it on the porch while she was still up on the ridge. And the devil of it is, he didn't even have to worry about anyone seeing him. Half the town turned out for the search, and this place is so deserted, no one would have seen him anyway."

Leveling a somber look at Elizabeth, he scolded, "You

really do need to see about finding a place closer to town. You're just too vulnerable way out here by yourself.''

That was something she'd already decided for herself. ''Believe me, I'm not any more thrilled about it than you are,'' she told him. ''But this is Liberty Hill, not Denver. There's just not a heck of a lot of rental property to choose from. The only decent place I know of is the Aikman house on Main, and it's as big as a barn. Even if I could afford the rent—which I can't—just heating it would cost me a fortune. But I'll look around,'' she said quickly when both men started to scowl. ''If nothing else, I may be able to find someone who would be willing to rent me a room.''

Considering the lateness of the hour and the lack of any kind of hotel in the area, there was little else she could do for the moment, but neither man was satisfied with the arrangement. ''I'll make a few phone calls when I get back to the office and see what I can come up with,'' Nick promised as he popped the tape out of the answering machine and slipped it into the evidence bag. ''In the meantime I'll send this stuff off to the lab, but I'm not holding my breath that the lab boys'll find anything. There's no doubt that this guy's a real sick puppy, but he's no idiot. He knows how to cover his behind.''

Zeke agreed, and it was driving him crazy. As a special agent for Fish and Wildlife, he'd handled everything from a lovesick moose who mistook a Texas longhorn for one of its own kind to a poacher who killed bald eagles because he needed the feathers for an aphrodisiac. He knew all about animal behavior in man and the wild kingdom, and there was usually nothing he enjoyed more than investigating a crime with few, if any, clues. He liked the challenge, the thrill of the hunt, of chasing down the bad guys and figuring out what the creeps were going to do next before they knew themselves.

But this time Elizabeth was involved and in danger, and he didn't like it, dammit. He didn't like it at all! She was scared and hurting, and he'd never felt so helpless in his life. The bastard gave him nothing to work with, then taunted him by walking right up to her front door and terrifying her. And there wasn't a hell of a lot he could do about it—except stay close and wait for the jackass to make a mistake.

There was no doubt in Zeke's mind that it was only a matter of time before that happened—he hadn't run across a perp yet who didn't get cocky with his own success and end up shooting himself in the foot. And when this one screwed up, he could count himself lucky if the worst he'd done to Elizabeth was just scare her. If he so much as laid a finger on her, he'd have to pay.

"That's all right," he told Nick. "He can't keep this up forever. Nobody's that clever. He's going to outsmart himself, and when he does, we'll nail him. In the meantime let's check out the rest of the house. I want to make sure he didn't leave any other nasty surprises."

They searched the entire house, inside and out, and found nothing. All the windows and doors were locked, the snow around the house free of any footsteps. Satisfied that the jerk had just left the collar on the porch, then departed, the two men returned to the kitchen to find Elizabeth still at the table, her hands cupped around her coffee mug as color gradually seeped back into her cheeks.

"Everything checks out, but you still shouldn't be here by yourself tonight," Nick told her. "It's just too dangerous."

Scowling, he shot Zeke a pointed look that was totally unnecessary. He'd already decided he wasn't going anywhere. "She won't be alone," he said simply, and let it go at that.

It was a moment before the meaning of his words sank into Elizabeth's tired brain. When they did, she gasped softly. "Oh, you don't have to do that! I'm sure I'll be fine."

She might as well have saved her breath. The two men had already decided what was best, and they didn't spare her so much as a glance. "Good," Nick said as he headed for the front door with Zeke right behind him. "I don't think we have to worry about any trouble as long as someone's with her, but I'm not taking any chances. Until we can find her another place to live, I'm going to schedule regular patrols out here at night."

"I'll be on the lookout for them," Zeke promised. "If we have any problems, I'll give you a call."

And just that quickly Elizabeth found herself alone with Zeke for the night. In the silence left by Nick's leave-taking, she told herself not to be foolish and read anything into his offer to stay. This was small town America where people helped each other in times of trouble. If old Mrs. Johnson down the road had needed someone to be with her overnight, he would have been just as quick to volunteer.

Yeah, right, a cynical voice drawled in her head. *The man lives to spend the night with old ladies.*

Her heart thumping as she watched him lock the dead bolt in the front door, she said huskily, "This really isn't necessary. Nothing else is going to happen tonight. He wants to see me sweat, and he can't do that if he moves fast. So he'll sit back and let me think about how he killed Napoleon, how he's going to kill me, then let me worry awhile. It'll be days, maybe weeks, before he strikes again."

"I'm staying," he said flatly. "It's settled."

Nothing was settled, least of all her pulse, but she only had to take one look at his set jaw to know that it would be pointless to argue. The man had made up his mind, and she was going to have to find a way to live with it. He was spending the night.

Just the thought of that sent heat spilling into her stomach and hot, seductive images dancing before her mind's eye. Zeke, kissing her. Teasing her. Seducing her. Sweeping her off to bed and loving her until she was limp from the wonder of it. Stunned, her blood humming in her veins, she just stood there in the doorway between the kitchen and living room, transfixed.

"Elizabeth? Did you hear me? I asked what you wanted to do about supper. We could go into town to Ed's—"

Dazed, she blinked him back into focus and only just then realized she was staring at him as if she hadn't eaten in a week and he was the first course, entrée and dessert all rolled into one. Dear God, what was she doing?

Mortified, she whirled back into the kitchen, cursing the hot color she could feel staining her cheeks. "No, I'll make something. I forgot to get anything out of the freezer to thaw, but there's eggs and milk and bread. I can make French toast if you don't mind having breakfast for supper."

"No, of course not, but I can do it," he said with a frown, following her. "You look tired. Why don't you go lie down and put your feet up until I get everything ready?"

Her heart kicked just at the thought of lying down. "No! I'm fine. Really," she insisted when he looked skeptical. "And cooking always relaxes me. It take my mind off things." Like beds. "But you can help by setting the table if you like. The plates are in the cabinet above the dishwasher. Oh, and the syrup's in the refrigerator. If you like yours hot, you can heat it in the microwave."

She was chattering, but she couldn't seem to help herself. Why hadn't she ever noticed before how big he was? Or how small her kitchen was? He seemed to take up all the space, not to mention the air. Breathless, she flew around the room, hurriedly assembling the ingredients for French toast, and seemed to brush against him every time she turned. It wasn't until she had a platter of food ready that she realized fixing something quick might not have necessarily been a good idea.

Intimacy. It closed around them the second he sat across from her at the kitchen table and her eyes met his. The setting was nothing like the previous evening—there was nothing the least bit romantic about it. Where there had been exotic antiques and candlelight at Myrtle's, now there was only an old chrome table and chairs and an ugly ceiling fixture that put out a glaring light. It didn't seem to matter. They could have been outside at the picnic table, in Denver at Micky D's and surrounded by screaming kids, on a bus to Timbuktu and sharing a sandwich, and she still would have felt the same.

Helplessly she just looked at him. ''Zeke—''

''Eat,'' he said roughly.

She tried. She really did. She wasn't a great cook, but she had a few specialties, and French toast was one of them. Tonight, however, she had little appetite for it. She pushed it around on her plate, but what little she was able to manage to swallow tasted like sawdust. All she could think about was last night, the meal they shared and the kiss that followed. With a will of their own, her eyes followed every bite Zeke took.

Awareness set the very air between them humming with expectation. And he felt it, too. Oh, he didn't say anything, but she could see the heat in his eyes, the need he couldn't hide any more than she could. And with every beat of her heart, it only seemed to get worse.

Restless, she never knew how she sat there for so long

without going quietly out of her mind. They were both waiting for the meal to be over, both waiting for...something. And she couldn't take it anymore. Pushing her plate away, she jumped to her feet.

"I'm not really hungry after all. I'll make up the couch while you finish eating. I'm going to sleep there and let you have my bed."

"Oh, no, you're not!"

"It's no trouble," she said over her shoulder as she stepped into the hall to collect sheets and spare covers from the linen closet. "I slept there the first night I moved in because the landlord ordered new mattresses and they hadn't arrived yet. It's not bad—really. But it's too short for you. You'll be much more comfortable on the bed."

The matter settled, she collected everything she needed from the closet and turned back toward the living room. She took two steps and found herself facing a scowling Zeke. "You're not sleeping on the couch," he growled.

"I don't mind—"

"*I* do."

"But—"

His steely eyes, dark with purpose, met hers. "If I sleep in your bed, sweetheart, it won't be alone. Is that what you want?"

Startled, her heart bucked in her breast, and for what seemed like an eternity, she could do nothing but stare up at him with widened eyes. Was that what she wanted? she wondered wildly. Was that why she'd been as nervous as a teenager on her first date all evening? She wanted him to make love to her?

The answer should have been immediate and unequivocal. No! He might have charmed her into liking him, but she'd known what he was from the minute she first laid eyes on him, and that hadn't changed. A ladies' man. Too sure of himself when it came to women, too much like her father, he was everything she didn't want in a man.

And she wanted him more than she needed her next breath.

A week ago—last night, for heaven's sake!—that would have been enough to send her running for the hills. She wasn't a woman who threw caution to the wind and got naked with just anyone. The lovers in her life had been few and far between. But there was something about Zeke, about the feelings he stirred in her, that had, from the very beginning, been as inevitable as the rising and setting of the sun. She'd fought it, argued with herself over the tug he had on her emotions, tried to resist him. And lost.

Never had defeat felt quite so exhilarating.

Butterflies fluttering in her stomach, she arched a brow at him. "And if I do?"

"Then you won't need those covers," he retorted, nodding at the armful she clutched to her chest. "If you're cold, I'll warm you up."

And so it was decided. No promises were asked for, none given. She needed him tonight—nothing else mattered. Her smile sweetly provocative, she tossed the sheets and blankets aside. "I am a little chilly."

It was a comfortable seventy-six degrees inside, and they both knew it, but he was more than willing to play the game. His blue eyes gleaming in anticipation, he murmured, "We can't have that. We need to light a fire."

Braced for him to grab her, to haul her close and lay a brain-numbing kiss on her, she was caught completely off guard when he lifted his hand and simply traced the curve of her mouth with a touch that was as light as a whisper. Just that easily, he made her throb.

Stunned, she lifted dazed eyes to his.

Smiling gently, he leaned down and nuzzled her ear, then

trailed his mouth down the smooth column of her throat. Between one heartbeat and the next, she would have sworn her temperature spiked twenty degrees. Suddenly boneless, she leaned weakly against him. "Oh, my."

Growling low in his throat in approval, he gathered her close. How could he have known she was so sensitive? Did she have any idea what that did to a man? Knowing that he only had to touch her to make her burn? Nuzzle her neck to turn her to putty in his arms? He wanted her, dammit. Right here, right now, so badly that his teeth ached. Enough with the games, the teasing. He just wanted to sweep her up in his arms and carry her off to bed and lose himself in her.

But she'd had a hell of a day, and he couldn't rush her. Not this first time when he wanted her soft and melting in his arms and any thought of the outside world far, far away. He wanted to make her forget. For tonight, at least, he needed her to think of nothing but him and what he could do to her with a kiss, a caress, the warmth of his breath on her naked skin.

So he kept his hands gentle and his kisses butterfly soft, and couldn't ever remember needing a woman more. Outside, snow drifted soundlessly down, but inside, there was nothing but Lizzie, nothing but the fire he built in her with a patience he never would have thought himself capable of.

When they moved to her bedroom, her bed, he couldn't have said. Lost in the touch and taste and feel of each other, they just seemed to drift that way without any conscious effort. Clothes melted away, senses blurred, and he couldn't remember a time when he hadn't wanted her like this...bare and beautiful, aching, restless, flushed, her eyes heavy-lidded and dark with passion. His own needs tearing at him he kissed his way down her throat, over the graceful slope of her shoulder, the curve of her breast, and lower still learning the slender lines of her body, steeping her in pleasure until she moaned.

And still, he kept a tight rein on his own needs and liked to think he was in control. Then she reached for him, stroked slow, knowing hands over him, and he realized too late that he'd been fooling himself all along where she was concerned. He had no more control over the need that sparked between them than she did. She only had to touch him to tie him in knots, move under him to completely destroy him.

And she knew it. He saw the knowledge in her eyes, in the curve of the seductive smile that curled just the corners of her mouth. Her eyes locking with his in the darkness, she skimmed her hands over the hard angles and planes of his body with a touch that was as soft as a promise and he was helpless to do anything but groan.

Delighted, Elizabeth only just then realized how much she needed to know that she could make this man, who was so sure of himself with other women, weak with need for *her.* She wanted to be the one he reached for in his sleep, ached for in his dreams, called out for when what was left of his control shattered. Murmuring his name, she pulled his mouth down to hers for a long, passionate kiss that went on and on and on.

She'd never known loving could be so easy. He'd told her they needed to light a fire, and he had. But it wasn't a hot, raging forest fire; instead, it was a slow banked fire that warmed and heated a deep need inside her. Shuddering softly, she moved under him, sweet demand pulling at her, and took him inside.

In the darkness his eyes met hers, and an emotion she couldn't name filled her heart to overflowing. Defenseless, tears welled in her eyes and spilled over her lashes. With a quiet murmur, he kissed them away, then he was moving, stroking the fire, feeding it. Before they could do anything but gasp, they were consumed by the flames.

Chapter 9

Sprawled on her stomach and hugging more than her share of the covers, Elizabeth slept like a whipped puppy. She was worn out, poor baby, Zeke thought with a grin, and knew exactly how she felt. They'd spent the night reaching for each other, touching and stroking and loving each other until they were both spent. She'd drained every ounce of energy out of him, turned him inside out and made him forget his own name. He couldn't remember the last time that had happened, but the lady wasn't going to get any complaints out of him. It had been the most incredible night of his life.

The portable phone on the nightstand rang then, shattering the quiet of the morning. Elizabeth didn't so much as twitch an eyelash. Amused, Zeke could only marvel at her. She slept like the dead, but after last night he knew he only had to nuzzle the back of her neck to have her wide awake and reaching for him. For all of two seconds he actually considered that, but she was tired. And after the difficult events of yesterday, she needed her sleep.

Before the phone could ring again, he leaned across her and picked it up. "Hello?" he said quietly.

"I was hoping you would answer," Nick said in his ear. "How's Elizabeth?"

Frowning, Zeke checked the clock on the nightstand. It was barely six-thirty—dawn was still a promise on the eastern horizon. Nick didn't call at that hour to shoot the breeze. "Sleeping. We've got more trouble, haven't we?"

"Napoleon's body was found. At least I think it's him," he amended roughly. "It's hard to tell. The son of a bitch mutilated him. He's in pieces, Zeke."

Just as Elizabeth's tormentor had said. Swearing soft and low, he swung his legs over the side of the bed and stalked naked over to the far window. "And you need Lizzie to identify him."

It wasn't a question, but a statement of fact, one Nick didn't deny. "I'm not any happier about putting her through that than you are, but she knows that wolf better than anyone."

He had a point, but that didn't make Zeke like it any better. "Where'd you find him?"

"Out on Hawk Road by the old Larkin place. Looks like someone just tossed him out on the side of the road without even stopping. One of my deputies came across him about three this morning. It's not a pretty sight, Zeke."

No, he didn't imagine it was. And as much as he hated it, there was no way he was going to be able to shield Elizabeth from it. Not this time. There was no doubt the remains were Napoleon's, but a formal ID had to be made for the record. He wasn't taking any chances that the jerk who did this would get off on a technicality when he finally went to trial because he and Nick hadn't done their jobs.

Resigned, he said tersely, "I'll bring her in in about an hour."

He'd planned to spoil her with breakfast in bed, then afterward, make love to her until they were both too weak to move, but that wasn't possible now. She would want to know immediately that Napoleon had finally been found, then there would be no stopping her. As much as it would hurt her, she'd race into town as soon as he told her the news.

Knowing that, he didn't wake her then, but let her sleep while he grabbed a quick shower. Dressed and shaved, he returned to the bedroom twenty minutes later to find her just where he'd left her, dead to the world. Given the chance, he would have crawled right back in beside her. Instead, he sat on the side of the bed and gently swept her tousled honey-colored hair back from her face, his fingers lightly skimming over her. That was all it took to draw her from sleep.

Moaning softly, her eyes still closed, she stretched and curled toward him in a sensuous move that seemed to suck all the air right out of his lungs. Swallowing a groan, he caught her hand when she blindly reached for him. "Lizzie? Wake up, honey. We need to talk."

At his rough growl, her eyes flew open, and hot, vivid memories of the night came rushing back in a flood. Sweet madness. There was no other way to describe it. She'd never been so…insatiable…with a man in her life, but before she could be embarrassed, before the awkwardness of the morning after could set in, she noted his clothes, his freshly shaved jaw, his somber expression, and all thoughts of the loving they'd shared flew right out of her head. He looked that grim only when something was seriously wrong.

Alarmed, she sat up, clutching the covers to her breast,

and she knew. After listening to the vicious message on her answering machine last night, she'd known Napoleon's killer wouldn't be able to resist torturing her with the wolf's bloody remains for long. "Napoleon's body's been found, hasn't it?"

Not surprised that she'd guessed, he nodded. "Nick called. He needs you to come into the office and identify him."

"Where?" she choked.

"Out on Hawk Road."

He started to say more, only to hesitate, and she knew there was more. "What? You might as well tell me the rest. I'll have to know eventually, anyway, and if it's bad, I'd rather deal with it all at once."

"The body's been mutilated," he said finally, bluntly. "This won't be easy for you, sweetheart."

She flinched, the images that came to mind turning her blood to ice. The monster had carried through on every one of his threats so far. So what was next on his agenda? Coming after her?

She shivered at the thought and was furious with herself for the weakness. The man was a devil, a treacherous bastard who took pleasure in murdering animals and threatening anyone whose views were different from his own. There was no way she was giving a piece of trash like that the power to terrify her.

Her jaw set determinedly, she reached for the robe at the foot of the bed. "Give me a few minutes to get dressed, and then we can go."

Nick was waiting for them in his office when they arrived. Elizabeth took one look at his face and knew that the next few minutes were going to be every bit as difficult as Zeke had warned her they would be. She'd never seen

Nick look so grim. Bracing herself, she said, "Where is he?"

"In the back room," Nick replied. "But I can't let you go walking in there thinking you're going to see the body of the same wolf you saw running across the ridge a few days ago, Elizabeth. He's in pieces," he said curtly. "There's not a lot to identify."

She was, she told herself, prepared for that. Even if her stomach was already roiling at the thought. "I can handle it," she said stiffly. "Let's get it over with."

The back room Nick led them to was normally used as a storage room. Small and windowless, it held discarded desks and chairs, office supplies, and boxes of records. An old scarred table in the middle of the room had been cleared off, and there, under a sheet, was Napoleon's remains, such as they were.

Her heart hammering against her ribs with dread, Elizabeth gratefully latched on to Zeke's hand when he wrapped his fingers around hers. With a nod to Nick, who stood across the table from her, she signaled that she was ready. Without a word, he swept back the sheet.

The sight before her was gruesome. Literally hacked to pieces, the poor animal could have been a wolf or a coyote, or even a dog. But even as bile rose in her throat, Elizabeth knew in an instant it was Napoleon. In the stark light from the bare bulb overhead, the fur that wasn't tainted with dried blood had the same faint sheen of blue that had always made it easy for her to pick Napoleon out of the other wolves.

Her fingers tightened in Zeke's, but she didn't cry. Instead, a hot fireball of fury burned in her gut. "That's Napoleon," she said coldly. "The blue in his coat is a genetic cast that none of the other wolves have." The identification made, she turned and walked out.

Seething with anger, she turned on the two men the second they joined her in Nick's office. "Whoever did this isn't going to get away with it," she said icily.

"I agree," Nick said. "The man's a psychopath. I don't mind telling you that just thinking about what he's capable of scares the hell out of me. He's enjoying himself too damn much, and next time, he won't be content with killing a wolf. And you're the one he's got his sights set on, dammit!"

"I think it's time we stirred things up with a reward," Zeke said. "Leaving threatening messages on Lizzie's machine is one thing. Killing and dismembering a wolf, then dumping it on the side of the road, is a whole other ball game. Somebody had to see something, hear something. With a little incentive, they just might come forward and talk."

Taken aback, Elizabeth said, "Are you saying that someone knows who killed Napoleon and they're just sitting on that information? While the monster plans to kill me?"

It was a sad fact of life, but it was true. Moral outrage seldom loosened tongues. Money, on the other hand, could turn a mute into a chatterbox if the numbers were high enough. "We'll give people the benefit of the doubt and hope that anyone who might have seen or heard something wasn't aware that a crime was being committed," he told her. "They will be, once the reward is posted. Then we'll see who comes forward."

He and Nick discussed the amount and agreed that five thousand dollars was more than an adequate incentive to get people talking. "I'll call Denver and get it okayed, then work up a flyer."

"My men'll help post it," Nick promised, then gave him a hard look. "You realize this is going to up the ante, don't you? Once news of the reward gets out, the bastard's going to start feeling the heat. And he's going to lay the blame for that right at Elizabeth's feet. If he was mad before, he's going to be downright ballistic now.''

''If he even thinks about coming after her, he's going to have more trouble than he can handle,'' Zeke said coldly. ''She's not going to be alone—not even for a second. Between you and me and your deputies, he's not going to be able to get near her.''

''We'll have to set up a schedule. I can keep an eye on her while she's here in town—''

Amazed, Elizabeth listened to them arrange her life and said dryly, ''Do I have anything to say about this schedule? Or am I expected to go meekly along with whatever decisions the two of you come up with?'' When both men just blinked at her, she rolled her eyes. ''I have a job, guys, and it doesn't involve sitting in an office all day long. I spend half my time out in the mountains with the wolves, and that's not going to change just because some jackass is threatening to kill me.

''That doesn't mean I intend to go off by myself,'' she said when Zeke started to scowl, ''but you might as well accept the fact that I can't always be with one of you two or a deputy. I can't even promise that Tina and Peter will be around, for that matter. Our job is to track and study the wolves as they establish their territory now that they're back in the wild, and they seldom stay together. When they split, so do we.''

''I don't like it,'' Zeke growled.

''I'm not wild about it, either,'' she admitted, ''but if I have to tie myself to the office all day, then we might as well fold up our tents and call it quits right now because this project will never succeed without me in the field. I can't direct things from behind a desk in town. I'll be careful, but I'm not letting Napoleon's killer sabotage what's left of this project by scaring me into not doing my job."

Her chin set stubbornly, this wasn't something she was willing to bend on, and both men, like it or not, had no choice but to accept it. Nick, recognizing a woman who had her heels dug in when he saw one, knew when to give in. "Keep your eyes open whenever you leave the office to make sure you're not being followed," he told her. "And keep your cell phone handy. If you're the least bit scared, even if you don't see anything threatening, I want you to call my office immediately."

Zeke wasn't nearly so gracious. "And one of us should know where you are at all times," he said roughly, his blue eyes dark with irritation. "I don't care if you just stop by the grocery store on your lunch hour, I want to know about it."

He looked so disgruntled that Elizabeth couldn't help but grin. "Yes, Zeke. Whatever you say, Zeke. I wouldn't want to worry you, Zeke."

"See that you don't," he growled. And ignoring Nick's presence, he hauled her close for a scorching kiss.

It was over almost before it had begun, but when he reluctantly drew back, she was flushed and breathless, and he didn't want to let her go. "C'mon," he said huskily. "I'll follow you to your office, then come back here and get started on those flyers." Ignoring Nick's broad grin, he took her hand, and led her outside.

How she was able to think clearly enough after that to drive, she never knew. It was only a short distance, but she found herself watching her rearview mirror, watching Zeke and thinking about last night. Earth-shattering. There was no other way to describe it. He'd turned her world upside down and shown her a side of herself she hadn't known existed, and she didn't know if she'd ever get over the experience. Not when, hours later, she was still feeling the aftershocks from just a kiss.

She had to think…about Zeke, about herself, about the emotions she didn't seem to have any control over any longer…but the day that stretched before her was packed to the brim with things that needed to be done. Now that Napoleon was beyond her help, she had to find Queenie and make sure she—and her pups when she had them— was all right. But first and foremost, she had to find another place to live. Despite the fact that Zeke and the memories he'd given her last night had gone a long way toward making her forget the horror of finding Napoleon's bloody collar on her front porch, she never wanted to spend another night in that house as long as she lived.

Tina and Peter arrived at the office the same time she did, so Zeke didn't even come inside once he saw she wouldn't be there alone. Waving, he turned around to head right back to Nick's, leaving Elizabeth to tell them about the discovery of Napoleon's body and the threats made against her and the other wolves.

"So watch your backs," she warned. "So far, he seems to be focusing on me, but there's no telling what the man's capable of."

"We'll be fine," Peter assured her. At six foot four and two hundred plus pounds, he was more than capable of handling anyone who made the mistake of coming after him or his wife. "You're the one I'm worried about. I don't like the idea of you living out there in the country all by yourself."

"Why don't you move into town with us?" Tina suggested. "I know the apartment's small, but we can make do."

If their place had been big enough, Elizabeth wouldn't have hesitated, but small was an overstatement when describing their place. Little more than a minuscule loft over a two-car garage, it and the old Murphy place had been the only two rental properties available when they'd all moved to Liberty Hill for the duration of the wolf project. Tina and Peter had had no choice but to take it, but they couldn't turn around without bumping into each other with just the two of them living there. There was no way they could squeeze in a third person.

"I appreciate the offer, guys, but I just don't see how we could manage it without killing each other. But I am going to move. I'm going to call the Realtor right now."

Not surprisingly, the town's only Realtor couldn't help her much because there just wasn't anything available. The town was too small, and when people moved there, they had a habit of staying put. There were no motels, no apartments, nothing but two run-down old shacks that hadn't been lived in in years. Stuck, Elizabeth asked her to check rental property in Spring Canyon, the next closest town, but although the woman agreed to get back to her, she couldn't hold out much hope that she would find anything. Thirty miles away, Spring Falls wasn't much bigger than Liberty Hill and was just as sedentary.

Desperate, Elizabeth then called Ed at his diner and the postmistress. Between the two of them, they saw just about everyone in town over the course of a given day, and if anyone would know who had a place they might be willing to rent or someone who even took in an occasional boarder, it was Ed and Hilda.

Unfortunately she struck out there, too. She had a pleasant chat with both of them, but when she hung up a few minutes later, she was no better off than she had been before. Unless the Realtor came up with something in Spring Falls, she would be forced to stay where she was.

In the meantime she had a bigger problem to worry

about. Queenie was pregnant, her mate dead, and she was due to go into labor anyday now. When she did, she would be in serious trouble. Without Napoleon there to get food for her, she would have to do it herself, and if she picked the wrong spot to den, there was a possibility that her pups could be killed by predators or freeze to death before she could make her way back to them.

"She's moved back to the ridge," Peter said when Elizabeth checked the female wolf's radio signal. "She must have waited until everyone left yesterday, then made her way back to the area near the holding pen late yesterday afternoon. You think she's still waiting for Napoleon to come back?"

Elizabeth listened to the radio signal herself and shook her head. "Maybe initially, but not now. She's so close to dominoing—if she hasn't already—that her first priority has got to be her pups. I think she's denned."

"Then we'd better find her," Tina said, already reaching for her jacket. "I'll warm up the chopper."

The day was clear and cold, with no sign of the fog that had shrouded the mountains the previous morning. Lifting the chopper into the crystal-clear air, Tina headed north, toward Eagle Ridge, while Elizabeth adjusted the volume of Queenie's radio signal in her earpiece. The closer they drew to the meadow where Elizabeth had last seen the two wolves running free, the faster the signal beeped.

"She's got to be around here somewhere," she said into her headset over the roar of the rotors. "Try over there by those trees to the right. There's a lot of underbrush—she could have crawled in there to den."

Tina obligingly sent the chopper skating to the right until they were hovering directly over the trees, but the view was obstructed by the thickness of the foliage. Queenie's collar sent out the same rapid beat as before, but that only meant she was in the approximate vicinity. She could have been a thousand yards in any direction, and the signal would have been the same.

"Let's find the perimeter of the signal," Tina said and began to zigzag across the sky.

Twenty minutes later they had mapped out a thousand-square-foot area north of the meadow. Wild and untamed and dense with trees, it was just across the meadow from the holding pen and held all manner of places for an animal to hide.

Pushing on her sunglasses to cut the glare off the snow, Elizabeth gazed down with narrowed eyes at the rough landscape below, searching for the slightest sign of motion, but there was none. And still Queenie's radio signal beat frantically in her ear. The fact that the chopper hadn't scared off the pregnant wolf like it had the other animals in the area was all the proof Elizabeth needed that she'd denned—which was all the more reason that they find her soon, before something happened to her pups. Those pups were all Elizabeth had left of Napoleon and were the future of the project. They had to survive.

Swearing softly, she said, "See if you can set us down in the meadow. We're going to have to continue the search on foot." There was no other alternative.

Zeke had the reward approved by ten in the morning, and handbills designed within a half hour. By noon, he'd printed them out on Nick's computer at the sheriff's office and posted them all over town. Nick's deputies distributed them around the county, and by two o'clock the calls started coming in. Not surprisingly most people just wanted to chat and find out what was going on.

Manning the phones with Nick, Zeke winced when he

recognized the nasal voice of Dolores Ivy, his mother's third cousin. Loony as they came, Dolores had been known to stand on her rooftop and signal for aliens with a flashlight. If she knew anything about Napoleon's death, Zeke would swallow one of the reward posters whole.

"Hello, Dolores," he drawled, rolling his eyes at Nick, who was well acquainted with his cousin and her eccentricities. "What can I do for you?"

"You can tell me how I apply for this reward you're advertising all over town. Roger Harper plowed down my fence the other night when he came home drunk, and I need the money for a new one."

"It's not quite as simple as just applying for it like it's a bank loan, Dolores. We're trying to find out who killed that dead wolf that was found on Hawk Road early this morning. You wouldn't know anything about that, would you?"

"Well, of course not!" she huffed. "Abigail Smith lives out that way, and I wouldn't be caught dead anywhere near that woman! Do you know she told everyone at church that I had a screw loose just because I sleep with my glasses on so I can see my dreams better? I haven't spoken a word to her since."

Zeke seriously doubted that Abigail cared, but he only said soothingly, "I'm sure that's very wise of you. I wish I could hear more of the story, but I've got another call. If you hear anything about Napoleon's death, call me. Okay?"

"Okay, dear. But wasn't he killed at Waterloo?"

Swallowing a groan, Zeke explained that he was talking about the wolf and quickly hung up. When he looked up, it was to find Nick grinning at him. "Why am I getting all the nutcases?"

"Hey, she's your relative," Nick retorted, chuckling.

"And you just got a taste of what I have to put up with on a regular basis. Do you know she actually called me at three in the morning one night and wanted me to come out to her place to arrest an alien she swore was hiding in her basement? And I'm not talking about the illegal kind, either. She was convinced it was a Martian. I tried to explain that she'd probably just heard a mouse scrounging around for something to eat, but nothing would do but that I had to go out there and search the place myself. When I didn't find anything, she claimed he flew off right before I got there."

"I guess it's a good thing Napoleon's body wasn't found anywhere near her place or she'd have sworn the Martians did it," Zeke replied just as the phone rang again. Snatching it up, he said, "Sheriff's office. Zeke McBride speaking."

"Are you the fella looking for that wolf killer?"

The caller was elderly, his voice sharp and rough. Assuming it was another curiosity call, Zeke leaned back in his chair and began to doodle on his notepad. "Yes, sir, I am. I'm an agent with the U.S. Department of Fish and Wildlife. And you are…?"

"Lloyd Godwin," he said promptly, and rattled off his address.

"So what can I do for you, Mr. Godwin? Do you know anything about how the wolf died?"

"Well, I'm not quite sure about that," he said. "Maybe. What day was he killed?"

There was something about the old man's tone of voice that had Zeke sitting up straighter and motioning for Nick to listen in on the call. "We're pretty sure he was killed the day before yesterday, sir. Why? Did you see something suspicious?"

He hesitated, then drawled, "I don't know if I'd say it

was suspicious. Just kind of odd. Chester Grant was up on the ridge road in his wrecker late that afternoon, and the idiot almost drove me off the road. Normally, I wouldn't have thought a thing of it—he drinks, you know—but I got a good look at him as he passed me, and he was white as a sheet. If you ask me, he was running from something.''

Alarm bells clanged in Zeke's head. When he was first called in on the case, he sat down with Nick and came up with a list of people who were openly opposed to the wolf project. Chester Grant's name was on that list. An alcoholic with a short fuse, he had a reputation for blowing up at the least little provocation. In spite of that, though, Zeke wouldn't have thought he had the guts to actually kill one of the wolves in cold blood. From what he knew of the man, he was nothing but a bag of hot air.

"Could you see if he had a gun with him?"

"Well, of course he did," he retorted in a voice that implied Zeke shouldn't have even had to ask. "He always carries that .42 of his on the gun rack over the cab window of his wrecker. Claims that in his line of work, he never knows when he's going to run into trouble. If you want my opinion, I think he goes looking for it half the time, but I guess that's his business.''

It was going to be his business if he found out Chester had anything to do with Napoleon's killing or the threats left on Elizabeth's answering machine, Zeke thought grimly. "What time of day was this, Mr. Godwin?"

"Around four-thirty in the afternoon," he said promptly. "I was trying to get to town before the bank closed."

Four-thirty. It fit, Zeke thought. Five hours later, just about the time he was kissing Elizabeth at Myrtle's, the wolf's collar had started emitting the mortality code. "And did Mr. Grant have anyone with him in the truck?"

"I don't think so, but I couldn't swear to that. You got

to remember—I was trying to stay on the road, and it happened so fast that I didn't notice anything but his face when he raced past me."

"Where exactly did this happen on Ridge Road?"

"Right past the cutoff to the meadow where the wolf lady and her people set up that dang holding pen for the wolves," he retorted.

Across the desk, Zeke's eyes met Nick's. Bingo. Finally, they had a break! "Thank you for calling, Mr. Godwin," he said into the phone. "The sheriff and I will check into this, and if anything comes of it, I'll get back in touch with you about the reward. For your own safety, sir, I'd advise you to keep this conversation to yourself. The incident may have been completely innocent, but until we know that for sure, you could be in danger for coming forward."

"Don't you worry about me," the old man retorted tartly. "Chester Grant's not the only one that carries a .42 in his pickup."

Great. Now he had to worry about a shootout at the OK Corral. Shaking his head, Zeke hung up and reached for his jacket. Already on his feet and ready, Nick raised a brow. "Your car or mine?"

"The patrol car," Zeke said, grinning. "We want to make an impression."

Chester's Garage was the last building on the south end of town and the bane of his neighbor's existence. Cars in various states of disrepair crowded the parking area near the street, while at the back of the lot, junkards that looked like they hadn't been driven in decades sat rusting under mounds of snow. To make matters worse, a general air of filth permeated the area. Even the snow was greasy.

It wasn't the kind of establishment that Zeke's family would have ever taken their vehicles to, but there were plenty in town who did. As Nick pulled up before the garage, a half dozen men stood inside the open bay door shooting the breeze while Chester fiddled under the hood of a three-year-old Chrysler. Everyone of them knew Zeke and Nick by name, had grown up with them, knew their families, but at the sight of the patrol car, they stiffened like men who had something to hide.

And Chester was the worst of all. As Zeke and Nick stepped from the car, he straightened abruptly, slamming his head against the hood of the Chrysler. He swore and nervously wiped his greasy hands on a rag, looking everywhere but at his visitors. He couldn't have looked more guilty if he'd been caught with his hand in the cookie jar.

Greeting him with a nod, Nick said, "We need to talk to you, Chester, if you've got a second. Maybe in your office?"

The blood drained from his face, leaving him pasty white, and for a second, he looked ready to bolt. But with Zeke and Nick in front of him and his customers blocking his back, there was nowhere to go. Throwing up his chin, he decided to bluster his way out of the situation. "You just can't come in here and expect me to drop everything so you can talk," he said irately. "I've got a business to run—"

"We can do it here, if you like," Zeke said smoothly. "The choice is yours."

Flustered, he sputtered, "N-no! I don't like, damn you! What do you want, anyway?" he demanded, glaring at Zeke. "You're not the sheriff here. You're not anybody but a damn McBride with more money than God. I don't have to talk to you if I don't want to."

Zeke considered himself an even-tempered man who didn't lose it often. But there were some things he didn't handle well, and name calling about his family from a perp with an attitude was one of them. Quick as a flash, he had his badge out and shoved in the garage owner's face. "Wanna bet? I'm a federal agent, Chester, and in case you haven't figured it out yet, you're not winning any Brownie points here. I suggest you cooperate before I forget I'm not allowed to shove my badge down your freaking throat."

In the stunned silence that followed that announcement, Nick said lightly, "What was it you were saying about that chat in your office, Chester? You've changed your mind? Good. I think that's a wise decision. Don't you, Zeke?"

"The smartest one he's made all day," he said curtly, never taking his gaze from Chester's beady-eyed glare. "Some things should be discussed in private."

Not as dense as he appeared, Chester obviously didn't have to be hit over the head with a two-by-four before he got the point that this was one fight he couldn't win. Grumbling, he turned toward his office. "If this takes longer than ten minutes, you can explain to Mrs. Eisenhauer why she won't be getting her car back today."

"Trust me, Mrs. Eisenhauer is the least of your problems right now," Nick told him dryly as he closed the office door behind the three of them. "Where were you Wednesday afternoon at four-thirty?"

It was a simple question, one that an innocent man wouldn't have batted an eye at. Sucking in a sharp breath, Chester almost swallowed his tongue. "What d-do y-you mean?"

"It's not a complicated question," Zeke growled. "Everyone was somewhere at four-thirty Wednesday afternoon. So where were you?"

"I—I—" Desperate, he looked frantically around the small, cluttered room for an answer. "I was on a call!" he blurted out finally and nearly wilted in relief. "Yeah, that's it. Now I remember. An out-of-stater blew a fan belt and needed a tow.''

''Where?''

Confused, he blinked. ''Where'd he need a tow to? The garage, of course!''

Praying for patience, Zeke counted to ten and forced a smile. It never reached his eyes. ''We figured you'd bring him here, Chester. What we're trying to find out is where the man broke down.''

''Oh.'' He hesitated, and Zeke could almost see the wheels working in his slow-thinking head. ''It was down by Johnsonville. By the lake.''

He was lying—a blind man could have seen it—and Zeke and Nick both had perfect vision. ''Then I guess whoever thought they saw you up on Eagle Ridge the day that wolf was killed was mistaken,'' Nick retorted casually, watching him like a hawk. ''You couldn't have been two places at the same time, could you?''

''N-no! C-course n-not!''

''You had this problem with stuttering long, Chester?'' Zeke asked with exaggerated concern. ''I never noticed it before. Maybe you should see a doctor.''

''I—I am. I—I mean I've already g-got an appointment w-with someone in Colorado Sp-Springs. In the m-morning!''

''That's good,'' Nick said. ''You can't let things like that slide. Now that we've got everything straightened out, you can get back to Mrs. Eisenhauer's car. Oh, and Chester,'' he said just as he reached the door, ''you will let us know, won't you, if you remember being up on Eagle Ridge for any reason on Wednesday?''

''S-sure,'' he croaked. ''But I don't think I—I'm going t-to remember anything l-like that.''

''Selective memory,'' Zeke drawled as they walked out

and shut the door behind them. "It's a wonderful thing, isn't it?"

"He's in this up to his neck," Nick replied. "You notice his .42's not in his wrecker?"

"Yep. Saw it right off."

"As long as I can remember, Chester's never been anywhere without that gun. You think he acted alone?"

Climbing into the patrol car, both men glanced back at the window of the garage office, where Chester was staring back at them with wide, frightened eyes. "Not a chance," Zeke retorted. "The man's afraid of his own shadow. Whoever left those messages on Elizabeth's answering machine and mutilated Napoleon was no coward. No, Chester didn't do it, but I'll bet next year's salary that he knows who did."

That was a bet Nick wasn't willing to take.

The second the patrol car pulled out of the parking lot and headed back toward town, Chester snatched up the phone and punched in a number with fingers that were far from steady. "Be there. Be there, dammit!" he whispered harshly to himself, then almost wept when the line was answered on the third ring.

"The sheriff was just here!" he said frantically. "And that damn Zeke McBride. They know, dammit! I'm telling you they know. You've got to do something!"

"Get ahold of yourself!" the man on the other end of the line ordered sharply. "They don't know jack squat or they would have arrested you. They were just trying to rattle you, and it looks like they did a good job."

"But they knew I was up on Eagle Ridge that day. Someone must have seen us." A sob of panic rose in his throat at the thought. "God, what am I going to do?"

"Nothing," the other man said coldly. "Absolutely nothing. You're going to leave everything to me."

"But—"

"Shut your mouth and listen. There's no reason to panic. All the evidence has been taken care of. There's nothing to link the killing of that damn wolf to anyone. And it's not against the law to drive up to Eagle Ridge. The sheriff was just fishing."

Trying to remain calm, Chester dragged in a shuddering breath. "Fishing. Yeah, he was just fishing. Looking for someone to blame."

"That's right. And we know who's really to blame, don't we?" he asked silkily. "That hotshot little biologist. She's the one who brought the damn wolves in here in the first place without asking us. We're paying her salary, but did she listen to us when we told her to get those killers out of here? Hell, no! She's causing problems for all of us, and we're not going to stand for it anymore. She's got to go."

His heart pounding, Chester nodded like a parrot. "She should have been run out of town months ago."

"I'll take care of the bitch," the other man said coldly. "You just make sure you have an alibi for tonight. Tonight, Ms. Davis gets what's coming to her."

Chapter 10

Standing in the cabin of the forest-service lookout tower, Elizabeth aimed her binoculars at the huge old pine in the distance that towered over the other spruce and pine in the area. At the base of its trunk, nearly concealed by the tree's low-hanging branches, was the rocky depression where Queenie had chosen to den. Studying it, Elizabeth had to admit that Napoleon's mate had chosen wisely. The thick branches of the pine acted as an umbrella, shielding the den from bad weather, and the surrounding rocks were as protective as a stone fort. With the small opening to the den, Queenie could, if she had to, put her pups behind her and fight off any predator that threatened her or her offspring.

There were wolf pups once again in southwestern Colorado!

Her heart expanding at the thought, Elizabeth didn't know if she wanted to laugh or cry or dance a jig. Finally, after years of preparing the way for them, fighting for their very right to exist in their native habitat, native-born pups could claim the area as their own. Napoleon's pups.

The tears came then, welling in her eyes, but they were tears of happiness rather than sadness. He had done his job and sired the next generation of wolves. Now it was her duty to see that nothing happened to those pups while they were still too young to protect themselves.

Her binoculars trained on the base of the tree, Elizabeth would have given anything to catch sight of one of them, but they were newly born and wouldn't, she knew, leave the den for weeks. And even if one of them had accidentally wandered to the mouth of the den, it would be well hidden. In their searching, she and Tina had come within thirty yards of that old pine at least three different times without once suspecting what was concealed at its base. Only when they heard the faint whimper of the pups, quickly silenced by their mother, did they realize they had finally found Queenie.

At that point she and Tina had quickly backed off. A mother wolf would fight to protect her pups, but if she felt she might not survive an attack from an enemy, she would abandon her pups to later have another litter.

Elizabeth was determined that that wasn't going to happen. Queenie was under enough stress as a single mother without having to worry about the curiosity of humans. Still, Elizabeth hadn't been able to bring herself to leave. Not yet. So while she kept watch over things, she'd sent Tina back to the office for food.

Down below, in the parking lot of the tower, she saw Tina pull up in her car, and wasn't surprised to see Zeke pull in right behind her in his truck. Gazing down at him, she felt a smile bloom on her face and was helpless to stop it. Even though no one could possibly sneak up on her in the tower without her being aware of it, she'd called him to let him know she was there alone, but safe. She should have known he wouldn't be able to resist checking out the situation for himself.

He and Tina looked up and waved, then moved to the trunk of Tina's car to remove the carcass of a dead coyote. With Tina showing Zeke the way, he carried it into the trees toward the tall pine in the distance where Queenie had denned.

Through her binoculars, Elizabeth watched every step they took through her binoculars. "Careful," she muttered. "Not too close. You don't want to scare her. She's got a good nose—she'll smell it if you put it anywhere within a couple of hundred yards. That's it. Right there!"

Relieved, she watched Zeke toss the roadkill as far as he could from where he stood, so that Queenie wouldn't be put off by the scent of humans any more than she already was. Then he and Tina quickly faded back into the trees. Her gaze still trained on the thick shadows under the pine that concealed the den, Elizabeth found herself holding her breath and silently urging Queenie to accept the food. If she didn't, she and her pups would have to be recaptured and held in the holding pen until the pups were old enough to fend for themselves.

"Come on, girl," she urged, "dinner's ready. You've got to be hungry. Go for it."

But nothing moved in the shadows under the pine.

Down below, Tina signaled that she was returning to the office, and Zeke started up the long flight of stairs to the tower's observation cabin. Elizabeth moved to unlock the door, then returned to the wide bank of clear glass that overlooked the den in the distance. Untouched, the dead coyote lay right where Zeke had thrown it.

"Beggars can't be choosers, Queenie," she muttered. "It isn't as if you haven't eaten roadkill before. That's all you had for the three months you were in the holding pen, and it didn't seem to bother you, then. So what's the problem?''

It was the pups, and Elizabeth knew it. Instincts kicked in after whelping that weren't there before. So while she might reluctantly accept roadkill from humans when she was penned, she would be suspicious of that same food now, if she thought it was somehow a threat to her litter.

The door opened behind her and Zeke stepped in. Only slightly winded from the long climb, he immediately joined her at the window, his own binoculars hanging around his neck. ''She take it yet?''

''No. And I'm afraid she's not going to. She probably picked up our scent, and after what happened to Napoleon, she's got no reason to trust us, especially now that she has pups to protect.''

''It's early yet,'' he said. ''Give her some time. She's a first-time mother in foreign territory and still getting the lay of the land. She's probably just scoping the situation out. If she's hungry enough, she's not going to be able to resist the smell of that food for long.''

Elizabeth wanted desperately to believe him, but there'd been little to be optimistic about over the past few days. And as seconds turned into minutes and time dragged, she found it harder and harder to be positive. Then, just when she was about to turn away in defeat, she thought she saw something move in the thick shadows under the old pine. ''Did something move? There! To the left of that boulder that looks like it was split by lightning. Is that Queenie's nose sticking out? It is! Look, here she comes!''

Barely discernible in the concealing shadows that protected her den, Queenie sniffed the air warily, still not sure she was ready to trust the handout being offered her. Through narrowed eyes, she inspected the surrounding forest, searching for predators, but nothing moved. Elizabeth couldn't be sure if the wolf was satisfied that she was safe or that she was just so hungry that she could no longer resist the lure of food, but suddenly she streaked out from under the pine and through the trees to the dead coyote.

She didn't stay long—just a few minutes was all it took for her to swallow a few hulking bites—then she was racing back to her den and her pups.

"All right!" Zeke said with a broad grin. "Atta girl!"

"She did it!" Elizabeth said with a laugh and threw herself into his arms, babbling with excitement all the while. "I was so afraid we were going to have to put her back into the holding pen until the pups got bigger. But she'll eat now. We've got nearly a freezerful of roadkill at the office, but it won't take her long to go through that since she's nursing. I need to call Nick—his deputies can keep a lookout for fresh meat. Oh, that sounds horrible, doesn't it, but—"

Suddenly realizing that she was chattering and he was grinning down at her while he held her close, she felt her heart lurch in her breast and had no idea how she'd come to be in his arms. Had she moved or he? She couldn't think, couldn't remember. She just knew that it seemed as if she'd been waiting all day to find her way back to him, and she hadn't even known it until now.

Shaken, she stepped back. Because she had to. Because there was a heat in his eyes that called to the longing in her heart. Because if she didn't put some distance between them, she was going to melt against him and lift her mouth to his and give herself up to the madness that had gripped her last night.

"I guess I was rattling on, wasn't I?" she said huskily, and only had to see the amusement curling his mouth to know that he knew exactly what was going on inside her head.

"A little," he said, chuckling. "But I'd say you're entitled. If Queenie had refused that food, you'd have had a major problem on your hands."

"I know. For a minute there, I was really starting to worry, but she's going to be fine now. Thank God something's finally starting to go right!"

"It seems to be a day for it," he agreed. "Nick and I posted the reward posters and got a very interesting phone call this afternoon."

"You got a break in the case?"

"It looks like it." He told her about Chester Grant and his wild driving up on Eagle Ridge the afternoon before Napoleon's collar switched to the mortality code. "Chester's always been more bark than bite, so it's doubtful that he actually killed Napoleon himself. But the little worm knows more than he's telling."

Elizabeth didn't doubt that. She'd taken her car to Chester one time and she'd never taken it back. He was a sly, cunning little man who'd made her skin crawl. It didn't surprise her at all that he would associate with the monster who'd killed Napoleon and still threatened her.

"You think he actually knows who the killer is?"

"The man was so scared he was stuttering, darlin'. Oh, yeah, he knows. Now we just have to get the truth out of him. Nick's getting a search warrant to check his garage and house, but it's so late in the day he probably won't be able to find a judge to okay it until morning."

"So we have to wait. Again."

"It won't be long. You know how these things work—we've got to follow procedure or we'll never be able to put these jerks away."

"I know. It's just frustrating. Because of them, I have to find another place to live, and there's just not anything available."

His gaze sharpened at that. "You talked to the Realtor?"

Nodding, she turned to stare glumly out to the west, where the sun was already starting its descent toward the mountaintops in the distance. "She couldn't come up with anything. She promised to check Spring Falls, but since I haven't heard from her, I think it's pretty safe to say she wasn't successful. I guess I'm just going to have to stay where I am for now. I don't know what else to do."

"I do. You can stay with my mother."

Even as the words popped out of his mouth, he wanted to take them back and suggest she stay with him at Joe's, instead. He wanted her with him, in his arms, in his bed. After just one night, he needed to know that if he reached out for her, she was there with him, and safe.

But Liberty Hill was a small town, and he knew from experience just how much people loved to talk. He wouldn't subject her to that, wouldn't put her through it. No, his mother's was better, he reasoned. The homestead had five bedrooms, and with his mother and Janey using only two of the five, there was plenty of room for Elizabeth.

And she'd be safe at Twin Pines. The main house was right in the middle of the ranch, three miles from the highway. Anyone who tried to get to her there would not only have to pass by Joe's house near the ranch entrance, but they'd have to chance running into any one of a dozen ranch hands who would be alerted to keep an eye out for anyone who didn't belong there.

The more he thought about it, the more he liked the idea. Dammit, he wanted her with his family. Now. Always. It was where she belonged.

The thought slipped up on him from behind, blindsiding him. Stunned, he felt as if he'd been hit in the head with a rock. When had he started thinking of *always* and Lizzie in the same breath? How could he not have seen this coming? Right from the beginning, he'd—

"I can't just show up at your mother's uninvited," she said, whirling to face him.

Still caught up in his turbulent thoughts, he blinked her into focus. "You wouldn't be. I just invited you."

"But it's your mother's house! You can't arrange for me to live there without even discussing it with her, for heaven's sake! What will she think of me?"

That she was beautiful and bright and perfect for him, he thought, knowing his mother. But he couldn't tell her that. Not until he'd decided what he was going to do about it. "She'll love you," he said with gruff honesty, and meant every word.

"Zeke, she doesn't even know me!"

Unperturbed, he shrugged easily. "So she'll get to know you."

She tried not to smile and failed miserably. "It's not that simple and you know it."

"Sure it is," he insisted, and marveled she would be so shaken at the idea of meeting his mother. Teasing her, he said, "You don't throw your gum on the floor when you've chewed all the sugar out of it, do you?"

"Of course not! I don't even chew gum, and I certainly wouldn't throw it on the floor."

"And you don't talk with your mouth full—I know, because I've eaten with you. And I bet you even bathe every day just like rich folks."

"Zeke!"

Wicked laughter danced in his eyes. "Am I right or am I right?"

"Of course you're right, silly."

"Then what's not to like?"

He watched her flounder for something about herself to

criticize and grinned broadly. "Well? Cat got your tongue" You're beating a dead horse, Lizzie, honey. Just about everything about you is damn well likeable. Even this hairy mole on your chin," he teased, drawing her close to kiss her perfectly clear chin. "And that real beak of a nose o yours," he added, dropping another kiss on her pert nose "And then there's this thin, passionless mouth of yours. That really is enough to send a man running in the opposit direction. I just don't know what we're going to do abou that."

She was laughing when he playfully kissed her smack on the lips. Then he drew back, her eyes met his, and suddenly neither of them was smiling. How, he wondered, had he gone all day without kissing her? Loving her?

"Come here," he growled, and pulled her back into hi arms.

This wasn't the time or the place. Somewhere in the back of his head, the thought registered. He had to help her collect her things, then get her to his mother's so he could res easy tonight knowing she was safe. And even if there' been time, which there wasn't, the lookout tower wa hardly set up for a romantic rendezvous. There was no bed nothing but a thin cot for a ranger who found himself wit fire duty in the middle of the summer. It wasn't made fo two and didn't even have a blanket on it. She deserve better, dammit.

But with her mouth hot and hungry under his, her arm clinging to him, and every sweet inch of her pressed close none of that seemed to matter. He had to have her. Now Here. On top of the world, where there was no fear, no on to bother them, nothing to distract them from this crazines that had sparked between them the first moment they'd lai eyes on each other.

"I want you," he rasped, reaching for the hem of he

weater. In one quick move, he had it up and over her head.
efore it hit the floor, he'd found the snap of her bra, and
heartbeat later, her breasts spilled into his waiting hands.

She moaned, stunned pleasure in her eyes, and swayed
ward him. "Yes."

She couldn't manage anything else, just that one simple
ord, and had no idea what she did to him. No woman had
ver made him so hot, so hard, so fast. She was a wildness
 his blood, a burning need that grew more desperate every
me he just thought about her. And he thought about
er...about this, about touching her, loving her...con-
nually. Knowing that he could make her want him just as
uch as he wanted her, with nothing more than the stroke
 his fingers on her breasts, destroyed him.

A rough groan rumbling low in his throat, he tore at what
as left of her clothes, ripped at his own and knew, the
cond he had her naked, that he was never going to make
 as far as the cot. Crushing his mouth to hers, he wrapped
er close and carried her with him down to the floor.

Ravaged. Her head spinning, her heart thundering, Eliz-
eth felt ravaged, consumed, devoured. And she loved it.
ow could she have lived all these years and never expe-
enced the wonder of driving a man right to the edge of
s control? It was wonderful, heady, intoxicating. And she
anted more. She wanted everything. She wanted him
eak for her, wild, crazy with need, out of his head with
anting...for her.

Murmuring his name, she pushed him to his back and
lled with him and had the satisfaction of surprising him.
eeling the tension that gripped him and knowing she was
sponsible for it, she smiled down into his eyes. "I thought
d indulge myself," she said huskily. "Do you mind?"

He'd never be able to stand it. Even before she touched
m, he knew that he'd never be able to hang on to what

was left of his tattered self-control once she laid her hand
on him. But he could no more have denied her than he
could have denied himself his next breath. His jaw clenched
as he resisted the need to sweep her under him and bury
himself deep; he linked his hands behind his neck and gave
her a tight smile. "Indulge yourself all you like, sweet
heart," he said thickly. "I'm yours for the taking."

Hers. The thought wrapped around her heart and
squeezed gently, tempting her beyond bearing. How long
had she wanted him to be just hers and hadn't even known
it? How long had she been fooling herself into thinking it
could happen? It wouldn't. He, like her father, was too
much of a ladies' man to ever be satisfied with just one
woman, but for the first time she realized why her mother
let her father charm her time and again even though she
knew he would eventually hurt her again. When she was
in his arms, she could pretend she was the only one.

She wasn't her mother. She couldn't live like that. But
knowing that this was all she was ever going to have, she,
like her mother, could pretend.

Ducking her head, she buried her face against his neck
and drew in the scent of him. Old Spice. She always loved
the clean, fresh scent of it, and now she would never again
smell that familiar scent without thinking of him. Murmuring approval, she moved over him, indulging fantasies she
hadn't even known she had. She stroked and teased and
rubbed against him and loved the way sweat broke out on
his big, hard body. With a touch, she learned what made
him shudder. With a kiss low on his belly, she had him
cursing and fighting the need to reach for her. Laughing
softly, her own body humming with need, she moved lower
and discovered just what it took to break his control.

"Enough!" he growled, and with a lightning-quick
move, he reversed their positions.

Startled, her eyes met his, and then there was no time for laughter, for teasing, for anything but the lust that had their breath tearing through their lungs and their bodies burning for release. He moved over her, she parted her thighs, and with a groan that seemed to come all the way from his soul, he surged into her liquid warmth, filling her, claiming her body, her heart, her very soul. With a broken cry, she arched under him, then he was moving, his hips pumping, control lost. Driven past reason, she couldn't think, couldn't do anything but feel him loving her, taking her in a way no one ever had. Need tightened like a fist deep inside her, then, when she couldn't bear it another second, she heard his hoarse shout and pleasure hit them like a tidal wave, sweeping them under.

Cradled in Zeke's arms, her head nestled on his shoulder and her heart beating in time with his, Elizabeth would have given anything to lie just like that for the rest of the evening. But the sun was already sinking behind the mountains to the west, and with twilight just a promise away, she still didn't know where she was going to spend the night.

"It's getting late," she murmured.

Still, she couldn't bring herself to pull out of his arms. He lazily stroked her bare arm, and with a sigh, she nestled against him. Just another few minutes, she promised herself. Just until she worked up the strength to leave him.

"I want you to go to my mother's," he said quietly. "I wasn't kidding when I said she would love to have you. The house has five bedrooms, and it's just her and Janey there. Joe and Merry each have their own place, so it's not like you'd be putting anyone out. There's plenty of room."

After her earlier arguments, she knew he expected her to say no. It was an imposition, asking his mother to take her in, when she didn't know her from Adam. But the loving she and Zeke had just shared had changed everything. She had fought it with every fiber of her being, but she could no longer deny the truth. She was falling in love with him.

She didn't know how it had happened, how she'd *let* it happen, but she had to do something fast, before he broke her heart. She had to get her feet back on the ground, and the only way she could think of to do that was move in with his mother. Families had a habit of telling stories about a person, of exposing them for what they really were—not viciously, but honestly. By staying with his mother and sister, right in the middle of the family ranch, she would hear about all the old girlfriends, the women, the fiancée who had broken off their engagement just weeks before the wedding. And if that didn't strip the rose-colored glasses from her eyes and kill the crazy feelings she had for him, nothing else would.

"You're sure she won't mind?"

Stunned that she was actually considering the suggestion, he pulled back to look down at her in pleased surprise. "Of course. So you'll do it? You'll stay at the ranch?"

Grimly she nodded. What other option did she have if she wanted to protect herself from a broken heart? "Until I can make other arrangements." Like how to live without him the rest of her life.

The matter settled, they dressed and started down the long flight of stairs to the parking area below, just as the first faint stars appeared in the evening sky. "If you'll just drop me at the office, I'll pick up my car and drive out to my house to pack some things," she said as they reached his truck. "While I'm doing that, you can go ahead and clear things with your mother."

Frowning, he stopped in the process of opening the passenger door for her. "There's nothing to clear. I told you she'll love having you."

"I'm sure she will. But I'm not showing up at her house with my suitcase in my hand when she doesn't even know I'm coming," she said stubbornly. "You have to at least warn her, Zeke."

"So I'll call her."

"In person," she insisted. "She's your mother. You can't just foist some strange woman off on her without doing her the courtesy of discussing it with her in person first. That's rude."

Scowling, he rolled his eyes. Women had such weird ways of looking at things. "You're not strange. Hard-headed, maybe, but not strange." When she just looked at him, he sighed in frustration. "Look, I'll call her, okay? Will that satisfy you?"

"No."

"Come on, sweetheart, be reasonable about this. I don't like the idea of you going out to your place alone."

"But it's in the opposite direction from the ranch," she argued, "and it's silly for you to go that far out of your way when I won't be there ten minutes. All I'm going to do is grab a few things, stuff them in an overnight bag and get out of Dodge. Nothing's going to happen. And while I'm doing that, you can be talking to your mother…in person. If she's not thrilled at the idea of having company, you'll be able to see it on her face, and we'll make other arrangements."

He could have told her that Sara McBride would never turn away anyone in trouble, but that was something she would discover for herself. Struggling for patience, he tried to see things from her perspective and had to admit she had a right to be concerned with appearances. She was coming into a strange house, asking someone she didn't know for hospitality, and that could be awkward. If it took a face-to-face discussion between him and his mother to make her more comfortable with the situation, then by God, he'd do it. He wanted her to like his mother, to be at home in the house where he'd grown up. Because if he had his way, she was going to be staying much longer than a while.

"All right," he said with a sigh, giving in. "I'll talk to my mother. *In person.* But I want your word that you won't take any chances at your house. You get in and out as fast as you can, and if something doesn't look right when you get there, you don't even go inside. And *don't* check your answering machine. If anyone has anything important to tell you, they can call you at your office.

"Twenty minutes, sweetheart," he growled. "I'm giving you twenty minutes. If you're not back at the ranch in twenty minutes, I'm coming looking for you."

"I'll be there in fifteen," she assured him. "I promise."

His thoughts wrapped up in Elizabeth, Zeke walked through the front door of the homestead and was four steps into the living room before he noticed the balloons and streamers. Stopping in his tracks, he groaned. His mother's birthday! The family had a big party for her every year and invited everyone they knew—it was a tradition.

Damn, how could he have forgotten? Elizabeth was going to walk in just about the time the first guests started arriving, and he hadn't thought to invite her. Swearing under his breath, he could just imagine how she would feel about that. If she'd balked at the idea of moving in without him getting a personal okay from his mother first, there was no way in hell she was going to crash a birthday party.

"Oh, there you are, dear," his mother said as he strode into the kitchen and found her with her hair still in curlers and hurriedly putting the last-minute touches on her own cake. ''Joe could use some help stringing some lights outside, then you'd better hurry up and get dressed. We all seem to be running a little late this year—''

Suddenly noting his distraction, she broke off abruptly. ''Where did I lose you, honey? You look a million miles away.''

Another man might have tried to blame his forgetfulness on stress or his job or problem with a woman, but his mother would have seen through that in a heartbeat. So he gave her the truth. ''I forgot all about the party.''

''Is that all?'' she said, laughing. ''It's no big deal, sweetheart. You have plenty of time to change.''

''No, changing isn't what I'm worried about, Mom,'' he replied somberly. ''Sit down. We need to talk.''

Pulling out a chair for her at the old oak kitchen table that had been in the family for as long as anyone could remember, he sat across from her and told her about the messages left on Elizabeth's answering machine, the threats, the bloody radio collar left on her front porch. ''It's not safe for her to live there by herself any longer, but there's no other rental property available. So the only other option is a motel—''

''A motel!'' she gasped. ''But the closest one is in Gunnison! Zeke, don't you dare let that girl do that. She'd spend half her time on the road commuting. She can stay here, of course. I hope you told her that.''

Smiling, he reached over and squeezed his mother's hand. She really was the best. ''Actually, she's packing right now and should be here in about fifteen minutes. But she's afraid of imposing, and I had to promise to clear everything with you in person first.'' Glancing pointedly at the cake, he grimaced wryly. ''That brings up another problem. Since I forgot all about the party, I never actually invited her. She's going to walk in right in the middle of it and feel like she's crashing.

"I know," he said when she started to grin, "we don't stand on ceremony around here, and anyone who wants to come is welcome. But Elizabeth's going to feel like she's imposing."

"I'll talk to her," Sara said, and saw more than Zeke realized. "I've heard so much about her that I feel as if I know her already. But she doesn't have to join the party if she doesn't feel comfortable. She can go on up to her room and no one will think a thing of it. We'll have plenty of time to visit later. Okay?"

Satisfied, he rose and drew her up for a bear hug. "I don't care what people say about you," he teased, "you're a pretty darn good mom."

"Scamp!" Laughing, she hugged him back, then pushed him toward the door. "Go on and get out of here and help your brother get those lights up. We've got a party to get ready for!"

Elizabeth pulled up before her house and braked to a stop, her heart knocking loudly against her ribs. Complete darkness had fallen since she'd left Zeke, but in the glare of her headlights, nothing appeared to have been touched since she'd left that morning. The windows were locked and shut, the front door bolted. There were no tracks in the snow except hers and Zeke's, nothing to show that anyone had been anywhere near the place all morning.

Relieved, she glanced at the clock on the dash and grabbed her keys. If she was going to make it to the Twin Pines Ranch in fifteen minutes as she'd promised, she was going to have to hustle.

Hurrying inside, she locked the front door after her and flipped on lights as she rushed into her bedroom, shivering slightly as silence engulfed her. Next to her bed, the answering machine blinked, but she ignored it and turned to her closet for her overnight bag.

Grabbing whatever was at hand, she took all of two minutes to throw things in the bag, stuff her makeup in and head for the door. She fumbled with the lock and cursed fingers that were anything but steady. There was, she tried to tell herself as the lock finally gave, no reason to be afraid—she was completely alone. But by the time she hit the porch, she was running. It wasn't until she was back in her car, the doors all locked, that she could finally draw a calming breath. Even then, her heart didn't return to a halfway normal rhythm until she pulled onto the highway and turned toward town.

Darkness engulfed her, and with a sigh of relief she noted that there wasn't another soul on the road. Settling back, she increased her speed and switched on the radio for noise. Fiddling with the channel selector, she never saw the car come flying out of the dark behind her until he was bearing down on her, his lights blinding.

Suddenly he was right on her rear bumper, shadowing every move she made, the sharp glare of his headlights pinning her in front of him. Startled, her heart thundering, she hit the accelerator, sending her car rocketing down the road, but he stayed right behind her with alarming ease. It was just a stupid kid trying to intimidate her with his fast car, she told herself. As soon as she reached the double lane at the climb ahead, he could get around her and gladly leave her in his dust.

But when she flew around a curve and swung over into the right-hand lane provided for slower traffic, he mimicked her every move and followed her. Fear crawled into her stomach, and it was then she knew she was in trouble.

Her fingers curling tightly around the steering wheel, she

didn't dare take her eyes from the road as the dark countryside flew past her window in a blur. Liberty Hill was just a mile down the road. All she had to do was call Nick, and he'd grab this jerk as he chased her through town.

She reached for her phone, but before she could dial the number to the sheriff's office, the driver behind her suddenly backed off. Surprised, she lifted her eyes to her rearview mirror...just as what sounded like a gunshot exploded behind her. A split second later, her right front tire blew.

She screamed—there was no time to do anything else as the car swerved sharply to the right. The wheel jerked in her hands, and suddenly she was careening off the road. Trees danced in front of her. Gasping, she wrenched the wheel to the right...and sent the car crashing down into a ravine.

"Oh, God. Oh, God." That was all she had time to whisper before she slammed sideways into what looked like the Rock of Gibraltar. The air bag exploded—and her head slammed into the window of the driver's door. The pain was immediate and sharp. She moaned and tried to lift her hand to what felt like blood at her temple, but it was too late. Darkness hit her like a ton of bricks, and without another sound, she collapsed in a boneless heap.

Chapter 11

She was late.

Guests—invited and uninvited—milled about, talking and laughing and enjoying themselves, and there was no sign of Lizzie. Checking his watch for the tenth time in as many minutes, Zeke told himself there was no reason to worry just because she was twenty minutes late. She'd said she was just going to grab a few things, but he didn't know a woman alive who could pack that fast. She'd have to make sure things matched, find her best underwear, collect her makeup and shampoo and a hundred other things that women needed to make themselves beautiful. She didn't need all that stuff, of course—she was gorgeous just the way she was—and he'd tell her so just as soon as she got there. Which would, he assured himself, be any second now.

But when the doorbell rang a few minutes later, and he rushed to open the door to a horde of more party-goers, Elizabeth wasn't among them. Or in the next group that came streaming inside a few minutes after that, shedding coats and bearing gifts. And with every tick of the clock, the knot of worry in his gut tightened. Something was wrong.

To hell with it, he thought. He was calling her, and if he didn't get her, he was going looking for her.

Fighting his way through the crowd that had logjammed in the hall outside the kitchen, he was trying to make his way to the phone in the study when Joe struggled to his side. Zeke took one look at his grim face and braced for bad news. ''Something's happened to Elizabeth.''

He nodded somberly. ''Nick just called. She had an accident. The paramedics are rushing her to the hospital right now.''

The news hit him like a blow from a sledgehammer, stopping his heart dead in his chest. ''How bad is she?'' he asked hoarsely.

He shrugged. ''Nick just said she was unconscious at the scene.'' Digging in his pocket, he pulled out his keys. ''Take my truck—it's out back by the barn. Yours is blocked in. I'll tell Mom and the girls.''

Zeke didn't wait to hear more. Shouldering his way through the crowd, he made his way into the kitchen and rushed out the back door without bothering to grab a coat. The cold night air slapped him in the face, but he didn't notice. All he could think of was Elizabeth. All this time he'd been waiting for her, she'd needed him. His blood cold with fear, he ran for Joe's truck.

She was lucky to be alive. If the young intern who patched her up in the emergency room of the Falls County Hospital told Elizabeth once, he told her a dozen times she had to be living under a lucky star. There was, he felt sure, no other explanation for her continued good health. Not that she'd come out of the accident scot-free, he acknowledged—she had a concussion, sprained wrist and bruised back muscles that were already starting to tighten up. Tomorrow she was going to feel as though she'd been flattened by a Mack truck, but considering the severity of the crash, she'd gotten off lightly. If her personal angels hadn't been quite so diligent, she could have been as totaled as her Jeep.

Elizabeth knew he was just trying to make her feel better, but he was wasting his time. All she could hear was the sound of a gunshot just seconds before her front tire exploded.

He'd tried to kill her, she thought in horror. Did he know he hadn't succeeded? Was he plotting even now a way to get to her to finish the job?

Terror clawed its way up her throat, threatening to choke her, even as she assured herself there was no reason to panic. She was safe. Nick was right outside in the hall, and he had deputies stationed all around the hospital. No one was going to get her here.

She knew that, and tried to take comfort from it, but her fear cared nothing for logic. Feeling like she was going to fly apart any second, she told herself to focus. If she could just think about the pain and nothing else, she'd be fine.

For a while it worked. But then a commotion in the hall had every muscle in her body tightening in panic. Alarmed, she struggled to sit up just as the door to her room burst open and Zeke came striding in, looking furious, with Nick right behind him, trying to soothe the ruffled feathers of the nurse who insisted that both men wait outside until the doctor had cleared the patient for visitors.

"We'll just be a moment," Nick told the older woman.

"Speak for yourself," Zeke retorted, heading straight for

Elizabeth. His eyes, dark with concern and hot with temper, met hers from across the room. "I'm staying right here."

"Sir, you can't!" Indignant, the nurse scurried around him to plant herself right in front of him. As lean and tough as a drill sergeant, she shot him a look that just dared him to take one more step. "Am I going to have to call security?"

Nick choked on a laugh. "Ma'am, that's not necessary."

"You're darn right it's not necessary," Zeke retorted, scowling. With a muttered curse, he pulled out his badge and flashed it at her. "You want security, you got it, lady. I'm a special agent with the U.S. Government, and the gentleman choking on his own amusement is the sheriff. Now if you'll excuse us, we got business to discuss with Ms. Davis."

Far from beaten, the nurse sniffed and sailed toward the door with her nose in the air. "We'll just see what the doctor has to say about this."

Not the least bit concerned, Zeke turned back to Elizabeth, his scowl deepening as he took in her colorless face, pain-darkened eyes, and the bandage at her temple. Ten seconds, he raged. That was all he needed with Chester Grant to take the miserable worm apart.

Aching to sweep her into his arms and hold her until the color returned to her cheeks and he was sure she really was all right, he had to content himself with taking her hand instead. "Nick told me what happened," he said huskily. "Are you all right?"

She'd never been less all right in her life, but the second his fingers closed around hers, the fear that tore at her eased. Clinging to his hand, fighting sudden, foolish tears, she gave him a watery smile. "Yeah. I guess I'm running a little late getting to your mother's, huh?"

"Just a little," he said with a half smile that wasn't any

steadier than hers. "Next time you decide to take a little detour down a ravine, try to avoid the rocks, sweetheart. They're hell on a car's body work."

"Mine, too," she replied with a chuckle, only to wince as the pounding in her head intensified. Sucking in a sharp breath, she went perfectly still and rode out the pain, waiting for it to ease. Even when it did, though, her head throbbed dully.

Her hand clutched his tightly as she asked weakly, "Do you think you could see about getting me out of here? I'm sure I'll feel much better at your mother's."

Zeke thought of the crowd, the noise and laughter of the party, and swallowed a silent groan. She needed peace and quiet, and it would be hours before all the guests left, but there was no way in hell he was taking her anywhere else. Not when he'd come so close to losing her. She could rest upstairs—no one would bother her there—and he could leave her there and know that she was safe with his family while he went to hunt down Chester.

"I'll go check it out right now, sweetheart," he assured her. "I'll be right back."

Motioning for Nick to join him in the hall, he waited until the door shut behind them before he said coldly, "I'm going after Chester, Nick. Don't try to stop me. The bastard almost killed her, and this time he's going to pay."

Nick took one look at the rigid set of his jaw and didn't even try to discourage him. "I'm going with you. I called Judge Fischer from the scene of the accident and got him to agree to the warrant to search Chester's house and garage before he has a chance to destroy any evidence. As soon as you get Elizabeth discharged, I'll run by Fischer's place and pick up the paperwork while you take her out to your mother's. We can meet back at the office and leave for Grant's from there."

A muscle jumping in his jaw, Zeke nodded. "Stay with her while I hunt down her doctor."

Not surprisingly he ran into Lizzie's battle-ax of a nurse in the hall. "Since you won't listen to me, I talked to Dr. Wells," she said smugly. "He'll be here any second to discuss Ms. Davis's condition with you."

"Good," Zeke retorted. "Then he can release her. I'm taking her home."

"Oh, but you can't!" the older woman said, shocked. "She's concussed. She can't go home!"

The doctor tended to agree with the nurse when he put in an appearance a few minutes later, but Zeke had no intention of taking no for an answer. "If you want to keep her an hour or two to make sure she's okay, that's fine," he told the younger man. He'd just get one of Nick's deputies to watch over her while he and Nick went to Chester's. "But she's in a great deal of danger, and she'll be safer at my family's ranch. If you're concerned that she'll need medical attention during the night, I'm sure my sister will be happy to look in on her as often as you like. She's an R.N. at the nursing home and will see that Elizabeth gets the same care at home that she would here."

Put that way, the doctor didn't have much of an argument for keeping her. "There's no doubt that she'll rest better at home," he admitted, "but she does need to be watched carefully. If her headache worsens or she experiences any vision problems or nausea, she needs to be brought back here immediately."

Zeke assured him he would never take any chances with her health, and within fifteen minutes he was carefully wheeling Elizabeth outside in a wheelchair to Joe's '58 Chevy truck.

"I can walk," she protested, frowning as he scooped her up to deposit her in the pickup. "Where's your Suburban?"

"Back at the ranch," he said easily as he gently pushed her hands aside when she reached for the seat belt and buckled her in himself. "It was blocked in, so Joe let me use his truck."

He knew he would have to tell her about the party and wasn't looking forward to it. Not only would she shrink from the idea of intruding on a family gathering, she was going to hate walking into a houseful of people in her present condition. But he didn't want her to worry about that until she had to.

"You should feel honored," he said with a grin as he shut her door, then walked around the cab to climb in under the wheel. "He doesn't let just anybody ride in this thing, you know. He must like you. I'll have to watch him, tell him to get his own girl. You're taken."

He said it to tease her, to get her mind off his truck and her injuries, and he succeeded. Color bloomed in her pale cheeks, and for a startled moment, her eyes locked with his searchingly. He could have told her then he meant every word. She was taken. She was his. He didn't know when or how it had happened, he just knew he wasn't letting her go, now that he'd found her. One day soon they would have to discuss it, but not now. Not when she was weak as a kitten and he couldn't take her in his arms and show her just how he felt about her.

So he reached for her hand instead, pressed a kiss to the back of it and said huskily, "Close your eyes, honey, and rest. I'll get you home as fast as I can."

Her heart thumping, she did as he said because she was tired and when she closed her eyes the pounding in her head wasn't quite as bad. And, she silently acknowledged, because she was a coward and didn't have the nerve to ask him if he was serious.

It had been a roller coaster of an evening, and she would have sworn her senses were in too much of a spin for her to sleep, but when she laid her aching head against the passenger window and sighed, exhaustion just slipped up on her in the dark and dragged her under. She never noticed how carefully Zeke drove, avoiding potholes so he wouldn't jar her awake, or the worried glances he kept throwing her. The next thing she knew, he'd parked in front of his mother's house and was easing open the passenger door to help her unbuckle.

Blinking sleepily, she frowned at the fingers he held right in front of her nose. "How many?" he growled.

"Two," she said, and only just then noticed that the house was ablaze with lights and surrounded by what looked like every vehicle in the county. Startled, she sat up abruptly and instantly regretted it when her head felt as though it was going to fall off her shoulders. "Oh, God!" she groaned, and grabbed her head.

"Easy, sweetheart. There's no reason to be alarmed. We're just having a little party for my mother's birthday."

"Birthday?"

"Don't sound so horrified. You're not intruding on some kind of exclusive family gathering. My mother throws herself a party every year and opens the house up to whoever wants to come. I would have invited you myself last week, but I forgot all about it until this afternoon when I left you to talk to Mom about you staying here for a while."

"You hit her with that when she was getting ready for a party for half the county? Oh, no, Zeke!"

"Will you stop?" he said, laughing. "When you get to know my mother, you'll realize she takes everything in stride. She didn't even blink at the thought of a houseguest.

In fact, she's really looking forward to getting to know you. So calm down, okay? Everything's going to be fine.''

Marveling that he could say such a thing with a straight face, Elizabeth could only groan. The man obviously didn't have a clue that this was hardly the circumstances under which she wanted to meet his mother.

"But it's a party, Zeke! And I can't walk in there looking like this.'' She cringed at the very idea. Her sweater stained with blood and her head bandaged, she looked as if she'd just escaped from a war zone. ''Look at me. I'm a mess! My suitcase was left in my car, and even if I had something to change into, I'm not in any kind of shape to socialize with people. I think I'd cry if I even had to try.''

She didn't mean to complain, to be a whiny baby, but she was exhausted, her defenses shattered. Silent tears spilled over her lashes to trail down her cheeks, and she didn't even have the strength to blink them away. Sniffing, she slumped against him and laid her aching head against his shoulder.

With a quiet sound, he shushed her and eased his arms around her. ''Shhh. It's okay, baby. Nobody expects you to join the party, especially my mother. I'm sure Joe has told her by now what's happened and she's already got a room ready for you upstairs. I'll take you up the back stairs and you won't even have to see anyone. Okay?''

He made it sound so easy. And she was so tired. ''Your mother's going to think I'm horrible,'' she murmured as her eyes drifted shut. ''What kind of guest sneaks up the back stairs?''

''The kind my mother will love,'' he said softly, but she didn't hear. Limp in his arms, she was already asleep.

Given the chance, he would have held her the rest of the night, but that wasn't an option. She needed to sleep, and Nick was waiting for him at the office. So he eased her the

rest of the way into his arms and carried her up the back
stairs to the old bedroom he'd had as a child. Just as he'd
suspected, his mother had the covers pulled back invitingly
on the bed and a light softly burning on the nightstand.

"There you are," his mother whispered, letting herself
into the room just as he gently laid Elizabeth on the bed.
"Joe thought he heard you drive up. How is she?"

"Lucky to be alive," Zeke replied quietly, and gave her
a rundown of Elizabeth's injuries. "She was afraid she was
going to ruin your party."

"Oh, Zeke, the poor girl! As if that's important after all
she's been through tonight." Fussing over her, she helped
Zeke get Elizabeth's shoes off, then pulled the covers up
over her. "Do you know who did this to her?"

He nodded grimly. "I've got a pretty good idea. Nick
and I are going to question him as soon as I get back to
town." Needing to leave, but reluctant to let Elizabeth out
of his sight, he reached down to gently brush her hair back
from her face. "The doctor says she needs to be watched."

"I'll talk to Janey," Sara assured him. "She'll check in
on her. We all will. If there's any change, we'll get her to
the hospital immediately."

He'd known he could count on his family, known they
would protect Elizabeth as if she was one of their own. No
one would harm her while she was in their care. But just
hearing the words allowed him to shift a load of worry from
his shoulders. "Thanks, Mom," he said gruffly, and pulled
her into his arms for a fierce hug. "I'll be back as soon as
I can."

"Just be careful," she cautioned softly as she followed
him to the door. "We don't want anyone else getting hurt."

That wasn't going to happen. At least not to him. He
wasn't, however, making any promises about Chester

Grant. After what he'd done to Elizabeth, the bastard deserved whatever he got.

Chester lived in a small, wood-sided house two blocks from his shop. As ratty looking as his garage, the house was little more than a shack that should have fallen down years go. It listed to the right and appeared to be standing solely because of the front porch that anchored it to the ground.

Pulling up before it in his patrol car, Nick frowned at the cars that lined the street in front of the house. "What the devil's going on? It looks like your mother's not the only one having a party."

Zeke snorted at that. "Chester have a party? If he keeps his house anything like he does his garage, it's a wonder it wasn't condemned years ago. I can't imagine too many people wanting to step foot in that kind of grunge, let alone party in it."

Despite that, there was no question that the man had company. Every window in the house was ablaze, and when they approached the front door, they could hear raucous male laughter from inside.

The sound of it grated on Zeke's nerves like ground glass. He growled, "I hope he's in there gloating over nearly killing Elizabeth. Then I can tear his head off his shoulders, and there's not a jury in this country that would blame me."

"Nobody's tearing anybody's head off," Nick warned him. "Unless he does something stupid like try to resist arrest when we finally get enough evidence to nail his sorry butt. Then we do what has to be done."

His lean face stony with purpose, he banged on the front door. "Open up, Chester," he ordered sharply. "This is Sheriff Kincaid. I've got a warrant to search this place."

Inside, silence fell like a stone, then they heard the scrape of chairs being hurriedly pushed back and men arguing in furious, panicky whispers. Nick and Zeke exchanged knowing glances. Without a word of warning, Nick stepped back, then kicked the door in. Guns drawn, they rushed inside. "Freeze!"

Zeke half expected to find Chester scrambling to hide the gun he'd used to shoot out Elizabeth's front tire. Instead, he and five other well-known lowlifes in the county froze in the act of scooping up scattered cards and cash from the middle of the kitchen table and stuffing it into their shirts.

Immediately recognizing a poker game when he saw one, Nick swore and holstered his gun. "I ought to run the lot of you in. Dammit, Chester, the next time I tell you to open the door, you'd damn well better do it and be quick about it!"

"You didn't have to kick it in!" he whined. "Now I'm going to have to get a whole new door."

"Where have you been all night?" Zeke demanded. "And don't say right here, because we know better."

"But it's true," Carl Merchant said, frowning in confusion. "We started the game about four-thirty at the garage, then brought it over here when Chester closed up for the night. We've all been right here ever since."

"And Chester never left to answer a call with his wrecker?" Nick asked suspiciously. "Or go to the store for more beer? He's been here the entire time?"

The other men nodded. "Hell, I wish he had left," Brian Ackers grumbled. "Maybe then the rest of us would have had a chance to win a hand or two. If I hadn't brought the cards myself, I would have swore he was playing with a marked deck. He's been damn lucky."

He'd been lucky, all right, Zeke thought, swearing under

his breath. Too lucky. It had been his experience that a man like Chester, who didn't have the brains God gave a rabbit, didn't conveniently have an alibi right when he needed one unless he was warned in advance that something bad was about to go down.

"So just how long have you guys been getting together for a game or two?" he asked casually. "A couple of months? A year or so? What?"

"Today was the first time," Carl answered innocently, not seeing the warning glance Chester shot him. "Though I guess it'll be my last, once my wife finds out about this. You gonna arrest us, Sheriff?"

Studying the lot of them long enough to make them sweat, Nick finally shook his head in disgust. "Not this time. But if I ever catch you at it again, your wives won't be the only ones you'll have to worry about. Go on. Clear out."

Given the opportunity, Chester would have slid right outside with his friends if Zeke hadn't been standing at the door to stop him. "Oh, no, you don't," he said silkily. "You're not going anywhere. We've got some business to conduct with you, a little search of the premises. If you're lucky, the place'll still be standing when we're through."

Heady with the success of his alibi, the other man gave him a smile that Zeke would have given anything to mop the floor with. "Go ahead," he said flippantly. "I got nothing to hide."

That, unfortunately, turned out to be the only truth that Chester Grant told all evening. Zeke and Nick went over the small house with a fine-tooth comb, and even went so far as to search the backyard to see if he'd buried anything that might link him to Napoleon's death or the recent attacks on Elizabeth, but Chester was squeaky clean, at least when it came to evidence. After hours of searching, they found nothing but dirt.

Disgusted, they had no choice but to give up the search for the moment, but Zeke wasn't about to admit defeat. He could smell the guilt all over the miserable little wretch. "Elizabeth Davis was almost killed tonight," he said harshly. "She lost control of her car and ran off into a ravine."

If he hadn't been watching him closely, Zeke never would have seen the shock that flared just for a second in his eyes before he quickly recovered. "So?" he said with a shrug that might have been convincing if sweat hadn't beaded his brow. "She's not from around here. It's not my fault she doesn't know how to drive in the mountains."

"I don't know about that," Nick said. "That depends on whether or not you knew the bastard who shot out one of her front tires. If you knew what he was going to do, and you did nothing to stop him, that makes you an accomplice to attempted murder. You could go to jail. And you weren't even there."

Zeke watched him turn green and gave the screw another twist. "I'd think about that if I were you, Chester. Paying for a crime you had nothing to do with, spending the rest of your life in a cage. Is that what you want?"

"N-no!" he stuttered.

"Then tell us what you know now," Zeke pressed. "Work with us. We know you're involved. Maybe you didn't mean for things to go this far, but now it's turned nasty and you're caught up in something you didn't plan on. You don't have to let it ruin the rest of your life. Come clean now, and it'll be a lot easier on you in the long run."

For a moment, Zeke actually thought he was going to confess. Pale as a ghost, his skin clammy, he opened and closed his mouth like a fish, searching for words. Then, just when Zeke wanted to hit him on the back and tell him to spit out whatever was stuck in his throat, he took a step back, flattening himself against the wall.

"I don't know nothing!" he cried desperately. "Why do you keep hounding me? You heard the guys. I was here all night playing poker. That's it. End of story. I don't know nothing about a wreck or a shooting or anything else. And that's all I'm going to say!"

He meant it, and there was no getting anything else out of him. Stubbornly keeping his mouth shut, he refused to answer any more questions. Without any evidence to link him to Elizabeth's wreck, Zeke and Nick were left with no choice but to leave. Warning him they'd be watching his every move, they stalked out, slamming the door behind them.

Left alone with his fear, Chester finally spoke. "No one was supposed to get hurt."

The doctor was right, Elizabeth thought with a groan as she lay in bed the next morning and finally summoned enough energy to open her eyes. She did feel like she'd been flattened by a semi. Every bone in her body ached.

The night had passed in a blur. She had no memory of how she'd gotten upstairs and only vague memories of Zeke's sisters helping her change into the pretty pink flannel gown she wore. His mother, too, had appeared at her bedside during the night to check on her, and once she thought she'd opened her eyes to find Zeke himself slumped in a chair next to the bed. But there was no one with her now, no chair next to the bed, and she couldn't be sure she hadn't imagined the whole thing.

Careful not to move her head and awaken the pain that had rumbled like thunder in her head for most of the night, she looked curiously around and realized that the room must have been Zeke's as a child. There was a rock collection on the maple dresser, wildlife posters on the walls, and a bookcase full of books on everything from true crime stories to bald eagles to cowboys in the Old West. All too easily, Elizabeth could see him there as a boy with mischief in his eyes and holes in the knees of his jeans from playing with his brother on the ranch. He would have been a daredevil, a scamp, a tease who drove his sisters crazy.

Smiling at the image, she started to drift back to sleep to dream of him, when there was a quiet knock at the door. The tease himself poked his head around the door, saw she was awake and grinned. "So Sleeping Beauty's awake. Good. You can eat breakfast with me." And pushing the door open with his shoulder, he stepped into the room with a breakfast tray loaded with enough food to feed a small army.

Feeling anything but beautiful—she'd seen herself in the mirror and winced at the yellowing bruise that curled around her left eye—she still couldn't stop her heart from fluttering at the sight of him. "You must have been the one who took a hit on the head last night if you think bruises are beautiful," she said. Lifting her nose in the air, she sniffed delicately. "Something smells wonderful."

"French toast, scrambled eggs, ham and hash browns," he said promptly, and leaned over her to set the bed tray across her lap. "Since you missed supper last night, Mom thought you might be hungry." His hands free, he held up three fingers in front of her face. "How many?"

She'd been asked that question so many times during the night that it had followed her into her dreams. Rolling her eyes, she grinned. "A hundred and five."

"Aha. Somebody's feeling better." And before she could guess his intentions, he leaned over and gently kissed her.

With a quiet murmur of need, she pulled him close, poignancy tugging at her heart. Was this what it would be like to wake up in his bed morning after morning? she wondered. Slow kisses and quiet murmurs and the rest of the world far, far away? Her heart thudding, she desperately wanted to believe that it could be just like this for the rest of their lives. But she couldn't. Because it was only a matter of time before another woman caught his eye, his attention. Her mother might have found a way to live with that, but she couldn't. It would break her heart.

No, this was all they had, all they could ever have, and she couldn't deny herself what precious moments they had left. Giving herself up to his kiss, she let herself float on the sweetness of it. When he finally let her up for air, she couldn't have said if it was seconds or eons later. Limp, her arms draped around his neck, her heart thudding, she smiled into his eyes. "Good morning."

He felt the kick of that smile all the way to his toes. "Good morning to you, too," he growled, and just barely stopped himself from giving in to the temptation to kiss her again. God, she was beautiful! Battered and bruised and still weak as a kitten, she only had to smile to turn his heart over in his chest. And she didn't have a clue what she did to him.

After his broken engagement he'd sworn that he would be old and gray before he'd ever let a woman get close enough to hurt him again, but he knew now that, right from the beginning, he'd never stood a chance of walking away from Elizabeth. With an ease that was staggering, she'd stolen his heart, and he couldn't imagine life without her. She belonged here—in his family home, in the bed that he'd slept in as a child—but soon it would be time for them both to go back to their separate worlds, and he panicked at the thought. He wouldn't, couldn't lose her.

He almost told her then. He needed her to know just how much he loved her, but even as he opened his mouth to tell her, he realized that he couldn't. Not now. Not when a member of his family could walk in on them at any time and he didn't even have a ring for her. He had to give her time to heal, had to give himself time to make some plans. He intended to ask her to spend the rest of her life with him, and a man didn't do that on the spur of the moment. That would be a memory they would both carry with them for the rest of their lives, and it had to be perfect.

Forcing himself to be patient, he drew back and said teasingly, "Enough of this, woman! You keep tempting me, and I'm going to crawl into bed with you, and then where will we be if my mother decides to come up here and check on you?"

She giggled, healthy color spilling into her cheeks. "I don't know—you tell me. She's your mother."

"In hot water, that's where. Now eat like a good girl so I know you really are feeling better." And picking up her fork, he scooped up some eggs and held it up to her mouth.

Amused, she grinned. "I can feed myself."

"So can I. So humor me."

Without a word she opened her mouth.

He fed her because it made her smile and because he wanted to baby her and because even though she tried to hide it, he could see that she was definitely feeling the aftereffects of the accident. She ate, but not much, and was careful not to move much.

"Back hurting you?" he guessed.

She grimaced. "That and my head and just about every bone in my body."

"Then it's time for a pain pill," he said, and rose to set the breakfast tray aside.

"But I don't have any tolerance for those things," she

complained as he shook one out of the brown plastic bottle on the bedside table. "It'll knock me out, and I want to visit with you."

"Wah!" he teased, and drew a reluctant smile from her. "Come on, honey, don't pout. The doctor said you need to rest, and you can't do that if you're in pain." Holding the pill out to her in his palm, he wheedled, "Take it and I promise I'll stay with you until you fall asleep."

"And you'll come back later and eat lunch with me?"

Laughing, he agreed. "That's blackmail, but it sounds good to me. Now will you take the pill?"

Grinning, she took the pill and glass of water he held out to her and swallowed it in one gulp.

Not only was he back for lunch, just as he'd promised, but he carried her downstairs to the couch in the living room so that she could visit with his mother. He would have stayed to talk, but word had gotten out about the circumstances surrounding Elizabeth's accident, and people were outraged. Nick's office was getting flooded with calls about that and the reward for information about Napoleon's killer. If they were lucky, today would be the day they got a break and the right person would call in.

"I don't know when I'll be back," he told Elizabeth as he propped pillows behind her sore back and covered her with an afghan he retrieved from the back of the couch. "If you need me, just have Mom call me. I can be here in ten minutes."

"She'll be fine, dear," Sara McBride assured him with an affectionate grin. "There's no one here but the two of us, and if she gets tired, she can take a nap right there on the couch."

"Stop worrying about me," Elizabeth told him when he

still lingered. "Believe me, I'm not going anywhere. I'll still be sitting right here when you get back."

"All right, all right. I'm going." And unmindful of his mother's presence, he leaned over and kissed Elizabeth goodbye. She was still blushing when he rose, kissed his mother on the cheek and headed out the door.

In the silence left in his wake, Sara McBride chuckled as she sank into the rocking chair in front of the fire Zeke had built in the fireplace. "Don't be embarrassed, dear. Zeke has never cared who was around when he wanted to kiss a pretty girl."

Here it came, Elizabeth thought. The conversation about all the old girlfriends, the past loves, just as she'd known it would. She didn't for a minute think his mother made the comment to hurt her—not when she'd opened her home to her and cared for her during the night like she was one of her own daughters. Sara McBride was a kind woman— and an honest one. And Elizabeth appreciated that. Because as much as her heart wanted to deny it, she needed the truth about him as only his family could give her.

Settling back, she said wryly, "And there must have been a lot of them. He's a very attractive man."

Sara couldn't dispute that. "He has his father's charm," she admitted with twinkling eyes. "Lord, that Gus was a flirt. He had dimples like Zeke, and he knew just how to use them to make a girl fall head over heels in love with him. I was twenty-one when I met him, and he had half the women in the county chasing him." Grinning, she shook her head. "He thought he was God's gift to the ladies, and so did they. I was sure he'd never look twice at me."

Stunned that she could talk about her deceased husband with so much affection, when he'd obviously been as big ladies' man as her father, Elizabeth blurted out, "And that didn't bother you?"

"What? That he flirted with all the girls before he fell in love with me? No—"

"No, I mean afterward. After you were married."

Shocked, Sara stopped in mid-rock. "Excuse me?"

"I'm sorry," Elizabeth said quickly, cursing her wayward tongue. "I shouldn't have said anything. It's really none of my business. I just assumed it must have been painful for you—"

"Painful?" Confused, the older woman frowned. "Elizabeth, are you asking me if my husband was unfaithful?"

Trapped, it was too late to change the subject. Miserable, she nodded. "I'm sorry if I offended you."

Far from offended, Sara stunned her by laughing. "I'm sorry," she choked. "I don't mean to laugh—I just don't know how you ever came to such a conclusion about Gus. Oh, yes, he liked the ladies," she said with a dismissing wave of her hand. "But that was before he met me. From the day he fell in love with me, he never looked at another woman.

"The McBrides are a loyal lot, Elizabeth," she said with quiet conviction. "Gus was, and my children are. Once they give their heart, it's forever. That's why Joe never remarried. He loved Belinda with all his heart, and he's never gotten over her...or the way she left him. It'll take a very special woman to make him forget that."

She sounded so sure—not only of her husband, but of her children. Confused, Elizabeth said, "But what about Zeke? The first day I met him I heard all about how he was engaged to one woman and caught with another. If commitment means that much to him, how could he have betrayed his fiancée?"

Sara had heard the same tale and all the other stories that

had circulated about her youngest son over the years, and normally she wouldn't have lowered herself to comment on something so ridiculous. But Zeke cared a great deal about this young woman. And whether she knew it or not, she cared just as much about him.

"Zeke and Rachel got engaged during her last year of medical school," she explained. "He was finishing up his Ph.D. in California, and she was in Iowa. Neither one of them had much money, so naturally, they didn't get to see each other very often. Then Zeke got a chance to surprise her on Valentine's Day and flew in without telling her he was coming. He caught her with another man."

"Oh, no!"

"It was awful," the older woman said quietly. "He broke things off, and for the longest time, wouldn't even tell the family what had happened. People talked, of course, and because he wouldn't answer any questions and everyone knew he was a flirt, it was assumed that *he* was the one caught playing around. Nothing could have been farther from the truth. He's just like his father. The woman who wins his heart will get his undying loyalty and devotion or he'll never ask her to marry him."

There was no doubting Sara's sincerity, no doubting that she knew her son better than anyone. And too late, Elizabeth realized that she'd been as bad as the friends and neighbors who had judged him so wrongly. She'd assumed that because he was a man to whom flirting came easily, he had to be like her father and went around breaking hearts wherever he went. But if that had been the case, the women in town would not have cared how charming he was, they would have hated his guts. And Elizabeth knew for a fact that wasn't the case. She'd seen the way his old girlfriends flocked to him—they still adored him. Because he was man with principles who, unlike her father, hadn't betrayed their trust.

Horrified at what she'd done, needing to talk to him, she pushed herself up from the couch and hardly felt her battered body tighten in protest. "Where's the phone, Sara? Please, I need to call Zeke. I need to talk to him."

"In the kitchen, dear," she said, startled. "Sit down. It's a portable. Let me get it for you."

That was as far as she got. She turned toward the kitchen, took two steps, and came face-to-face with a man who had just slipped through the back door without a sound. In his hand was a revolver, and it was pointed right at Elizabeth.

Chapter 12

"Get out of the way, Sara," he rasped coldly. Madness glinting in his pale blue eyes, he motioned her aside with the gun. "I got no beef with you. She's the one I want."

Furious, she never budged. "Butch Jenkins, what the devil are you doing? Have you lost your mind? Put that thing away right this minute!"

"The hell I will! I told her to get rid of those damn wolves. They're not wanted here. *She's* not wanted here. gave her a chance to pack up and get out of town and take those murdering monsters of hers with her, but she wouldn't listen. Now she has to pay."

Her heart threatening to beat right out of her breast, Elizabeth never took her eyes off the gun. It was trained right between her eyes. Beside her, she could feel Sara hesitate and it terrified her. *Don't!* she wanted to cry. *Don't play hero! You can't win.*

They couldn't even call for help. There was no one to call. Zeke was in town, and Joe, thinking they would b safe there on the ranch, was checking the fence for downed wire. It would be hours before he and the hands returned.

"It's all right, Sara," she said quietly. "Just do what the man says and maybe we can find a way to talk this out."

"Shut up!" he snarled. "I'm tired of all the damn talking. The lies! If you'd have just died last night like you were supposed to, this would all be over with now. But you had to make things difficult. You have from the very beginning. Well, now I'm calling the shots. Let's see how you like that."

Reaching into his pocket, he drew out a two-foot length of rope and threw it at Elizabeth. "Tie her up," he ordered harshly, nodding at Sara.

"Butch, please don't do this," Sara pleaded. "I know you're upset, but this isn't the way. Let me call Joe and Zeke. We can all sit down and discuss this and see if we can find a way to work it out. No one has to get hurt."

"*You're* not going to," he said pointedly, "as long as you don't stick your nose into something that's none of your business." His eyes cold, he turned back to Elizabeth. "Tie her up. *Now!*"

Fear a thick lump in her throat, Elizabeth didn't dare disobey him. There was madness in his eyes, a rage that destroyed rational thought. His finger twitched on the trigger of the gun, stopping her heart dead in her breast. Given the chance, he would kill them both. He was just looking for an excuse. She'd be damned if she'd give it to him.

Moving over to Sara, she started to tie her hands in front of her when he said sharply, "Behind her! And you'll do it tight if you know what's good for you. I'm not taking any chance on her getting loose and calling for help."

Without a word, Elizabeth stepped behind her and began to wrap the rope around her wrists. Her head bent over her task, she racked her brain for a way to tie Sara so that she would be able to get undone just as soon as she had an opportunity, but all she could think of was Zeke coming home and finding his mother shot dead on the floor. With a will of their own, her fingers tightened the binding around Sara's wrists until it was snug and inescapable.

"I'm sorry," she whispered in a low voice that carried no farther than the older woman's ears. "I can't put you at risk. Zeke would never forgive me."

The older woman nodded imperceptibly, and with a soundless sigh of relief that she understood, Elizabeth stepped away from her. "She's tied," she said flatly.

He checked, just as she'd known he would, and made no attempt to hide his disappointment that she hadn't given him an excuse to shoot her. "Too bad you can only follow orders when you've got a gun pointed at your head. C'mon," he growled. "We're going for a little ride."

"No!" Sara cried. "Damn you, Butch, you can't take that girl out of this house. Think what you're doing! You're in enough trouble already. Do you want to add kidnapping to all the other charges against you?"

"When a man's protecting what's his, he does what he has to do," he said with frightening logic. "You know what those damn wolves did to us before, Sara. To my daddy. I saw him do it. Did you know that? I saw him blow his brains out. Because of the wolves. Because they cost us everything. I won't let it happen again. Even if I have to kill her and every one of those damn bastards. *I'm not losing my ranch!*"

His face contorting with fury at the possibility, he jerked open the door to a nearby closet and pushed Sara inside. He slammed the door in her face and turned to grab Elizabeth by her hair. "You even look at me wrong, and you're history," he warned her, and shoved her toward the front door.

Pain streaking down her bruised back muscles like a hot flame, Elizabeth swallowed a moan and stumbled outside with him. A battered pickup sat in the drive, its motor still running. Muttering curses when she didn't move as fast as he wanted her to, he dragged her over to the passenger side and jerked open the door. "You're driving," he growled. "Get in."

Don't do it! a voice in her head cried. *If you leave the ranch with the monster, you'll never live to see Zeke again.*

But what other choice did she have? she wondered frantically. The man had lost it; he was totally out of touch with reality. No matter what she did, he was going to kill her. The question was when? If she went along with him peacefully, she could buy herself some time and hopefully come up with a way to get away from him.

It was, she knew, a slim hope, but it was the only one she had at the moment. Not uttering so much as a whimper, she climbed up into the seat and slid over under the wheel. Seconds later, following his terse orders, she drove to the ranch's main entrance and turned right. And all the while, his gun was jammed into her side.

It was one of those days when the whole world seemed to be going crazy. The phone was ringing off the wall at the sheriff's office with calls from indignant people who felt sure they knew who had tried to kill Elizabeth, and Zeke could have used at least three more people to help him handle them all. But there was a traffic accident out on the interstate, a train off the rail in the northern part of the county and a domestic disturbance that all had to be dealt with. With one deputy out with the flu and the other two investigating the accidents, Nick had to deal with the disturbance complaint, leaving Zeke to handle the phones. And they were ringing off the wall. There were three lines, and he couldn't hang up from one call without another coming in almost immediately. Everyone had to be put on hold and wait their turn to speak to him, but people didn't complain. The attempted killing of Elizabeth had shaken people, and they were just beginning to realize that someone in the community, one of their neighbors, had a serious problem. They wanted him caught, and they called in with the most trivial information, hoping they could help. And Zeke was thrilled. People were talking, and eventually someone would realize they knew more than they thought they did.

Taking the next call, he said, "Sheriff's office. McBride speaking."

"Zeke! Just the man I wanted to talk to," Hazel Abbot said briskly. The town librarian, she was prim and proper and didn't suffer fools lightly. She'd been ruling over the bookshelves in the old Carnegie Library for forty years and could, to this day, intimidate grown men who dared to raise their voices above a whisper in its rooms. "It's about that reward you've got everybody talking about. I think I have some information you might be interested in."

Surprised, Zeke said, "And what might that be, Miss Abbot?"

"I saw two men throwing something off the Beaver Creek bridge out on Thomasville Road," she told him, all business. "I was driving out that way to visit my sister and came around the curve, and there they were. I couldn't see what they were throwing, but they quickly turned away when they saw me, as if they had something to hide. I don't know if that's much help to you, but I thought you should know."

"You did the right thing," Zeke assured her, jotting down notes. "What day was this? Did you get a look at either one of the men?"

"It was late in the afternoon last Tuesday," she said promptly. "The library closes at two that day, and I always visit my sister."

"And the men?"

She hesitated, then admitted, "I don't like the idea of naming names when I didn't get a good look at either one of them, but a little farther down the road, Chester Grant's wrecker was parked on the side of the road."

"And he wasn't with the vehicle?"

"No. I guess this doesn't sound like much, does it?" she said regretfully.

Zeke started to tell her she'd been a big help when he looked up to see Chester Grant himself walk into the office with Nick. "It could be important, but I can't tell you for sure until I check it out," he told her quickly. "I'll get back to you."

"Look who I ran into outside working up the nerve to come in," Nick told him as he hung up. "I think Chester's got something he wants to say to us. Don't you, Chester?"

Numbly, the other man nodded, then he just stood there, inside the door, looking like death warmed over. Exchanging a glance with Nick, Zeke went to the coffeemaker and poured a cup of coffee. "You look like you had a rough night, Chester," he said, holding the cup out to him. "Why don't you sit down and tell us about it?"

He took the cup and wrapped his hands around it, only to frown down into the black brew. "Nobody was supposed to get hurt."

"Who got hurt, Chester?" Nick asked quietly. "Who're you talking about?"

"That lady, the government one." Looking up sharply at Zeke, his eyes were tortured. "I didn't do nothing, Zeke. I want you to know that. I didn't lay a hand on her. You know me. I wouldn't do something like that. I thought we were just going to scare her. That's all it was supposed to be. At least in the beginning.''

Burying his hands in his armpits to keep from reaching for him and pounding him into a bloody pulp just for thinking about scaring Elizabeth, Zeke growled, ''Who's *we*, Chester? Who are you mixed up with?''

Looking sick, he swallowed thickly. ''He'll kill me for sure if I tell you. He's crazy! The wolf wasn't even supposed to get killed. Why do you think we left that meat with the strychnine in it *outside* the holding pen? We just wanted her to know we could've killed all of them if we'd wanted to.''

''Where'd you get the poison? You steal it?''

''Oh, no! We wouldn't do nothing like that. He had some for killing rats and so we'd use it to make her think we really meant business. But we didn't mean for any of the wolves to get hurt. Then that big one ran out in front of us that day up on Ridge Road and I had to swerve to miss him. H-he hit his head on the windshield, and the next thing I knew, he was grabbing my rifle from the gun rack in my wrecker and he shot him. Just like that.'' He tried snapping his fingers, but they were slick with sweat and he failed miserably.

''We took the carcass up into the mountains,'' he continued hollowly. ''I thought we were just going to dump it, but he pulled out his hunting knife and cut it up.'' Hugging himself, he shuddered. ''When he threatened to do the same thing to the Davis woman if she didn't cancel the project, I didn't think he was really serious, since we threw my rifle in Beaver Creek. But then last night he tried to kill her, and I just can't stand by and let him do that. Next time he might really do it.''

''Who?'' Nick persisted harshly. ''Dammit, Chester, we

can't do anything if we don't have a name! Give us the bastard's name!''

Pushed to the limit, he couldn't take any more. "Butch Jenkins!" he shouted. "It's Butch Jenkins!"

Swearing, Zeke whirled to grab his jacket from the coatrack near the door. "I'll kill the son of a bitch!"

"Dammit, Zeke, hold on!" Nick snapped, then cursed when the phone rang.

Jerking it up, he didn't even have time to identify himself before Sara McBride said shakily, "Nick? Let me talk to Zeke. It's an emergency."

His gaze flew sharply to Zeke. "You'd better take this," he said grimly. "It's your mother. She says it's an emergency."

"What?" In two quick strides, he crossed the room and took the phone. "Mom? What is it? What's wrong?"

"Zeke, thank God!" she sobbed. "It's Elizabeth, honey. Butch Jenkins was just here—"

"Did he hurt her?"

"He took her, honey. I tried to stop him, but he had a gun and he wouldn't listen to reason. He made her tie me up—"

"Are you all right?" he asked quickly.

"Yes, but he took off with her in his truck. He's going to kill her, Zeke!"

"Then he's a dead man," he said coldly. "Tell me exactly what he said. Did he say where he was taking her?"

Dragging in a calming breath, she let it out shakily. "No. Just that they were going for a ride, and that he'd kill her and every one of the wolves before he'd take a chance on losing his ranch. Be careful, son," she warned. "He's made up his mind what he's going to do, and he'll shoot anyone who tries to get in his way."

"Oh, I'll get in his way, all right," he promised furiously. "I'll get right in the bastard's face."

After making sure she really was okay and telling her to track down Joe on his cell phone so he could stay with her until Zeke was able to get back to the ranch, he hung up and turned to face Chester with barely controlled rage blazing in his eyes. "Where's he taken her?"

Pale, the other man scrambled to his feet, knocking over his chair as Zeke advanced on him purposefully. But he was too slow, and Zeke was on him like a dog on a rat. "Where are they, dammit? Where's the slimeball taken her?"

"I don't know!" he cried. "Honest!"

"Don't give me that garbage," Zeke growled, grabbing him by his shirt and snatching him up on his toes to shake him. "You know him, know how he thinks, where he likes to hang out and plot his twisted revenge. You said he took Napoleon up in the mountains after he killed him. Where, dammit!"

"The o-old m-mine shaft off Deer Mountain Road," he gasped, his head bobbing back and forth as Zeke gave him another threatening shake. "We used t-to go up there to drink and sh-sh-shoot off our guns. H-he might have g-gone there."

It was a place to start. "If he's not there, I'm coming back for you," Zeke promised with a snarl. Dropping him, he headed for the door with Nick just two steps behind him.

He should have told her he loved her.

His jaw rigid, Zeke sat silently in the passenger seat and stared straight ahead as Nick raced out of town with sirens blazing. Grabbing his radio mike, he called for backup to meet him and Zeke at the old abandoned mine in the mountains west of town, but all Zeke saw was Elizabeth's face that morning when he'd kissed her. He'd known right then that he wanted to spend the rest of his life with her, and he hadn't said a word. And now he might never get the chance.

Swearing, Nick took a curve too fast and had to slow down or risk losing control. "I should have known it was Butch. He came to every damn town meeting and just sat there, never saying a word, never acting like he cared one way or the other whether there were wolves in the area or not, and that should have tipped me off right there. He saw his father blow his brains out, didn't he? Because the wolves were running in packs back then and feeding on cattle?"

Zeke nodded curtly. "I remember my father talking about how bad it was. There was a drought and the elk moved farther north to feed. Instead of going with them, the wolves stayed here and turned on the cattle. Everyone took a hit, some more than others. Butch's family lost everything. But then, so did some others. You didn't see any of them picking up a gun and kidnapping a defenseless woman."

"We're going to get to her in time," Nick said. "Elizabeth's smart. She'll do whatever she has to, to buy herself some time. You've got to believe that."

Zeke didn't doubt that. It was Jenkins that had him worried.

A mile from the cutoff to the mine, Nick cut the siren. His deputies, scattered around the county, radioed that it would be another fifteen to twenty minutes before they could reach the mine, but Nick only had to look at Zeke's set face to know that he wasn't waiting on anyone to go in after Elizabeth. Cautioning his men to come in quietly and expect gunfire, he pulled off into the trees a hundred yards from the entrance to the mine. Seconds later, with their guns drawn and Zeke in the lead, they soundlessly made their way on foot to the mine.

"You thought you were so smart, hiding out at the McBrides'," Butch taunted as he forced her deeper into the mine. "Did you think I was too stupid to find you? Any moron could have done it. All I had to do was call the hospital and tell them I was a florist and had some flowers to deliver. They told me where you were, just like that," he said with a snap of his fingers.

"I would have guessed eventually, anyway," he confided as he set the flashlight he was carrying on the ground and pointed it up at the roof of the mine. "You've been hanging out with McBride ever since he hit town."

Plopping down on a rock, he casually pointed the gun at her, as if he didn't have a care in the world now that he had her right where he wanted her. "He would have hurt you, you know. He likes to play around. Of course, you don't have to worry about that now that I'm going to kill you, but I really hate to see a man take advantage of a woman."

The statement was ludicrous, coming from him, but he didn't seem to realize that. Dressed in nothing but the pink flannel gown and house shoes she'd been wearing when he'd forced her into his truck, Elizabeth shivered as the cold air of the mine skated over her skin. He was crazy, she thought, staring at him in horrified fascination. Certifiably nuts. One second he acted like a big brother looking out for her best interest, then in the next breath, without an ounce of regret, he casually added that she was going to have to die. And she didn't doubt for a second that he meant it. The question was When? Was he just stringing out the torture, making her sweat, or did he even know himself when he was going to pull the trigger?

Keep him talking, she told herself. How long had it been since he'd kidnapped her? An hour? Two? Surely Zeke knew by now that she was missing. He would come for her. As sure as she knew she loved him with all her heart, she knew he would come for her. All she had to do was hang on. Somehow he would find her.

Standing well back in the shadows, every muscle in her body tight with fear and pain, she glanced around at the rough-hewn walls of the mine and pretended an idle interest in its construction. And all the while, her eyes furtively searched for a way out. "I've never been in a mine before. How deep does it go?"

"Deep enough for your grave," he retorted, his grin sinister in the weakening light of the flashlight. "If you're worried about the animals getting to you, don't. I'll take you down into one of the tunnels and wall you up. You can rest there for eternity, all nice and cool and quiet."

He was so smug, she wanted to smack him one. And although she knew she shouldn't, she couldn't just stand there and let him think he was going to get away with murder. "I can't stop you from killing me," she told him curtly, "but there's no way in hell you're going to leave my body here to rot and just walk away like nothing ever happened—"

"Shut up!"

"Sara's told Zeke by now that you took me, and he's going to tear these mountains apart looking for me," she taunted, lifting her chin defiantly when he raged at her in fury.

"Zeke McBride couldn't find his ass with both hands tied behind his back!"

"He's not looking for that. He's looking for you," she

jeered. "And if you don't think he'll find you, you're crazier that I thought."

"I'm not crazy!" he screamed, jumping to his feet to wildly wave the gun at her. "Shut up, you bitch! I'll kill you. I swear I will!"

"And then what? You can't go back to that precious ranch of yours—that's the first place Zeke'll look. So you'll have to run, to hide like a snake-in-the-grass. And everywhere you go, you'll have to constantly look over your shoulder for Zeke. Is that what you want? Think about it."

Leaving the entrance of the mine behind, Zeke inched his way down the main shaft in the dark with Nick at his side and went weak with relief as Elizabeth's voice carried back to him in the all consuming darkness of the tunnel. She was alive! Thank God! Then her words registered, and he swore silently. He was, he promised himself furiously, going to kill her himself the second he got his hands on her. Dammit, what the devil was she doing? Trying to goad the creep into shooting her?

His heart hammering with fear for her, he made his way deeper into the mine, feeling his way down the shaft as it dipped and curved without warning in the darkness. Then, just when he thought he was never going to find Elizabeth and Butch in the all-concealing blackness, the shaft took a hard right turn, and suddenly there they were. Standing in a weak pool of light fifty yards in front of him and Nick, they circled the light like wrestlers, each looking for a chance to bring the other one down.

Every instinct Zeke had shouted at him to rush into the light and snatch her out of harm's way. But Butch was waving the gun like a madman and far closer to her than he was. The second he stepped into the light, he'd shoot her.

He had to take the bastard out from where he stood, he decided. Butch was distracted and, thanks to Elizabeth's taunting, too furious to notice that they were no longer alone. All Zeke needed was one shot, and the jerk would never hurt Elizabeth or anyone else again.

His gun drawn, he motioned to Nick that he was going to take the shot from where they stood, then quickly took aim. But even as he lined up the shot, he knew he couldn't take it. Jenkins was too close to Elizabeth, the shadows that danced between them magnified by the flashlight on the floor between them, and neither of them stood still for longer than a second. He couldn't get a clear shot without possibly hitting Elizabeth, and that wasn't a chance he was willing to take.

Swearing silently, he lowered his gun and shook his head at Nick. Understanding, the sheriff moved to the opposite side of the tunnel to wait for a better shot, but in the darkness, he couldn't see the loose gravel underfoot. He took a step, skidded on the rocks, and the sound was like a shout in the echoing darkness of the mine shaft.

Her heart in her throat, Elizabeth froze, her eyes wildly searching the darkness that extended beyond the boundaries of the flashlight's dim glow. "Zeke!" He was there, somewhere in the shadows between her and the mine's entrance. Without a thought, she ran toward the darkness.

She never made it. With a snarl, Butch turned on her and caught her by the hair, nearly jerking her head off her shoulders. She shrieked, her back on fire with pain, and hardly recognized her own voice for the roaring in her ears. This was it, she thought, sobbing. The final reckoning. It was either her or him, and by God, it wasn't going to be her!

Somewhere in the distant reaches of her consciousness, she thought she heard Zeke yell something, but the words didn't register. Screaming, her only thought to get back at the monster who tortured her, she turned on him like a she-cat and caught him off guard. His one hand still wrapped in her hair and the other trying to steady the gun, she launched herself at him before he could take aim, and they both went down hard. Blindly, she grabbed for something to hit him with, but all she could come up with was a handful of gravel and dust. She threw it right in his face.

"You bitch!"

She never saw the blow coming. Releasing her hair, he backhanded her, and pain exploded in her face. Before she could do anything but moan, Butch was on his feet and pointing his gun right at her heart. He never saw Zeke step up behind him until it was too late.

"Give me a reason to use this," he said silkily, pressing his own gun to the underside of Butch's jaw. "Just one. I'm begging you. C'mon. Make my day, tough guy."

For all of ten seconds, the bastard actually considered it. Zeke could feel the tension in him and was braced to pull the trigger at any second. And Butch obviously knew it. He hesitated, then abruptly decided this wasn't a fight he could win. Hatred glittering in his eyes, he threw down his gun.

Zeke would have liked nothing more than to beat him to a pulp, but he kicked the gun away instead and handed the bastard over to Nick. Before he even had him cuffed, Zeke was reaching for Elizabeth. With a sob, she threw herself into his arms. Only then was the nightmare truly over.

Her hand caught in Zeke's, Elizabeth didn't know if she could ever bring herself to let go of him again. Through all of Nick's questions about her kidnapping, through another exam at the hospital to make sure Butch's blow to her head hadn't worsened her concussion, over the course of the ride back to his mother's, she never let go of Zeke's hand.

And he didn't seem any more inclined to let go of her than she was of him. He only did so once—to hug his mother and assure himself that she really was all right—then he was reaching for Elizabeth again, keeping her close even when his brother and sisters rushed forward to hug them both in relief, and there was nowhere else she would have rather been.

She should have been in bed, but when Sara insisted that Zeke take her upstairs and let her get some rest, his fingers tightened around hers in protest. "In a little while, Mom. First I have to show her something," he said gruffly.

"But, Zeke, the poor girl's exhausted!" she protested in surprise as he headed toward the front door with Elizabeth in tow. "Can't it wait?"

His jaw stubbornly set, he kept walking. "No. It won't take long. I just can't put it off any longer." And with no other explanation than that, he led Elizabeth outside and helped her into his truck.

When he drove past the house, deeper into the ranch instead of toward the entrance, Elizabeth lifted a brow in surprise. "Where are we going?"

"Someplace special," he promised. "If you're up to it." Concern darkening his eyes to slate, he frowned down at her pale face. "You've been through hell. I should have listened to Mom. You need to be in bed."

"I'm fine," she assured him. "The pain pills the doctor gave me helped, and I can rest later."

Not convinced, he stared down at her searchingly, but something in her eyes must have convinced him that she really was okay. With a nod, he turned his attention back to his driving. "When I found out Butch had taken you, all I could think about were the things I hadn't said to you yet," he said huskily, gazing straight ahead. "I promised myself if I ever got you back, I was going to tell you the first chance I got. This is it."

Her heart doing flip-flops in her breast, Elizabeth couldn't manage a word as he turned off the ranch road and bounced over the rough ground to a spot in the distance where two gnarled old pine trees stood all alone on a rocky knoll that had been swept bare of snow by the wind. The highest spot for miles in every direction, it offered a breathtaking view of the mountains to the west.

Pulling up between the two pines, facing the mountains, Zeke cut the engine. His eyes on the view, he confided, "When I was a kid, my father told us kids that when we were grown, we could each build a house anywhere on the ranch we wanted. I picked here."

Elizabeth could understand why. It was spectacular. With no effort whatsoever, she could see a rock and log home there, with large windows to the west, bringing the mountains and sky inside. "It's beautiful," she said softly, and didn't want to picture who he would be sharing that home with. "I hadn't realized that you were planning on coming back here to live."

"Actually, there was a time when I had pretty much given up on that. I was engaged…" He sent her a sharp look. "I suppose you heard about that?"

She didn't deny it. "She was in medical school."

"I didn't play around on her, Lizzie. I know this may be hard for you to believe, considering the way the gossips talk in this town, but she was the one who wasn't faithful—"

"I know," she said simply. "Your mother told me. I believe you, Zeke. You don't have to explain your past to me."

Just that easily, she gave him her trust and had no idea what that did to him. Emotion clutching his heart, he took her hand and twined his fingers with hers. "I don't want any secrets between us. Rachel and I were a mistake right from the beginning. She wanted a high-dollar practice in Chicago, and I thought I could live with that."

At her look of horror, he laughed. "I was under the misapprehension that I was in love. It didn't take me all that long to figure out that I was wrong."

"Thank God!" she said. "Somehow I can't see you in Chicago. Not that there's not wildlife in the big city," she added, her lips twitching, "it's just not the kind people normally get a Ph.D. in. You'd have been miserable."

"You're right," he agreed. "This is where I belong. Right here on this spot. I've known it since I was a kid. I'd just given up hope of ever finding a woman I could share it with. Until I met you."

Surprised, her eyes flew to his. "What are you saying, Zeke?"

"I love you," he said roughly. "That's what I needed to tell you when I found out that Butch had taken you." A tortured look passed over his face, and his hand tightened painfully around hers. "If something had happened, I'd have spent the rest of my life regretting not telling you when I had the chance. Because I knew this morning. I knew when I fed you breakfast and watched you fall asleep. And I never should have left you without—"

She stopped him with a kiss, her mouth sweet and hungry and loving on his. "Stop," she choked softly. "Nothing happened. I'm fine and we're together and I love you, too. Nothing else matters."

Careful not to crush her close the way he longed to and hurt her sore muscles, he kissed her and wished life was that simple. But they both had a past that they had to deal with if they were going to find happiness in the future.

Drawing back, he framed her face in his hands and laid

his heart on the line. "I want to marry you, sweetheart, and spend the rest of my life with you, but we've got to talk about your father. I know you think I'm like him, but I'm not, and there's no way to prove that to you except with time. I promise you I'll never play around on you or betray you in any way, but that's a promise you'll have to take on faith. If you have a problem with that, then tell me now. I need to know where I stand."

Tears welling in her eyes, she stared up at him and wondered how she could ever have been so blind when it came to Zeke McBride. Yes, he was a flirt, there was no question of that. He liked to tease, but he was just as likely to flash his dimples at seventy-eight-year-old Myrtle and make her laugh as he was at Ed's three-year-old granddaughter. And when it came to proof of just what kind of man he was, she already had it. Rather than destroy the reputation of his former fiancée in a town where most people didn't even know her, he'd taken the rap for something he hadn't even done and let friends he'd known all his life think the worst of him.

No, he wasn't like her father. He would never sneak around behind her back, never betray her or hurt her. He had too much integrity for that.

Her heart in her eyes, she said huskily, "I don't need proof of the kind of man you are. My heart knew it the first time you kissed me. I could have never fallen in love with you if I hadn't trusted you."

She kissed him then because she couldn't help herself, because she thought she would die if she didn't, and when she drew back just enough to catch her breath, they were both smiling. "Now, about this house we're going to build. I think you should know that we're going to need lots and lots of bedrooms."

Lifting a brow at her, he grinned. "Oh? And why is that?"

"Because we're going to have lots and lots of babies, so we'd better get started."

"On what?" he teased, dragging her closer. "The house or the babies?"

Mischief dancing in her eyes, she grinned and lifted her mouth to his. "Guess."

Epilogue

One year later

From the forest-service lookout tower, Elizabeth and Zeke stood side by side and watched one of Napoleon's now-grown pups try to woo a female yearling from the newest pack of wolves released that spring. His tail held high, he pranced around in front of her as if to say, "Look at me, sweetheart. Aren't I something?" Far from impressed, she stared off into the distance, apparently bored to tears. But every once in a while, when she thought he wouldn't notice, her tail twitched in interest and she sneaked a peek.

Laughing, Zeke slipped an arm around Elizabeth's waist and tugged her close, his hand coming to rest on her belly and the place where his baby was just beginning to grow. "Conniving female! Look at her, playing hard to get."

"Her!" she gasped indignantly, her green eyes dancing. "What about him? The flirt. He thinks he only has to look at her and she's going to drop at his feet? I don't think so.''

"I don't know about that," he teased. "It worked for me."

"Oh, really?" she said archly. "And just who dropped at whose feet?"

Eye-to-eye, they grinned, knowing they'd both been lost the second they laid eyes on each other. There'd never been any question that they belonged together, and over the course of the past year, the love they shared had only grown stronger, richer, more wonderful. In full view of God and family and most of the population of Liberty Hill, they'd married on the hilltop where they planned to spend their life together. Then they'd spent the next ten months building their house, complete with plenty of room for children, including the one that was already on the way.

Any fears for their children had died with the conviction of Butch Jenkins and Chester Grant for the roles they'd played in the killing of Napoleon and terrorizing of Elizabeth. Because he'd cooperated in the end, Chester had gotten a lesser sentence and would only spend the next ten years of his life behind bars. Butch, on the other hand, would never hurt Elizabeth or anyone else again.

With the trial over, they'd finally put the past behind them and gone on with their lives. Their home was on the ranch now, and they hadn't wanted to take any chance that their jobs could pull them away from each other or Liberty Hill. So they'd both quit their jobs to open up a wildlife refuge for injured animals right there on the ranch. And every chance she got, Elizabeth took time to track down Napoleon's babies and keep an eye on the next generation. Life didn't get any sweeter than that.

Gazing down at the two wolves, who were now nuzzling

each other playfully, Zeke nodded toward the scene below. "Looks like Napoleon's son has found his mate."

"So have I," she said huskily, turning in his arms for a long, mind-numbing kiss. "So have I." And like the wolves, it was for life.

* * * * *

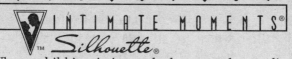

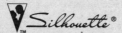

If you enjoyed what you just read,
then we've got an offer you can't resist!

Take 2 bestselling
love stories FREE!
Plus get a FREE surprise gift!

Clip this page and mail it to Silhouette Reader Service™

IN U.S.A.	**IN CANADA**
3010 Walden Ave.	P.O. Box 609
P.O. Box 1867	Fort Erie, Ontario
Buffalo, N.Y. 14240-1867	L2A 5X3

YES! Please send me 2 free Silhouette Intimate Moments® novels and my free surprise gift. Then send me 6 brand-new novels every month, which I will receive months before they're available in stores. In the U.S.A., bill me at the bargain price of $3.57 plus 25¢ delivery per book and applicable sales tax, if any*. In Canada, bill me at the bargain price of $3.96 plus 25¢ delivery per book and applicable taxes**. That's the complete price and a savings of over 10% off the cover prices—what a great deal! I understand that accepting the 2 free books and gift places me under no obligation ever to buy any books. I can always return a shipment and cancel at any time. Even if I never buy another book from Silhouette, the 2 free books and gift are mine to keep forever. So why not take us up on our invitation. You'll be glad you did!

245 SEN CNFF
345 SEN CNFG

Name	(PLEASE PRINT)	
Address	Apt.#	
City	State/Prov.	Zip/Postal Code

* Terms and prices subject to change without notice. Sales tax applicable in N.Y.
** Canadian residents will be charged applicable provincial taxes and GST.
    All orders subject to approval. Offer limited to one per household.
    ® are registered trademarks of Harlequin Enterprises Limited.

INMOM99   ©1998 Harlequin Enterprises Limited

This August 1999, the legend continues in Jacobsville

DIANA PALMER

LOVE WITH A LONG, TALL TEXAN

A trio of brand-new short stories featuring three irresistible Long, Tall Texans

GUY FENTON, LUKE CRAIG and CHRISTOPHER DEVERELL...

This August 1999, Silhouette brings readers an extra-special collection for Diana Palmer's legions of fans. Diana spins three unforgettable stories of love—Texas-style! Featuring the men you can't get enough of from the wonderful town of Jacobsville, this collection is a treasure for all fans!

They grow 'em tall in the saddle in Jacobsville—and they're the best-looking, sweetest-talking men to be found in the entire Lone Star state. They are proud, hardworking men of steel and it will take the perfect woman to melt their hearts!

Don't miss this collection of original Long, Tall Texans stories...available in August 1999 at your favorite retail outlet.

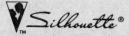

Silhouette ®

Look us up on-line at: http://www.romance.net

PSLTTT

Coming in June 1999 from

Silhouette Books...

Those matchmaking folks at Gulliver's Travels are at it again—and look who they're working their magic on this time, in

HOLIDAY Honeymoons

Two Tickets to Paradise

For the first time anywhere, enjoy these two new complete stories in one sizzling volume!

HIS FIRST FATHER'S DAY   Merline Lovelace
A little girl's search for her father leads her to Tony Peretti's front door...and leads *Tony* into the arms of his long-lost love—the child's mother!

MARRIED ON THE FOURTH   Carole Buck
Can summer love turn into the real thing? When it comes to Maddy Malone and Evan Blake's Independence Day romance, the answer is a definite "yes!"

Don't miss this brand-new release—
HOLIDAY HONEYMOONS: Two Tickets to Paradise—
coming June 1999, only from Silhouette Books.

Available at your favorite retail outlet.

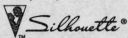

THE MACGREGORS OF OLD...

#1 *New York Times* bestselling author

NORA ROBERTS

has won readers' hearts with her enormously popular
MacGregor family saga. Now read about the MacGregors'
proud and passionate Scottish forebears in this
romantic, tempestuous tale set against the bloody
background of the historic battle of Culloden.

Coming in July 1999

REBELLION

One look at the ravishing red-haired beauty and Brigham
Langston was captivated. But though Serena MacGregor
had the face of an angel, she was a wildcat who spurned
his advances with a rapier-sharp tongue. To hot-tempered
Serena, Brigham was just another Englishman to be
despised. But in the arms of the dashing and dangerous
English lord, the proud Scottish beauty felt her hatred
melting with the heat of their passion.

Available at your favorite retail outlet.

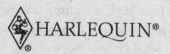

HARLEQUIN®

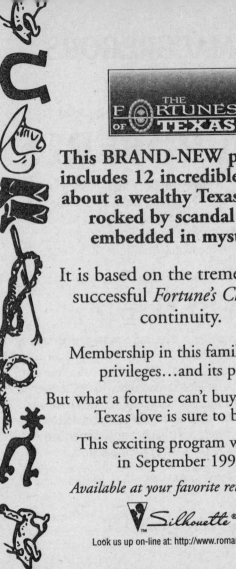
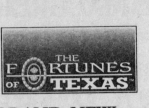
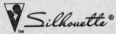